A LIVING NIGHTMARE

It was still dark when Sarah woke up in her bed with the taste of blood on her tongue. Josh was snoring quietly beside her. The sheets smelled fresh, like they had just been washed. Sarah screamed.

She kept screaming even when Josh woke up and wrapped his strong arms around her. Even when he began to rock her back and forth and stroke her hair.

"It's okay, Sarah. It was just a bad dream. Everything's okay."

Sarah checked Josh's neck and chest. Then she checked her own. There were no wounds, no blood. She dropped her head onto Josh's shoulder and began to weep.

"That sick bastard. You don't know what he did to me. He killed us. You were dead. We both were. The new neighbor ... that guy ... Dale ... he murdered us!"

"It was just a dream."

"No! It wasn't a dream!"

Other *Leisure* books by Wrath James White:

SUCCULENT PREY

The
Resurrectionist

WRATH JAMES
WHITE

LEISURE BOOKS NEW YORK CITY

To Mom

A LEISURE BOOK®

December 2009

Published by

Dorchester Publishing Co., Inc.
200 Madison Avenue
New York, NY 10016

ISBN 10: 0-8439-6312-3
ISBN 13: 978-0-8439-6312-0
E-ISBN: 978-1-4285-0776-0

The name "Leisure Books" and the stylized "L" with design are
trademarks of Dorchester Publishing Co., Inc.

Printed in the United States of America.

10 9 8 7 6 5 4 3 2 1

Visit us online at www.dorchesterpub.com.

ACKNOWLEDGMENTS

Special thanks to Monica O' Rourke and Kelli Dunlap for their much needed last minute assistance in proofreading this book; to Tod Clark, my dedicated reader, for his honest opinions; to Larry Roberts of Bloodletting Books for being the first to publish my first novel; to Brian Cartwright for the beautiful work on the limited edition; and Brian Keene, Maurice Broaddus, my wife Christie, and my son Sultan for their constant support and encouragement. Oh, and special thanks to Jack Staynes for his rabid enthusiasm. Here's a little bit of siction for ya.

The
Resurrectionist

CHAPTER ONE

Dale walked slowly down the hall, yawning and rubbing his eyes as he tiptoed to his parents' bedroom where the screaming was increasing in intensity, growing ever more shrill and agonized. He shivered despite his flannel pajamas and held his comic book clenched tight in his fist like a security blanket, rolling it up and squeezing it until the pages creased and wrinkled and the cover tore. He hadn't slept yet. He'd been lying in bed reading *The Man of Steel*, trying not to fall asleep until the fighting was over.

Just as he had every night, he'd lain awake listening to the wet smack of knuckles striking flesh, the roar of his father's angry voice and his mother's own shrill, defiant retort, not backing down until the blows began to fall without relent. Then, when his mother had been beaten into silence, that horrible sound would come. That squishy, rhythmic smack of flesh against flesh mingled with grunts and groans and his mother's muffled sobs. A part of him had always worried that someday his father would go too far and he would wind up an orphan. A part of him figured it was inevitable.

When Dale heard that new sound, wetter, more violent, less rhythmic, cries and screams that turned into a gurgling wheeze, he knew that his mother was dead before he ever walked into the bedroom.

His mother was swimming in a river of blood. It poured off the bed as Dale's father continued to stab her. He was still inside of her, raping her as he did every night, eyes glittering, high on crystal meth. The steak knife in his hand rose and fell over and over again, stabbing in rhythm with his own thrusts. Dale's mother had stopped screaming. Still, she continued to struggle beneath him, trying to escape. But even her struggles had lost their urgency. Her arms and legs pinwheeled in slow motion, her fingernails clawing the bloody sheets as Dale's father fucked her from behind and stabbed her in the back again and again, wrenching the knife free from her shoulder and flinging blood onto the white walls up to the ceiling before clenching the knife in both fists and bringing the blade down again with all his strength.

When her movements finally ceased, his father rolled her over onto her bloodied back. Her head wobbled loosely on her neck, which had been hacked and cut so that her vertebrae were visible through the back of her neck. Dale thought that this meant the assault was over and his mother would finally have some peace, but his father reinserted his erect penis into his mother's blood-slickened vagina and continued stabbing her in her breasts, throat, and face until she was nearly unrecognizable.

His father didn't say a word as he viciously unmade Dale's mother. He grunted occasionally with the effort and exertion as he simultaneously fucked and stabbed her. His father finally ejaculated, his body hitching and jerking. His eyes rolled back in ecstasy. A grin ripped across his bloodied face. He looked over at his son and smiled wider. For a moment, Dale thought his Dad was going to hold up his hand for a high-five.

His father was still breathing hard and smiling when he looked back down at the ruin he'd made of his wife. Blood and sweat ran down his father's face and Dale watched as his dad wiped the sweat from his eyes with his forearm, replacing the perspiration with blood, looking pleased with himself, as if he had just painted a work of art or played some complicated piece of music. His father looked at the knife in his hand and the blood that covered his fist and arms, then looked back down at Dale's mother and began to cut on her again.

Dale watched the entire thing without saying a word. He knew that this was much worse than the beatings. He knew that his mother was dead and that she would never be coming back, but he just could not connect with it all somehow. He felt as if he were watching a movie and not the sadistic murder of the woman who had given birth to him, who had been feeding him macaroni and cheese just hours ago, before tucking him into bed.

He walked into the living room and picked up the phone. He could hear tearing and ripping sounds coming from his parents' bedroom. He gritted his teeth, wincing each time he heard the sound of skin ripping away from muscle. Dale finally began to sob as he dialed 911.

"Police emergency line. What is your emergency?"

"My . . . my daddy just killed my mommy and . . . and he . . . he's cutting her up."

He closed his eyes and tried his best to block out the sounds coming from the bedroom. He didn't want to go in there again, didn't want to see his mother butchered, reduced to meat. What he'd already seen and what he was imagining in his head was bad enough. Dale didn't want to know what his father had been doing with that knife for the last twenty minutes. He waited on the couch with his hands clamped over his ears until the police arrived.

"Police! Open the door!"

Dale opened the door for the police and was whisked outside and into the arms of a female officer who placed him in the front seat of a squad car. The policewoman told him her name. Linda? Lydia? Lila? He had forgotten it immediately after hearing it. He was too busy thinking about his mom.

Everything was happening so fast. His mind was having a hard time catching up. Somehow, he'd gone from eating mac and cheese, watching *Afro Samurai* on TV, and kissing his mom and dad good night to sitting in a cop car while policemen stormed the house to arrest his dad, who'd just murdered his mother. Dale's mind was having a hard time making the adjustments. He could not connect with this reality.

He watched the other officers enter the house, heard the shouts and screams and then the gunshots. He began to cry again, screaming for his mommy when he saw the officers stagger out of the house, ashen-faced, some regurgitating on the front lawn, others just staring off into space. A couple of cops held each other and wept. It was seeing those cops crying for his dead mother that broke him, brought home the reality of his mother's brutal murder.

"Mommyyyyyy! Mooooommmyyyy!"

"Stay right here."

The female officer climbed out of the police cruiser and walked across the lawn into the house. It was less than a minute before she came running back with her eyes wide and terrified. Dale watched as she leaned against the trunk of the car and vomited into the street while crying hysterically.

"Oh my God! Oh my God! He tore her apart! How could he do that to his own wife? How could he do that to the mother of his child? He cut off all of her skin!"

Dale quietly left the police cruiser. He walked back across the lawn and into the house while the other officers stood by their vehicles comforting each other, calling for the coroner's van and the crime-scene unit, doing whatever they could to avoid going back into the house.

The bedroom was splattered red. The carpet was saturated with his mother's blood. It squished between Dale's toes as he crept barefoot toward the bed. What he saw splayed out on the sheets defied all sanity. His father had torn his mother's body apart. Her nightgown was pushed up around her neck and the skin had been flayed from her torso and piled up on the floor. She had been stabbed multiple times in the face, neck, and chest, puncturing both eyes, her cheeks and forehead, bisecting her mouth and nose. Her ears had been removed and she'd been scalped. Her throat had been cut so deeply that she'd been nearly decapitated. Dale's father had begun skinning her legs when the police had apparently burst in and shot him. His body was crumpled up on the side of the bed.

Dale crawled up onto the bed, slogging through his mother's blood, his chest hitching with emotion, and placed his lips to his mother's lips, trying to give her mouth-to-mouth resuscitation. He blew into her lungs, then inhaled deeply and blew again. He was about to give her another breath when he felt her blow back into his mouth. She was breathing.

Her breaths came slowly at first and then began to speed up, coming faster and faster as if she was hyperventilating. As Dale watched, her flesh began to knit back together. A fury of movement exploded beneath the thin sheet of skin that remained on her body. It looked as if her muscles had been filled with tiny insects that were all moving at once, warring within her flesh.

Severed veins, arteries, tendons, and sinews crawled like vines over exposed bone, slithering like a nest of worms within the lacerated meat, reattaching muscle to skeleton. Skin cells regenerated, reproducing at an astonishing rate as the skin grew back to cover her skeletal muscular system where the skin had been shorn away.

Her breaths came in quick, short bursts as her body remade itself, chest rising and falling rapidly. Long minutes went by before her breathing began to slow, relaxing into its normal rhythm. Slowly, her eyes opened and she sat up.

Dale's mother looked around at all the blood and skin and bits of flesh, then down at her husband's body. She screamed and immediately the room filled with police officers with guns drawn, shouting at her and ordering her to lie down on the floor.

"Get down! Get the fuck on the floor! Put your hands where I can see them!"

One of the police officers tackled Dale's mother and soon three cops were pinning her down and wrestling her arms behind her back. Once they had her in handcuffs they lifted her back to her feet.

"Now, who the fuck are you? How did you get in here?"

Blood obscured her features in a mask of red.

"I live here. What are you doing in my house?"

"Where's the body? What did you do with the body?"

"What body? I don't know what you're talking about! What happened to my husband?"

She was in a panic. Dale clung to her legs, hugging her tight.

"There was a woman's body lying in this bed with her head almost cut off and half her skin removed. You've got her blood all over you. Now what did you do with the body?"

Police officers surrounded Dale's mother, staring at her in horror and disgust. His mother's nightgown had been cut to ribbons. Her breasts and the triangular patch of brown hair between her thighs were visible through the rents in the fabric. Blood covered nearly every inch of her body.

"Who let her in here? Who was supposed to be watching this kid?"

"It's my mommy. She's okay. I made her better."

The officer who'd tackled her pointed at her shredded gown.

"Isn't that the same nightgown the dead woman was wearing? What the fuck is going on here?"

Two of the officers who'd handcuffed Dale's mother were now standing beside her, backing slowly away, looking at her as if she were a ghost. The fear in their eyes was like a light growing brighter until it radiated from them and filled the entire room.

The policewoman walked over to Dale and his mother. His mother was holding him tight, smearing blood onto his pajamas.

"What happened to my husband?"

"We had to shoot him. He was killing someone. We

thought it was you. Do you know where the girl went? The woman whose body was here in this bed?"

"I don't know what you're talking about."

"There wasn't anybody else in here. It was just my mommy. My dad hurt her real bad and then I gave her mouth-to-mouth like they do on TV and she was all better!"

The police officers all looked at one another, not knowing what to make of it. The officer who'd shot Dale's father, a fat Italian cop in his forties, was shifting nervously from one foot to the other, wringing his hands. He looked around at his colleagues for support.

"I'm Lisa . . . L-Lisa McCarthy. This is my house. What are you all doing here?"

"How are we going to explain why we shot this woman's husband without a body?"

Another officer with gold bars on the sleeve of his uniform looked down at the body on the floor.

"Well, he had a knife. And with all that blood it looked like he'd killed her."

The policewoman who'd taken Dale out to the police car was standing in the room, looking around at all the blood and then at the blood-soaked woman with the torn nightgown.

"No! This wasn't some kind of hallucination! We all saw what he'd done to her. He almost cut her head off! Her skin was removed. Look! It's still there. Her skin is still there! There has to be a body."

The officers dashed frantically around the house, trying to find the missing corpse. The policewoman continued to stare at Dale's mom, noting the blood matted in her hair, already coagulating, the slashes in her nightgown. The policewoman began to visibly shake. She looked from the bloodied woman to Dale and back.

Dale's eyes connected with the policewoman's and the officer clamped a hand over her mouth as she stared back at him.

"Oh my God. It can't be," she whispered.

The policewoman sniffled a couple of times, wiped the vomit from her lips with the back of her hand, then wiped the tears from her eyes and straightened her uniform. Dale watched as she nodded to the other officers, gave them a weak smile, and then knelt down, taking Dale's hand. The policewoman looked up at Dale's mom and then over at the other officers.

"Can I take your son outside so the officers can ask you a few questions?"

"Uh, sure, but I don't know what happened. I just woke up on this bed in all this blood. And . . . and then I saw Mikey dead."

"He killed you, Mom. You were dead and then I brought you back."

The policewoman looked at Dale for a long moment. Dale could feel her trembling as she held his hand. Her hand flew up to her mouth again and tears welled up in her eyes. Dale knew right then that she believed him.

"Let's get you out of here."

The policewoman took Dale outside, casting one last glance over her shoulder at the blood-soaked woman, the woman she'd seen just minutes ago with stab wounds in her face and half the skin stripped from her body.

Outside, Dale and the policewoman sat in the back of the police cruiser. The sky had gone from black to gray as the sun began to rise somewhere beyond the big houses and trees. Dale stared out the window of the police cruiser, watching the sunrise. When he turned back toward the officer, she was smiling.

"You . . . you healed her, didn't you?"

Dale nodded.

"How?"

"Like they do in the movies. Mouth-to-mouth re-sussisation."

"You mean 'resuscitation'?"

"Yeah, I breathed into her and she healed all up."

"But she was dead. You know that, right?"

"Yeah, just like on TV. She was dead and I saved her."

"But-but how did her wounds heal?"

Dale shrugged his shoulders.

"I don't know."

"And you're sure that's your mom in there? It's not some other woman that got in the house somehow?"

"No, that's my mom."

"And the woman who was on the bed when we got here, the woman who was all cut up, that was your mom too?"

"Uh-huh."

The policewoman smiled and wiped tears from her eyes.

"It's a miracle," she said.

Tears began to flow freely down her face and she began to laugh.

"It's a miracle!" she said louder.

Dale smiled back at her, confused but happy.

Moments later CSU arrived. They began collecting evidence, evidence that would confirm exactly what Dale had told the policewoman, evidence that they would all reject. A week later, when the lab came back with the DNA results, the blood on the bed and carpet and the skin recovered from the scene were all confirmed as coming from Dale's mom. The results were dismissed as some sort of lab error and the case was promptly closed.

CHAPTER TWO

Dale picked up the kitten from the crate. His hand gripped its head tightly as he slowly turned it like he were unscrewing a jar, twisting its neck. He could hear the bones crunching and sinews and ligaments ripping and popping as the kitten kicked and gurgled and scratched. Its tongue flopped out of its mouth and its eyes rolled sideways and came to a stop. Dale smiled as he watched its chest cease its rise and fall. He stared at the kitten for a moment, then breathed into its mouth. Once. Twice. He pulled his mouth away and smiled as the kitten began to breathe again and its heartbeat returned, unnaturally fast at first, then gradually slowing. The fur around the kitten's neck undulated and Dale could hear snapping and popping sounds as muscles, bones, and sinew rearranged themselves beneath the feline's skin.

The kitten purred as Dale scratched its tummy and behind its ears. It closed its eyes and rubbed against Dale's legs contentedly. Dale chuckled and shook his head in disbelief.

"Dumb. Dumb. Dumb."

He grabbed the kitten by the throat again and began to squeeze.

Dale could hear his mother and grandmother talking in the kitchen. They were talking about him. They were always talking about him. They tried to whisper but it was so still and quiet that he could still hear every word drifting through the open window on the warm spring breeze.

"I talked to the priest today . . . about Dale."

"Momma! I told you nobody is supposed to know about him. About what he can do."

"Oh, hush. I didn't give away your secret. It was in a confessional. He can't tell anybody. Besides, something ain't right with that boy and you know it. The dog won't even play with him. I find knives and clothes in his room with blood on them. And I have nightmares. I have these terrible nightmares about being stabbed and suffocated. I know it has something to do with Dale."

Dale's grandmother was an old Southern woman who'd grown up on a farm. She wasn't like those Southern belles you saw on TV sitting on the porch of some old colonial mansion sipping mint juleps. His grandmother had dropped out of school in sixth grade to work the farm. She was hard and coarse and always spoke her mind whether she was right or wrong and was more likely to be smoking a cigar than sipping tea.

"Shhhh! Keep your voice down, Momma. He might hear you."

"Ya see? You's afraid of him too."

Dale heard his grandmother pause and take a deep breath. He paused too, holding his breath, waiting to hear what she'd said to the priest about him.

"I told him all about what happened to you and what Dale did. How he breathed life back into you. The things I've seen him do around the house. How I watched him kill a butterfly in the garden and then bring it back to life. Then I asked Father Stanley why God would put a power like that in the hands of somebody evil."

"Momma! Dale's not evil."

"That boy has got the devil in him and you know it."

"He's just a little boy."

"And God help us all when he becomes a man. God help us all."

His mother let out a long sigh and Dale could almost see her rolling her eyes.

"What did Father Stanley say, Momma?"

"Oh, he's an old fool. He tried to tell me that God wouldn't give power like that to someone unless it was to fulfill his purpose somehow. He told me Dale must have some good in him, that God must be working through him in some way. Made Dale out to be some kind of saint. He wanted me to bring him to the church and set him up like they used to do with the revival tents and all. So he could heal people in Jesus's name."

"And what did you say?"

Dale continued to listen. He was fairly certain that whatever the old battle-ax had said about him, it hadn't been good.

"I told him that God gives power to evil people all the time. Hell, some of the most powerful people in this world are mobsters, drug dealers, pimps and gun runners, dictators and warlords. I asked him if God had some sort of plan for Hitler or Stalin or Mussolini or Saddam Hussein or that idiot that got us into the war in Iraq. That shut him up right quick. He came back with that old bullshit about God working in mysterious ways. It seems like whenever you point out God doin' something that just don't make no damned sense they always hit you with that. Maybe God ain't really all that mysterious. Maybe he just likes puttin' us through hell."

"Momma, you don't mean to talk that way."

"To hell if I don't. You explain it then. You tell me why God would give that kind of power to a boy like that. That boy got the devil in him, I'm tellin' you. He ain't got no conscience, no sympathy. You know damn well he ain't no good. He's just like his father and look how he ended up."

Dale squeezed the kitten tighter. Its tongue lolled from its mouth and it made a dry hissing sound as its legs beat at the air. His mother, his grandmother, none of them understood him. He didn't even understand himself. All he knew was that he was different and for some reason it felt good to kill things.

The smile marring his face turned cruel and the look in his eyes became one that battered women often saw in the eyes of their abusers. It was the look his dad had worn the day he'd taken a knife to Dale's mother. Dale grabbed the kitten's head with two hands. It began scratching, hissing, and kicking its legs, its entire body twitching and convulsing as Dale shoved his thumbs into its eyes. Blood poured down the kitten's furry face, soaking its whiskers, as Dale's thumbs dug into the feline's brain.

The kitten twitched and shuddered, then went limp. Dale withdrew his bloody thumbs from the cat's skull and wiped them off on his Levis. He stared down at the cat and tried to feel for a pulse in its throat. He wet the back of his hand with his tongue and held it up to the cat's nose to see if he could feel it breathing. It wasn't. Dale looked over his shoulder to make certain that no one was watching and then gathered the kitten into his hands. Its body was so tiny it barely filled his cupped palms. He held its face up to his lips and once again Dale exhaled into the cat's lungs, watching as its chest expanded and then began to rise and fall rapidly.

Its eyelids seethed with movement. A riot of activity was taking place in the empty sockets where its eyes had been. A wet crackling sound emitted from the cat's bleeding face as it regenerated. When the kitten's eyelids fluttered open, two flawless green orbs stared up at Dale. The newly resurrected kitten sat in Dale's palms, licking its own blood off its whiskers and grooming itself. It showed no fear as Dale began to stroke its fur. Just as before, it rubbed itself against him, purring contentedly. It had no idea of the things Dale had done to it.

Still holding the kitten, Dale removed a small penknife from his pocket. He stabbed the knife into the kitten's throat as the kitten howled and hissed, crying out in agony and spearing its tiny needlelike claws into Dale's hands. Its claws were still embedded in Dale's hands when it began to shake and convulse, spraying blood from its mouth. This time Dale whooped with excitement and laughed out loud as the little gray-haired Himalayan choked on its own life fluid.

He was still smiling when he placed his lips against the kitten's mouth for the third time and breathed part of his own limitless life force back into the cat. The smile grew wider as the kitten's legs began to kick again and the wound in its throat stitched itself closed and faded away. His smile fell to a hard, flat line when he looked up and saw his mother standing above him.

He spotted her there only seconds before the back of her hand collided with his mouth.

"What the hell are you doing? Do you think torturing a poor animal is funny?"

Dale fell backward, still holding the cat. His eyes filled with tears and widened in shock.

"I-I wasn't doing anything. I was just playing with it."

"Playing with it? I watched you kill it with that knife!"

His mother pointed angrily at the small blood-covered knife still clutched in Dale's hand.

"But I brought it right back to life! It doesn't even know what happened to it."

"How do you know that? How do you know it doesn't remember? And even if it doesn't, that still doesn't make it okay. Do you think it was okay, what your daddy did to me? Because you brought me back? Do you think that made everything okay?"

"But you don't even remember what happened and neither does the kitty. Look!"

Dale reached out for the kitten but this time it hissed and bit him on the webbing between his thumb and forefinger, then dashed across the garden and into the house.

"Ow!"

Dale seized his injured hand with his other hand and brought it to his mouth to suck away the blood.

"Oh, baby! Let me see that."

Dale's mother knelt down and took his injured hand in hers. There were two tiny puncture wounds where the kitten's fangs had pierced his flesh.

"Dale, listen. You're right. I don't remember what happened to me and hopefully I never will, but that still doesn't make it right. What your father did to me was terrible and he's going to rot in hell for it. I may not remember the pain now but from what those police officers told me they saw, it must have been horrible. Just because you can bring me back to life or bring that cat back doesn't make it okay for us to suffer like that. Just because we can't remember what happened doesn't make it any less . . . evil. It's still wrong."

Dale stared at his mother. His face betrayed his utter lack of comprehension.

"It's like those Christians that say that if there wasn't a God they'd be out there robbing, raping, and murdering folks. If that's true, and the only reason they aren't out committing crimes is because they're afraid to go to hell, then they aren't really good people. Deep down they're every bit as evil as the murderers and rapists . . . as evil as your father. There's this quote and I forget who said it. I'm not really good with that sort of thing. But it says that morality is what you do when no one is looking. It's what you do when you know you won't get caught. Do you understand? Even if no one knows what you did when you killed that kitten, even if the kitten doesn't even know, you'll know and it'll change you. It's not about what you're doing to the kitten. It's about what you're doing to yourself. Do you understand?"

Dale nodded and his mother gathered him into her arms and hugged him. But Dale hadn't really understood his mother at all. The part of him that might have understood, might have empathized, had died on those many nights that he'd watched his mother get beaten and raped by his father. It had been buried the night he watched him stab her to death, rape her, and skin her. Dale hugged his mother tight, still remembering what she had looked like bleeding on the bed until he'd resuscitated her. He didn't understand. Not at all.

CHAPTER THREE

Dale heard his grandmother wake up in her bed screaming.

"Oh my God! He killed me! He killed me!"

He heard his mother's slippered feet sinking into the old carpeting as she ran down the hall to his grandmother's room. Her voice was calm and soothing, the same way she sounded when she spoke to him.

"It's okay, Momma. You just had a bad dream."

"It was Dale. He strangled me. He choked me to death. He killed me!"

"You're not dead, Momma. Everything is okay. You're okay."

"No. No. No! He did it! I'm telling you he did it. He killed me and then he must have brought me back. Just like he did with that butterfly and that kitten you caught him torturing."

"But why would he do that? If he wanted you dead, then why would he bring you back to life? I think you just had a bad dream."

"It wasn't a dream. He touched me too. He undressed me and he touched me."

"Momma! Why would you say that?"

"He did it, I'm tellin' you! H-he ... he ... urrrrlllgh."

"Momma? Momma? Oh my God, Momma! Dale,

call the ambulance! Dale! Dale, call the ambulance! Your grandma is having a stroke."

Dale threw back the covers and stepped out of his bed. He walked up the hallway and into his grandmother's room. His mother sat on the edge of the bed cradling his grandmother in her arms while the woman turned blue and saliva foamed from between her lips and came frothing down her chin. She must have bitten her own lip or tongue because there was blood in her saliva. Her eyes had rolled up in her head so that only the whites were visible. As Dale stood there, her eyes rolled back down out of her skull and fixed on Dale. Her eyes widened and she began to tremble. Dale smiled. When he looked up at his mother she was staring right at him. There was a look on her face of terror and disgust. She had seen his smile. Dale walked over to the phone, picked it up, and dialed 911. He continued staring at his mother and grandmother as he spoke to the emergency operator and they continued staring at him.

Later that night at the hospital Dale's grandmother passed away. Dale was asleep when she went. He woke up when his mother grabbed him and began slapping him. It took a moment for him to orient himself and remember where he was, in a hospital, with his dying grandmother. But why was his mother attacking him? Dale covered his head to protect himself from the blows.

"Mom? Stop! Why are you hittin' me? I didn't do nuthin'!"

"Bring her back! Bring her back!"

The nurses looked confused when they rushed into the room and pulled her off her son. Dale was breathing heavy. There were bruises on his face and arms from where his mother had struck him. His mother was breathing hard too. She stared at him with something that looked very much like hate blazing in her eyes as the nurses held her back and she struggled in their grasp.

"Bring her back! Do it! Do it!"

"Mrs. McCarthy! There's nothing he can do for her. The doctors did all they can. No one can help her now. She's gone."

"But he can. He can bring her back!" She looked directly into Dale's eyes. Her eyes were so full of tears that he wasn't sure that she could even see him through them. "Why won't you bring her back? Why?"

Dale tried to think of something to say, something that would ease his mother's mind and make him sound compassionate and wise. He couldn't think of anything. The only thing he could think to say was the truth.

"I don't want to bring her back. She didn't like me."

The two nurses turned to look at Dale. His mother's mouth dropped open.

"You did this. Didn't you? You did this to her. It wasn't a dream. Was it? Get out of here! Get the fuck out of here! I don't want you anywhere near her!"

A big, burly black orderly arrived with security.

"Maybe you should wait in the lobby, little man. Your mom is just a little upset. Everything will be all right."

"Get out! Get out! Get out! You did this! I know you did this!"

Dale walked out of the hospital room with the orderly and the security guard. He hated to see his mother like this, but he was glad the old woman was dead. He began to whistle as he walked toward the lobby. He stopped himself, suddenly realizing how inappropriate it must have appeared. He looked up at the orderly who was exchanging looks with the security guard. Their faces were completely shocked. It struck Dale as funny. He started to laugh, which made their expressions turn to bewilderment, which caused Dale to laugh even harder. They walked him into the lobby and then walked away shaking their heads. A teenage mother sat in the lobby, bouncing an infant on her lap.

"What's so funny, kid?"

Dale wiped tears from his eyes and looked over at the girl. She was smiling at him, anticipating a really good joke.

"My grandmother just died." He turned away from her and continued to laugh.

CHAPTER FOUR

Dale sat in his room reading an old article in his dog-eared *Encyclopedia of Crime* about a serial killer who had been captured in Philadelphia in the 1980s. His name was Gary Heidnick and he had been kidnapping women, keeping them chained up in his basement for months, raping and torturing them. A few of the women Heidnick kidnapped had been murdered and buried in his backyard or in a nearby wooded area. At least one of them had been dismembered, her flesh boiled into a stew and fed to his dogs and the other women. Dale found himself aroused by the tale. He believed the only way he'd ever get a girl would be to kidnap one.

The girls at his high school paid no attention to him except when they teased him and called him a loser or nerd. A bad case of acne made Dale's face look like he were growing cranberries on it. Where his skin was not erupting with pimples it was sickly pale, and he was so skinny that the bones in his chest and shoulders stood out prominently through his skin whenever he dared to wear a tank top. It looked as if he hadn't eaten in months. His chest was concave and his cheeks were sunken in. His eyes stared out from deep in their sockets, giving his face a cadaverous skeletal look. He was the very antithesis of the athletes all the girls in his high school were chasing. He didn't have their tanned muscular physiques. He looked about as healthy as death smoking a cigar in a nuclear waste dump.

Dale turned next to a story about Ed Kemper but soon lost interest in it. He wasn't interested in reading about killers who murdered just for the sheer joy of killing. He knew that joy. That was the only joy he could ever remember knowing. Now that he was in the full swing of puberty and his hormones had begun to rage and riot, he was interested in other forms of satisfaction. He was more and more interested in the girls in his class and curious about what pleasures their young bodies might hold.

Dale could understand raping a woman and then murdering her to keep her silent. It had a sort of logic to it. He could even understand the idea of killing just for the pleasure of the act. But the idea of taking souvenirs home, pieces of their corpses, and masturbating with them, that made no sense at all. The only reason he could think of to rape a woman would be so you didn't have to masturbate. Raping a woman and then killing her was one thing, but killing her and then raping her was just twisted. Dale thought about his father and what he'd seen him doing to his mother's corpse. He had been getting just as much pleasure from skinning her as he had from fucking her.

Dale slammed the book shut when he felt an erection swelling in his shorts. He remembered how his father had stabbed his mother again and again and then slit her throat as he fucked her doggy-style. Dale was ashamed at how that memory made him feel. He knew it was wrong but he couldn't help the sensations that image aroused in his body. It was as if his own body was betraying him and his mother. Dale was terrified that he understood Kemper more than he'd realized. He thought about what his grandmother had said about God being crazy for giving the power of life to a person like him. He hated to admit it, but the old woman had been right. He wouldn't do anything good with this power.

In the next room, Dale's mother was taking a bath. Dale had heard her running the bathwater hours ago. She hadn't left the bathroom since. He wondered if he ought to check on her. She had been in the bath far too long and he had heard a splashing and thumping sound coming from in there twenty or thirty minutes ago. He was afraid she might have fallen and hurt herself. It didn't matter though. If she was dead, he would simply bring her back like he'd done before.

The hollow echo of solitary drops of water splashing down into a larger pool of water echoed down the hallway as Dale approached the bathroom he shared with his mother. He grasped the handle but the door was locked. It was one of those privacy locks that were about as useless as childproof caps on medicine bottles. Dale reached for the little metal pin that his mother kept above the doorway. All you had to do was slip it, or just about anything else that would fit into the little hole, in the center of the doorknob and the lock would disengage. It was more of a nuisance than a deterrent if someone really wanted to get in. The "key" wasn't there.

"Mom?"

There was no answer.

"Mom?" Dale spoke in a louder voice. "Are you all right in there?"

Still no answer.

Dale banged his fist on the door.

"Mom! Mom!"

All he could hear was the drip of the tub faucet.

Dale sighed and turned away from the door. He took his time walking back to his room to get a hanger. There was no hurry. He had learned through trial and error that even if someone had been dead for several hours he could still bring them back, as long as they hadn't begun to decompose. Once a corpse began to rot it was good and dead.

Once he had retrieved a wire hanger from his closet, Dale began straightening it as he walked back down the hall. He imagined he would find his mother drowned in the bathtub after slipping and hitting her head on the edge of the tub. Perhaps she had fallen out of the tub completely and cracked her neck. Whatever it was, he could fix it.

Dale slid the straightened hanger into the hole in the doorknob and disengaged the lock. The door popped open and Dale slipped inside. He wasn't prepared for what he found. Dale's mother lay in the tub just as he had expected, only she hadn't slipped and hit her head or broken her neck or drowned or had a stroke or a heart attack. She had slit her wrists. The bathwater was tinted red like fruit juice. She had made a mess of her wrists. She cut across them first; then she'd taken the blade and cut all the way up her forearms. Ghastly red crosses scarred her arms.

Her eyes were closed and she looked as if she'd simply fallen asleep. Her breasts were pale and flabby and had flopped to either side of her chest. Her legs were splayed immodestly but the amount of blood in the tub prevented Dale from seeing anything. Dale felt that uncomfortable stirring in his shorts again as he stared at his mother's nude dead form. This time he didn't shy away from it. There was no one around. No one to see what he was doing. Why not have some fun? he thought. He had never seen a real woman naked before, and even though it was his own mother, she *was* naked, and at least she wasn't just a picture in a magazine or on TV.

He reached out and hefted her big flabby breasts in his hands, then rubbed the nipples. The straining in his pants became more persistent. Dale knelt down and licked droplets of blood and bathwater from her nipples, then began to suck them. He pinched them hard, bit one, then brought his lips to his mother's mouth and prepared to breathe life back into her lungs. He was just about to exhale when he spotted the words written on the shower wall behind her.

Let me die.

Dale paused there, trying to decide what to do.

Let me die.

It was her do-not-resuscitate order.

But why does she want to leave me?

The idea of being alone terrified him. Maybe it was just a test? Maybe she knew he would bring her back and she was just testing him? Maybe she was warning him to be a good boy or she'd leave him forever.

I'll be good, Mommy. I'll be good. Just don't leave me.

Let me die.

"Noooo!"

He clamped his mouth onto hers and breathed into her lungs again and again until she began to breathe for herself. She let out a deep breath and then a sob. A wail of anguish came from her as she rose from the bathtub. Her eyes were wild and she pulled at her hair and scratched her face.

"Why? Why? Why, Dale? Why did you do this? Why didn't you let me die? Why did you bring me back? Why didn't you let me die?"

Dale looked confused.

"B-because I need you. I love you."

Dale's mother shook her head.

"No. No, you don't love me. You don't know what love is. You're not capable of feeling love. I don't know what you feel, or if you feel anything at all, but it isn't love. You're evil, Dale. You're some kind of monster. Now just leave me alone and let me die."

Tears welled in Dale's eyes. He couldn't believe his mother was saying these things to him. She had been looking at him suspiciously ever since his grandmother died. Now she'd finally said what she was really thinking.

Dale's brow furrowed and his voice lowered. He stood up and put a hand beneath his mother's chin, turning her head to look him in the eyes.

"No, Mom. I won't let you die, ever. I need you and I'm not going to let you go. You can kill yourself again but I'll just bring you back. I'll just keep bringing you back again and again. You can't leave me. You can't ever leave me."

The next day his mother set herself on fire and burned down the house. Dale awoke to a room filled with smoke and a bedroom door that was engulfed in flames. He'd had to crawl out of his window and jump down into the parking lot below to avoid being immolated himself. He had just barely managed to get out of the house alive. The firemen told him that there had been gasoline poured outside his door. His mother had tried to take him with her. This time, he was not able to bring her back. She had found a way to get away from him after all.

CHAPTER FIVE

Sarah Lincoln awoke to the smell of maple syrup, frying bacon, and the clash and clang of pots and dishes. She loved Saturdays. Saturday was the day that Josh felt guilty for working late all week and woke up early to cook her breakfast. Sarah knew that Josh had to work to support the family. She still hated it. She wished he could spend every day with her.

She loved being able to stay home and play the dutiful housewife, cooking and cleaning, decorating their home, clipping coupons, balancing the checkbook, and making herself beautiful for him, but she'd be lying to herself if she didn't admit that she resented it sometimes. Seeing Josh leave for work every morning before the sun rose, and sometimes coming home long after dark, working double shifts, ten-, eleven-, and twelve-hour days, awoke all of her jealousies and insecurities. Even knowing that Josh was hard at work, all Sarah could think about was that at least he had people to talk to there, and that many of those people were women.

Josh was a blackjack dealer at one of the largest casinos in town, and while she just could not imagine standing in place for eight hours shuffling cards—it would have been hell on her feet and her lower back—she could imagine all the interesting people he got to meet. Including drunk, flirtatious women looking for a Vegas fling.

Sarah didn't think Josh was cheating on her. He wasn't the type. But she knew he enjoyed his work. He enjoyed the social interaction. He enjoyed getting the chance to meet celebrities and millionaires and people from all over the world. Sarah didn't get to meet anyone except the clerks at the local grocery store and the sales people at Wal-Mart. She was alone. She had no friends in Las Vegas. She'd left her family, her friends, and everyone she'd grown up with back in Indianapolis. After living in Las Vegas for eleven years she still did not even know the names of her neighbors. With all the foreclosures, her neighbors kept changing before she got to know them. Josh was her only friend.

The acrid aroma of burning butter wafted up from the kitchen, followed by a few whispered curses and the whoosh and sizzle of cold water running into a hot pot. Sarah giggled. Josh was many things, a hard worker, a sensitive listener, an attentive lover, even a pretty good singer, but he was a terrible cook. As she did every weekend, Sarah crawled out of bed and decided to go downstairs and rescue Josh before he burned down the house.

A loud banging noise came from across the street and several loud voices began shouting, not angrily, just talking louder than was necessary. Sarah went to the window and looked out. There was a moving truck pulled up to the little single-story house that an old couple named the Jensens had lived in before their mortgage rates had gone up and they'd gone into foreclosure. Sarah felt sorry for them. They were the only neighbors she spoke to regularly and even then it was mostly just small talk on the way to the mailbox.

Three men in overalls were carrying large boxes out of the back of the U-Haul. A small, skinny guy with dirty blond hair, wearing a white polo shirt and jeans, stood by nervously. One of the movers dropped a box onto the ramp that led out of the back of the truck and it slid down into the street. Nothing appeared to be broken, but the skinny guy looked like he was about to scream. Veins popped out in his forehead, the muscles in his jaws were clenched tight, and his complexion had turned red, but when he spoke his voice was calm and measured.

"Would you please be more careful? I have some expensive computer equipment in these boxes. It's what I do for a living."

Sarah shook her head in disbelief. If it had been her stuff those clowns had dropped all over the street she would have flipped the hell out. She never understood why guys always felt like they were never supposed to show any emotion. Josh was the same way. If the house was on fire he'd be standing there trying to figure out how to wake her without raising his voice.

The skinny guy turned his head toward the sky as if praying that his stuff would all make it into the house unscathed. His entire body was tense and his eyes were closed. He turned his head toward the house slowly and opened his eyes. A full thirty seconds went by with him standing in his driveway staring up at her window. His face relaxed and he calmed down. For a moment, Sarah thought he was looking into her eyes. She was suddenly conscious of the fact that she wasn't wearing a shirt but she doubted he could see her through the blinds. Then the man smiled. The expression wasn't particularly perverted or threatening. It merely looked amused. Still, Sarah felt a chill race over her skin. She crossed her arms over her chest and stepped away from the window.

Sarah walked into the closet and picked out a shirt. She thought for a moment about getting dressed but didn't want to give in to paranoia and admit the man had spooked her. She threw the T-shirt back onto the shelf and walked downstairs into the kitchen wearing only her panties, pink cotton boy-briefs, and no bra. She was thirty-four but still had the body of a teenager thanks to long morning jogs and a couple marathons a year. She and Josh planned on having kids soon, which meant that in a few years she would no longer be able to walk around the house naked, and after a child or two would probably not want to. She hefted her breasts in her hands. They weren't the silicone-filled double-D cups every other woman in town seemed to have, but they were real and at a 36-C she thought they were just the right size. They hadn't begun to sag yet and were still fairly firm. Josh liked them, and that was all that mattered. She knew that after she had a few kids they probably wouldn't look quite the same and she'd become more self-conscious. She couldn't imagine walking around the house with stretch marks, sagging tits, and a paunch. But until then, she planned on enjoying her freedom, which meant that in her house, she wore as little as possible.

"Good morning, honey."

Josh turned toward her, smiling, then turned red when he saw her naked body. He was still such a prude. Sarah didn't know how any man could be married to her for ten years and still be so sexually inhibited.

"Do you have to walk around naked all the time? What if some pervert is looking through the windows with a telescope right now?"

"This is Vegas. If a guy wants to see a naked woman he can see better bodies than mine for a handful of ones and a two-drink minimum."

"But why would he if he can see yours for free?"

"I'd be flattered if someone were going through all that effort just to see me."

Josh walked over to the windows in the kitchen and then in the great room and shut the blinds. Sarah giggled.

"You really do think someone might be looking. That means you still think I'm hot. Wanna fuck?"

"I made pancakes."

Josh smiled wide like a proud parent as he held up a plate of crispy bacon, fluffy eggs, and three blackened pancakes.

Sarah smiled back. At least the bacon and eggs looked good.

"Thank you, sweetheart. Maybe we can fuck after breakfast?" She winked at him, then took the plate and plopped down at the kitchen table. She didn't even have to look at Josh to know that he was turning red again. He embarrassed so easily it never ceased to amaze her.

"Maybe you can lick butter and syrup off me?" She smiled at him and he fumbled a plate and almost dropped it. Sarah laughed.

"You are so wild." Josh laughed.

"That's why you married me." She winked at him again and shoved a piece of bacon in her mouth.

"There's someone moving in across the street."

"I know. I saw him when I was upstairs. It looks like it's just some guy moving in by himself."

"He didn't see you, did he? I mean, you had some clothes on, didn't you?"

"If he can see through the blinds, two stories up, in the daytime, then he's Superman."

"In other words, you didn't have a shirt on?"

"Relax, nobody saw me."

She thought about the way the new neighbor had looked up at the window and another cold chill ran over her.

"Well, do you think maybe we should go introduce ourselves?"

"I guess that means you don't want to fuck me?"

"Sarah, is that all you think about?"

He had concern in his voice when he asked the question, as if he thought Sarah was crazy, some kind of nymphomaniac. Josh had asked her many times in the past if she'd ever been sexually assaulted or abused. He had almost insisted that she had been. It was the only explanation he could think of for her powerful sex drive, using his self-help-book psychology. Men always figured that a woman had to be damaged in some way if she had a stronger libido than theirs. It was one of those male-chauvinist things that pissed Sarah off.

Josh was even worse than most men when it came to that because he himself had been molested as a child. He had told her about it once and then made her promise never to bring it up again. He had been one of the apparent thousands of young boys who had been molested by a priest. His mother had sent him to Bible camp for the summer and one of the camp counselors, a popular young priest, had dragged him out into the woods every night for eight weeks. The camp counselors would tell all the kids what to say in their letters home and then read each one before they mailed them, destroying any that mentioned sexual abuse or any displeasure at being at the camp at all. They had all apparently been in on it.

Josh had come home and told his parents. They had freaked out and sent him to a home for troubled kids, where he'd been abused again by one of the older boys who'd anally raped him at knifepoint and one of the youth counselors had forced him to perform oral sex. This time he told no one. Eventually, he had his growth spurt and beat the hell out of the older kid. The counselor had left him alone then too.

Nothing happened to the priest who'd started it all. He got away with what he'd done for twenty years, and then one day they'd been watching TV when his picture had flashed on the screen, along with a story about how he'd been accused of molesting young boys going back more than a dozen years.

"More than *twenty* years." Josh had corrected the newscaster. Then he'd told Sarah the story. It had explained a lot, his shyness and timidity in the bedroom and his defensiveness around the entire Catholic child-molestation issue. Josh was still religious but avoided church like the plague though he still called himself a Catholic. Sarah didn't get it.

"How can you believe in a God who would let his own representatives do this? If he does exist, he might as well not exist for all the difference it makes."

"God had nothing to do with that," Josh said.

"But I thought God had something to do with everything?"

"He didn't have shit to do with that! That was just a man. One sick, twisted, evil man."

"But didn't God create the man?"

"God gave man free will."

"How can there be free will if God is all-knowing?

If God already knows everything you will ever do from birth to death before he ever creates you, then he created you specifically to do those things because he could have not created you or created you with a different nature. I'm just saying, an omniscient creator and free will are sort of incompatible concepts. Omniscience is more compatible with determinism."

"You're going to have to dumb it down for me a little. I didn't go to graduate school. But it sounds to me like you're saying that God wanted me to be raped by a priest? Is that what the fuck you're saying?"

That discussion hadn't gone well. They never did. Sarah had tried to discuss his religious beliefs with him a few times but they had all turned rather nasty and ended in shouting matches. Eventually, they had agreed that that subject was taboo, as was any discussion of his molestation. And Josh had slowly begun to open up more and more sexually under her patient guidance and coaxing. Sarah had enjoyed the challenge. It had fed her own need for control.

Sarah had always enjoyed making men uncomfortable with her wantonness, and even knowing the reasons for Josh's rather conservative attitude toward sex, she still enjoyed teasing him and rarely felt guilty about it even though she knew she should have. Much of her sexuality was an act anyway. If Josh had sex with her every time she asked for it she'd have stopped asking. She considered it a sort of protest against the double standard. A man who wanted sex all the time was a stud. A woman who liked sex was some kind of slut or a victim. And sex abuse aside, she knew that Josh felt the same way. This was just one more annoying manifestation of Josh's puritanical Catholic upbringing that Sarah had yet to adjust to.

"After barely seeing you all week? Yeah, fucking you is all I can think about. When I stop thinking about fucking you, start worrying."

She knew that Josh didn't think it was ladylike for a woman to say "fuck." It was one of those things he'd learned to get used to. Sarah even suspected that it secretly turned him on. She was so different than his friends' wives. She was more like the wives in *Penthouse* Forum.

Sarah shoveled the eggs into her mouth along with the rest of the bacon and then stood up, still chewing. She walked over to the garbage can and scraped the pancakes off the plate into the trash.

"Hey!"

"I love you, honey. But there's no way I'm eatin' that shit. I do appreciate it though. You're sweet for trying."

"Thanks. Sweet is exactly what I was going for."

He looked truly hurt. He looked down at his own plate full of burned pancakes, then walked over to the garbage and tossed his uneaten breakfast in as well.

"Oh, well. I tried."

"And I love you for it."

Sarah stood up on her tiptoes and kissed Josh on the cheek. Josh was not a small man. He was six foot four and over 250 pounds. He'd played hockey in college and had once had aspirations of making an NHL team. That was until he'd lost his athletic scholarship and had to admit that he didn't have a hockey player's killer instinct. He still played hockey on the weekends whenever he didn't have to work or when Sarah didn't nag him into staying home with her, which she did often. After he'd worked all week, if he finally got a weekend off, she didn't want him spending it chasing a bunch of men up and down the ice with a stick. She wanted him all to herself. She knew it was selfish and she ought to have felt guilty about it but she didn't. Sometimes she tried to be supportive and went to watch him play. The hotel he worked at sponsored their league and they played against other hotels, bars, and strip clubs that all had their own teams. Sarah knew that it made Josh feel great to compete in those games. It was the closest to the NHL he'd ever get. And it was a good excuse for him to stay in shape. His size and muscles made Sarah feel safe and when he hugged her she felt like a child again, without a care in the world.

"Okay, I'll go put some clothes on and we'll go say hi to another neighbor that we'll probably never speak to again as long as we live here. But when we come back in I'm going to fuck you like I paid for you." She smiled mischievously, then skipped up the stairs.

Upstairs in the bedroom, Sarah began to sweat. Her hands shook as she reached for the T-shirt. She was shrugging into a pair of jeans and almost fell over. Her legs were trembling.

What the hell is wrong with me?

She began to hyperventilate. The room tilted and whirled like a carnival ride.

I think I'm having an anxiety attack. Either that or a stroke.

She held on to the closet shelves and took deep breaths, waiting for the moment to pass. She thought about calling Josh but her pride prevented her. Sarah didn't want her husband to think she was weak. She had always been afraid to show weakness around him or any man. She considered herself the rock of the relationship. She was the strong, steady one, the one who never worried, never panicked, never flipped out no matter how difficult things got. Josh was the one who panicked whenever they were late paying a phone bill and rushed to the doctors whenever he had a cough or a stomachache. Sarah always kidded her husband about being a hypochondriac. The last thing she wanted was for him to see her freaking out.

"Sarah? Sarah, you coming?"

After a few more breaths the trembling in her body stopped and her breathing settled back into a normal rhythm. She finished pulling on her jeans and slipped on a pair of flip-flops.

"Sarah!"

"I'm coming right now!"

Sarah trotted down the steps and met her husband at the front door.

"What took you so long? Why are you all sweaty?"

"Well, you wouldn't fuck me so I had to do it myself. You wouldn't want me meeting the neighbor when I was all horny, would you?"

Josh's eyes widened.

"You didn't."

"A girl's gotta do what a girl's gotta do."

Sarah walked out the front door, leaving Josh standing there with his mouth hanging open.

The moving truck was almost empty when Sarah crossed the street to greet the neighbor. Josh jogged across the street to catch up with her. The movers all stared at her like they hadn't see a woman in years. Josh draped an arm around her protectively, claiming his territory.

"You're jealous. That's sweet."

"Okay, let's just meet the guy and go home."

"He's the guy standing in the garage."

Sarah and Josh walked toward the garage where a skinny guy in a white polo shirt stood, holding a blender and looking around as if searching for an escape route.

"Hi! We're your new neighbors. I'm Sarah and this is my husband, Josh."

Sarah held out her hand and the man looked at it for a second as if he were afraid it was going to grow teeth and bite him. Sarah looked back at her husband, then back at the man and smiled. The skinny man reached out tentatively and gripped Sarah's hand.

"I-I'm Dale. D-Dale McCarthy."

Josh stepped up and stuck out his hand. The skinny man winced as if he thought Josh was about to strike him.

"Nice to meet you, Dale. This is a great house you've got here. We knew the previous owners. Nice old couple. They took great care of the place."

The skinny man shook Josh's hand and smiled nervously.

"Nice to meet you both. You live across the street?"

He looked at Sarah when he asked, then looked away, dropping his gaze toward the ground and grinning. Sarah once again felt a shiver race up her spine.

"Yeah, we live in the big two-story. So where ya from, Dale? What brings you to Vegas?"

"I'm from Mesquite originally but I just moved here from Henderson. I do Web design."

"I'm a blackjack dealer over at the Hollywood Galaxy Casino. The wife here just finished grad school and she's still working on her dissertation. It's a study of the sociological effects of pornography on society's collective unconscious or something like that. She's going for a doctorate in social science."

"Wow. Congratulations. You must be really proud."

He was staring at her breasts when he spoke little grin was widening. He was almost drooling.

"Thanks." Sarah folded her arms across her chest and crossed her legs, visibly uncomfortable. She looked at Josh and then back at the house and then back at the skinny little man in the white polo shirt.

"She's the brains of the operation. I'm hoping that soon she'll be the one taking care of me. They've already offered her a position at UNLV."

"Excuse me? Where do you want your TV?"

A large black man in gray overalls with LOW-COST MOVERS silk-screened across the chest stood holding a plasma screen in his enormous hands.

"Jesus! Be careful with that. Put it in the master bedroom."

"Well, Dale, I'll let you get back to moving. Nice to meet you."

"Nice to meet you too."

Once again Dale looked at Sarah when he spoke, then down at her breasts, then grinned awkwardly and looked away. Sarah turned and walked back across the street, anxious to get out of the man's sight. Something about the way the neighbor looked at her made her feel violated. She felt like she needed to take a shower. Josh had to almost run to catch up to her. He caught up with her just as she opened the front door and stepped inside. She shut the door behind him and locked it.

"What was that all about?"

Sarah closed her eyes and took several deep breaths, trying to slow her racing heartbeat.

"That fucking guy is weird. He creeps me the fuck out. He's got to be some kind of pervert or something. Why did you have to tell him I was home alone all day?"

"I didn't say that!"

"You told him that I was home working on my dissertation while you're at work. I don't want that weirdo knowing that I'm here by myself when you're at work."

"I'm sorry. I didn't think it was a big deal. I was just making small talk."

"It's okay. I'm probably just overreacting."

Josh smiled and gathered her into his arms.

"I've never seen you this agitated before. Are you sure you're all right?"

"I'm okay. It's just the way that pervert was looking at me. He kept sneaking peeks at my breasts. Did you see that? And he could barely make eye contact with me."

"The guy just looked like he was terrified. A lot of guys are just nervous around beautiful women. A computer geek like that has probably never been with a woman as beautiful as you without paying for her."

"Oh, thanks. That makes me feel better."

Josh brushed the hair from her face and kissed her on the lips. It was a long, deep kiss, sucking her tongue into his mouth, nibbling and sucking her bottom lip. Sarah had always loved the way he kissed her. Even after ten years of marriage it still made her knees weak.

"You want to go upstairs?" Sarah asked breathlessly.

"No. I want to fuck you right here on the floor."

Now it was Sarah's turn to blush.

CHAPTER SIX

Dale watched the couple walk back across the street. His eyes crept down to the woman's ass as if they had a will of their own. It was small but round and tight. She was beautiful. He had seen her standing in the window earlier. He couldn't really make out her features but he knew someone was there and now he knew that it had been her. She hadn't been wearing a bra when she met him. He could see her nipples poking through the fabric of her shirt. She had a lovely face too. Big doelike eyes, slightly slanted as if she had some Asian blood in her somewhere. She had high cheekbones and full lips. Her hair was shoulder length, a deep, lush black, with wild loose curls. Dale thought she looked more like a movie star than a doctor of sociology or social science or whatever it was she was studying. She looked a lot like his mother.

Her husband had said that she didn't work, but that he did. That would leave Dale and his new neighbor plenty of time to get acquainted. But Dale wasn't sure he could wait for the guy to go to work on Monday. Luckily he didn't have to. It didn't matter how big the guy was if he didn't know it was coming. And Dale was going to make sure that neither of them knew what hit them. An erection was already tenting the front of his jeans.

Dale spent the rest of the day organizing his things in his new home. The movers had all gone and boxes sat upon boxes in every room of the house. The house was small, only 1,300 square feet. But it was perfect for him. It had two bedrooms, two baths, and a den with a window that looked out onto the street. His neighbor had been right. The old couple who had owned the house previously had taken great care of the place. For such a small place they had packed it with expensive upgrades. They must have spent almost as much up-grading the place as they had on the house itself. They must have thought this would be their last house, the house they would die in. Then they had lost most of their retirement in the stock market and their interest-only loan had adjusted and they'd been forced into foreclosure. Dale had picked up the house for half of what it had been worth a year ago.

The appliances in the kitchen were stainless steel, the cabinets were cherry wood with brushed nickel handles and glass fronts. Dale thought he would have to get better dinnerware. His dishes were mismatched and half of them were stained or chipped. Not that he ever entertained but he still liked his place to look good just in case, and seeing his old cheap dinner plates through the glass cabinet doors made the house look cheaper. It made it look like he didn't really belong in such a nice place.

The knobs and hinges on all the doors in the house were also brushed nickel, like the handles on the cabinets. There were faux wood blinds, which matched the cabinets, on all the windows. The floors in the kitchen, living room, hallway, and both bathrooms were covered in twenty-by-twenty-inch travertine, white with or-ange, black, and brown veins running through it. The wood floor in the den was the same cherry color as the cabinets and shutters. The only things Dale didn't like were the white walls. With all the other upgrades you would have thought they would have painted the walls a different color, maybe an accent wall or two or a faux finish. He would have to take care of that later.

Dale walked into the den and began unpacking his computer. He moved his desk over by the window so he could look out at the house across the street while he was working. He began unpacking his printer, his scanner. He plugged in his digital webcam and the speaker on his computer and then began unpacking all of his books.

It took him almost two hours but Dale managed to unpack, organize, and decorate his den. His bookcases were filled with books on Web design, true crime, and detective thrillers, along with crime-scene investigation and police procedure and old erotic novels from Anais Nin, Leopold Von Sacher-Masoch, Henry Miller, and de Sade. In several boxes that remained unopened were black-market DVDs and old VHS tapes of vintage pornography, including S-and-M movies from the eighties and nineties and some more modern torture films.

His computer was up and working. A picture of his mom and dad hung on the wall opposite the window. He had even hung up a couple of movie posters from two of his favorite movies, *Pulp Fiction* and *Reservoir Dogs*. Dale loved Quentin Tarantino movies. Tarantino was his favorite director.

Dale had posters of several Russ Meyers films still rolled up that he was planning to hang in his bedroom. That would be his next project. The movers hadn't even put his bed together and his mattress and box spring were leaning against the door to the master bathroom. At this rate, he wouldn't be done until well after dark. That would just barely leave him time for dinner and a brief nap before it was time to visit the new neighbors.

CHAPTER SEVEN

Sarah watched Josh rinse the dishes and stack them in the dishwasher while she curled up on the couch waiting for *Real Time with Bill Maher* to start. Josh had made dinner tonight and she had to admit that it wasn't half bad. He'd found a recipe for enchiladas in one of those little recipe books you picked up at the supermarket and had baked her some, using tortillas, Monterey Jack cheese, fire-roasted red chilies, cream-of-mushroom soup, and Old El Paso green enchilada sauce. It was actually pretty good and Sarah had eaten half the pan. She'd have to do a long run tomorrow or else she'd be packing on the pounds. She knew Josh would love her even if she got fat.

"Would you still love me if I gained a bunch of weight?" It didn't hurt to ask.

"When you marry a woman, you always have to assume that she's gonna gain at least thirty or forty pounds. You've still got like twenty pounds to go."

"What? I'm still the same size I was when you met me."

"I don't know about that. You've been eating a lot of ice cream lately."

"You're a pig. You know that don't you? A male-chauvinist pig."

"That's just how you like me."

"Now you've got me thinking about ice cream. Why don't you run to the store and get us some?"

"Why don't you? I cooked dinner. Remember?"

Sarah hugged the afghan wrapped around her.

"But I'm so comfy."

"You're the one who wants ice cream. I'm just the guy who deserves it."

"You're such a jerk. I can't believe you're trying to make me feel guilty."

"Guilty for what? For not getting ice cream for your poor tired hubby after he's worked hard all week and then slaved over a hot stove all day to make you a nice meal? I did cook you breakfast *and* dinner."

"Well, I made lunch and you burned the pancakes this morning, so we're even. But the enchiladas were pretty good. I guess that's worth a trip to the grocery store."

"Wait until I finish with the dishes. I'll go with you."

"That's a good hubby."

"Don't push it, woman."

Josh and Sarah were arm in arm, looking like new love as they walked out of the house and climbed into their SUV. When they drove off, they glanced only casually at the house across the street. There was a light on in the den and Sarah thought she could make out the silhouette of the neighbor's head through the closed blinds.

An hour later they were curled up in bed with a couple pints of Ben and Jerry's ice cream, watching *Dexter* on Showtime. Sarah was asleep before the credits rolled.

Josh must have gotten up and turned off the television after she'd fallen asleep because the room was completely black when Sarah awoke suddenly to the sound of her husband choking. She reached out for him and her hand came back wet. Josh was bleeding. His throat had been cut. He was choking on his own blood. When Sarah's eyes adjusted to the darkness, she saw the new neighbor standing above her husband, stabbing him in his chest again and again.

"Oh my God! What are you doing? Josh! Oh my God! Josh! Get the fuck away from my husband! You're killing him! Heeelllp!"

Sarah grabbed hold of her husband and began scrambling off the bed, trying to drag him with her, away from the crazed man with the knife.

The neighbor put the knife, dripping with her husband's blood, against Sarah's throat and raised a finger to his lips.

"Shhhhhhh. Shut. The. Fuck. Up. I don't want to kill you but I will and I'll enjoy it." Dale smiled to emphasize the point. "I'm going to fuck you anyway. Dead or alive."

"Y-you-you killed Josh. Oh my God. You killed him!"

The neighbor's fist lashed out and punched Sarah in her mouth, knocking her back onto the bed.

"I told you to be quiet. Since you won't cooperate, I'm just gonna have to kill you first."

The neighbor climbed over her husband's corpse and straddled Sarah's stomach. He drew the knife across Sarah's throat, cutting through both her jugular vein and carotid artery and lacerating her windpipe all in one clean cut. Sarah watched her own blood spray out over her breasts. She was struggling to breathe, lungs filling with blood, drowning, as she watched the neighbor begin to undress. When she saw him remove his erect penis from his pants she hoped that she would be long dead before she felt that puny uncircumcised thing inside of her.

The neighbor was fondling her bloodied breasts and stroking his ugly little cock. Her blood squished between his fingers as he squeezed her breasts and pinched her nipples. Sarah was beginning to lose consciousness. The neighbor slid his cock between her breasts and was using the blood from her severed throat as lubrication as he fucked her tits. When he finally came, his cum splashing onto her neck and face and mingling with the blood in a sickening mess of red and white, Sarah had already begun to convulse. By the time the neighbor was hard again, she was already dead, sparing her from feeling his cock between her thighs and in her mouth.

It was still dark when Sarah woke up in her bed with the taste of blood and semen on her tongue. Josh was snoring quietly beside her. The sheets smelled fresh, like they had just been washed. So did Sarah. Even Josh smelled unusually clean. He smelled like Irish Spring and ammonia. Sarah screamed.

She kept screaming even when Josh woke up and wrapped his big, strong arms around her. Even when he began to rock her back and forth and stroke her hair and tell her that everything would be okay. She was still screaming as he kissed the tears from her eyes. His eyes were half closed and he was still blinking the sleep from his eyes and trying to clear his head but even half-asleep his first priority had been her.

"It's okay, Sarah. It was just a bad dream. Everything's okay."

Sarah checked Josh's neck and chest. Then she checked

her own. There were no wounds, no blood. She dropped her head onto Josh's shoulder and began to weep.

"That sick bastard. You don't know what he did to me. He killed us. You were dead. We both were. The new neighbor . . . that guy . . . uh, Dale . . . he murdered us!"

"It was just a dream."

"No! He stabbed me! He stabbed you and . . . and he raped me! It wasn't a dream!"

"Baby, you're okay. You're not dead. I'm not dead. It was a dream. That's all. A bad dream. Now go back to sleep. You're safe. I'm right here. I won't let anything happen to you."

Sarah laid her head down on the pillow and pulled Josh's arms around her. He snuggled up against her back, spooning with her as she slowly drifted back to sleep. He didn't notice the door across the street open and the porch light click off, but Sarah did. Sarah shivered and began to weep again. She buried her face in the pillow and shook her head back and forth.

"No. No. No. No."

It was a long time before she fell asleep again.

CHAPTER EIGHT

When Sarah woke the next morning she didn't remember anything that had happened the night before. Her mouth still tasted like pennies and the smell of soap and disinfectant still permeated the air, tickling the fine hairs in Sarah's nostrils. She stretched, looked over at Josh, who was already dressed and ready for work, and smiled.

"Good morning, lover."

"Good morning. That must have been one hell of a dream you had last night."

"What?"

"You woke up screaming in the middle of the night. You said you had a dream about that guy who just moved in across the street killing both of us?"

"That little skinny guy? I'd probably kick his ass."

"You said he raped you and stabbed us both to death."

"Wow. He must have really creeped me out the other day. I don't remember any of that."

Sarah looked over at the clock on the nightstand. It was seven thirty in the morning.

"Aren't you late for work?"

"I've got a few minutes. I just wanted to make sure you were okay before I left."

"I'm fine. Go ahead and get to work. I'll let you know if the neighbor tries to break in and kill me."

Sarah winked coyly and draped her arms around the back of Josh's neck and gave him a light kiss on the lips.

"You sure you don't want me to stay?"

"Not unless you're going to spend the day fucking me. But honestly, I'm still sore from yesterday. I need a few hours to rest up."

"You are incorrigible."

"Maybe dreaming about the neighbor all night made me horny."

"Dreaming about Santa Claus makes you horny."

"He does look good in those big leather boots and he carries a whip."

"You have problems."

"And you have fifteen minutes to get to work."

Josh bent over and kissed Sarah again.

"Good-bye, sweetheart."

"Bye, lover."

Sarah rolled back over and snuggled up against her pillow as she listened to Josh's footfalls descend the stairs and walk out the front door. The door closed quietly with just a slight click and then the garage door rose as Josh pulled the SUV out of the garage. Sarah squeezed the pillow and a small red dot appeared on the pillowcase. She threw back her sheets and the indentation of her body was outlined with blood that had seeped up through the mattress.

"What the hell?"

Sarah climbed from the bed looking at the bloody mattress and pillow. Vague, dreamlike memories, nightmarish flashes of blood and meat and pain drifted into her head, then fled almost as soon as they appeared, leaving terrifying afterimages and a horrible feeling of unease. Images of Josh with his throat cut open, the neighbor's face grinning at her, her own breasts splattered with blood. Bile rose in her throat, burning her esophagus.

"Oh, God. Oh, God. What's going on? What the hell is going on?"

Sarah ran into the bathroom and regurgitated into the toilet. The image of the neighbor fucking her blood-soaked breasts with his oily little cock invaded her mind and she vomited again and again until green stomach bile was the only thing that would come up. Sarah sat by the toilet, trying to catch her breath, the nightmares receding from memory. She stood up, walked into the bedroom, and began stripping the sheets from the bed.

The mattress looked like an abattoir. It was saturated in red. There was a small red puddle where she had lain. The blood had soaked through the sheets and stained the bottom of the comforter.

"What the hell?"

Sarah flipped the mattress, then took the sheets downstairs along with the stained comforter. Her hands shook and tears ran down her cheeks as she shoved them into the washing machine. She dumped a scoop of detergent into the machine, turned it on, and ran out of the room.

Scooping up her cell phone, she dialed Josh's number. There was no answer. He must have already been on the casino floor. The voice mail picked up after six rings.

"Josh? I think something's wrong with me. I'm bleeding. I mean . . . I think I am. There's blood all over the mattress. I don't think I'm on my period, but there's blood everywhere. And I keep seeing pieces of that dream, that nightmare. It just feels so real . . . and . . . and all the blood. Call me back. Please call me."

Sarah hung up the phone and sat down at the kitchen table. She tried to remember the dream from the night before but the images were growing increasingly faint. By the time she took the sheets out of the washing machine and put them in the dryer, the dream had been completely forgotten. She started the dryer, then piled the comforter into the washer. She dumped a scoop of laundry detergent into the machine and shut the lid.

Sarah gradually convinced herself that she'd simply started her period early and experienced an unusually heavy flow. She thought about going to the doctor's office. It couldn't be healthy to bleed that much but she supposed that that was the reason they made the jumbo-size tampons for "heavy-flow days." She'd never had a heavy-flow day before. It looked like someone had bled to death. Sarah tried her best to ignore all the elements of her menstruation theory that didn't fit. She walked into the kitchen and popped a multivitamin and an iron pill.

While the sheets were drying, Sarah decided to go for a run. She needed to clear her head, to get away from the house, to think about anything but blood and death and nightmares. Feeling the wind in her hair, her heart pumping hard in her chest, the steady rhythm of her own breaths synchronized with her footfalls always made her forget about everything else.

Sarah put in a panty liner just in case she started to bleed again; then she pulled on a pair of running shorts and a dry-fit tank top. Sarah grabbed her iPod and her Garmin GPS navigator and headed out the door. She went through a quick routine of stretches on the driveway, staring at the new neighbor's front door as if she expected him to burst out of the house and attack her on the front walk. The vertical blinds on the front window parted slightly and Sarah hit the play button on her iPod, squeezed the tiny headphones into her ears, and took off jogging down the street faster than she'd intended just as "Kerosene" by Miranda Lambert began to play.

"Light 'em up and watch them burn, teach them what they need to learn . . ." She sang out as she pumped her legs at nearly a full sprint. She was breathing hard after only three blocks. Sarah checked her Garmin and realized that she had just run three blocks in less than three minutes. She had to adjust her pace. It took her another two blocks to calm herself down and steady her breathing. She hated the fact that the guy freaked her out so much. She wanted to go knock on his door and kick his scrawny little ass just to get over it.

Sarah jogged briskly past rows of for-sale signs lined up like tombstones. Nearly every third or fourth house was abandoned. It had never occurred to Sarah before how deserted the neighborhood was becoming. When she and Josh had moved in the community was still under construction. New couples and families had been moving in daily. Then construction had slowed to a halt and a mass exodus had begun as home values plummeted and people began defaulting on their loans. Now, half the homes in the neighborhood were in foreclosure. Her morning jog had grown increasingly depressing as every day she noticed a new house with a for-sale sign in front of it. Most of the signs contained the ominous sub-caption BANK-OWNED.

Miranda Lambert clicked off and Revolting Cocks came blaring through Sarah's headphones screaming, "Let the bodies hit the floor!" Sarah had to resist the urge to start sprinting again. Something about that song always got her blood pumping and it struck her as oddly appropriate as she jogged through her dying neighborhood, which was turning into a ghost town little by little.

There was an elementary school a few blocks away and Sarah felt a stirring of her maternal instincts at the light, airy, high-pitched squeals of children's laughter. She stared at the joy-filled faces climbing on the jungle gym and running in reckless circles on the rubberized playground. Every time she passed the playground she reconsidered her decision to wait to have kids. She wanted to have Josh's babies. She just wasn't sure that she wanted them right now. She wasn't sure that she was ready to give up her carefree lifestyle, her freedom, and most of all, her figure. Sarah continued jogging past the school and soon the laughter faded into the background.

After another mile, Sarah passed an active-adult fifty-five-and-older age-restricted community that was also half built. Construction had been ceased once funding had run out and the real-estate market had frozen after only a quarter of the houses had been built. Finished homes stood interspersed with dirt lots. Yesterday, there had been an ambulance in front of one of the homes and Sarah had seen a gurney being carted out with a body covered in a white sheet. In this community, a for-sale sign didn't always mean a bank foreclosure.

Sarah checked her pace on her Garmin compared to yesterday's run. The little computer screen showed where she had been at this time the day before and she was nearly half of a block ahead of her previous run.

She picked up her pace, trying to put a full block between herself and the imaginary runner in her device, racing against herself.

An hour later, when Sarah made it back to her house, she was drenched in sweat. Josh had always told her that she sweated like a man. Her dry-fit tank top was completely soaked. She checked her Garmin and saw that she had shaved a full minute off her run and burned 620 calories. She looked across the street and the vertical blinds in the new neighbor's front window were swaying back and forth as if someone had just closed them. Sarah hurried into the house.

The dryer had stopped. Sarah gathered the sheets and dumped them into her laundry basket; then she wrestled the big down comforter into the dryer and set it on high. She was walking up the stairs with her laundry basket when the phone began to ring. Sarah ran up the last couple of stairs, dropped the laundry basket on the bed, and snatched up her phone.

"Are you all right?"

"Well, it's a good thing I wasn't passed out on the floor bleeding to death."

"Are you on your period?"

The way he asked the question infuriated her for no reason she could articulate.

"No. I just woke up in a pool of blood . . . my blood . . . I-I think. Maybe my dream was real. Maybe the neighbor really did stab us both to death."

"Are you serious?"

"No, I'm not serious. Do I sound like I'm dead?" Sarah shot back in an irritated tone. She couldn't explain why she was so annoyed with him today.

"Do you need me to pick you up some . . . um . . . some feminine products on the way home?"

"No, I've got plenty of tampons at home. Thanks. Next time answer the fucking phone." She hung up and sat down hard on the bed. She knew that she was wrong for lashing out at Josh but she also knew that in minutes he'd be so wrapped up in his work, laughing and joking with his customers, that he would have forgotten all about it. He was good that way. It was one of the things about him that annoyed the shit out of her.

CHAPTER NINE

They had just come upstairs after washing the dinner dishes. Tonight, Sarah had cooked dinner. She'd made Josh's favorite, a big, fat, juicy porterhouse from Omaha Steaks with cracked pepper pounded into it and blue cheese on top. It was her way of apologizing for acting like an asshole earlier.

Sarah sat on the edge of the bed reading a book. The light on the nightstand and the TV were on. Josh was lying beside her with a pillow over his head, trying to block out the light and noise.

"Will you please go to sleep? Are you still tripping about that dream?"

"No. Yes. I don't know. I just can't sleep."

Conan O'Brien was making fun of the audience for not laughing at his jokes. It was an odd sort of comedy that Sarah couldn't get into. She switched the channel to Spike TV and began watching an old replay of the Ultimate Fighting Championship. Matt Hughes was getting his ass kicked by an out-of-shape B.J. Penn. Sarah usually loved that type of blood sport but tonight she just wasn't in the mood. She turned to Comedy Central, then lay back on the bed as the gang from South Park pranced across the screen.

She opened her book, a novel about zombies on an old battleship written by a relatively new author named

Brian Keene. Normally she loved a good horror novel, and Brian Keene was one of her favorites, but it was just too gory for her tonight. She looked at an Edward Lee novel that sat unopened on her nightstand with a picture of a winged devil on the cover. *No way*, she thought. Instead, she picked up a book about the people you meet in heaven after you die. After only a few pages, she fell asleep with the television still on, Cartman and Stan singing about Christmas poo in the background.

Sarah slept fitfully, horrible images of knives and blood dashed through her mind, of Josh screaming in pain, herself being raped, mutilated, and abused. She woke up twice, exhausted and drenched in sweat. When she woke up in the morning she was convinced that there was more to these dreams than just her subconscious overreacting to a creepy neighbor.

"Josh? Wake up, Josh."

"Is it time for work?"

"No. I just need to talk to you . . . about these dreams I keep having. They're really starting to freak me out."

"You had another one? Like last night?"

"I think so. I can't really remember. But I think it was bad. Really bad."

"Do you want to see a psychiatrist or something?"

"No, Josh. I think something is really going on. I want to go to the cops."

"You can't call the cops because of a dream."

There were tears in Sarah's eyes when she looked over at Josh.

"But what if it isn't a dream? What if he's really doing things to me in my sleep?"

Josh turned over and faced Sarah. He rubbed the

sleep from his eyes and gave Sarah his full attention. He stared into her eyes for a long moment before he spoke, reading her expression as if he were trying to solve a complex equation.

"Then you wouldn't need to call the cops because I'd kill him myself."

Sarah smiled halfheartedly and hugged her husband tight.

"What time do you go to work today?"

"I work the swing shift today, four to midnight."

"I don't want to be here alone tonight."

"I made some extra money in tips last night. Some dot-com millionaire younger than my little brother tipped me three hundred dollars before he started losing. Why don't I take you to buy a gun? With the way the neighborhood is changing it's probably not a bad idea anyway."

"Are you serious?" Sarah lit up at the idea. "What kind?"

She swiped the tears from her eyes with the backs of her hands and sat up in bed.

Josh looked at her with a bemused expression on his face. He reached out and brushed the hair from her face.

"You really aren't like other women. You know that?"

"Why do you say that?"

"Most women would object to the idea of having a gun in the house but you can't wait to buy one. You're too eager, in fact. Should I be afraid here? You're not going to use it on me, are you?"

"Not as long as you keep fucking me when I want to be fucked."

She kissed him on his lips, then rubbed her hands over his shoulders and down his arms. His biceps were still hard and muscular despite the layer of fat he'd put on since moving to Vegas. He'd had less time to exercise and spent too much time at the buffets. She ran her hand over his belly, which had expanded quite a bit in the last few years. It jiggled as she rubbed it. She ran her hand back up to his chest. His pecs were still big and hard like a bodybuilder's. They were even bigger than they'd been in college. Josh had begun powerlifting the last few years because it was quicker. He'd pile as much weight onto the bar as he could, do two or three reps, do that for three or four sets and then he was done. His entire routine took him less than twenty minutes a day. It was all he had time for.

He may not have had one of those ripped-up bodies full of cuts and striations with veins popping out everywhere like Arnold Schwarzenegger, but these days neither did Arnold. Josh was still a big, strong man despite his growing paunch. Sarah ran her hands over his belly, then down between his legs where he was already hard. Josh was not a small man in any regard. She hated to admit that the size of his cock had been one of the things she'd first fallen in love with. She knew that women weren't supposed to care about the physical, especially when it came to what a man was packing. It was supposed to be all about being treated right and cared for and Josh was good at all of that too. He was patient and supportive and attentive and treated Sarah like a queen. But being hung like a porn star certainly didn't hurt.

"Mmmmm. Is that for me?"

She crawled beneath the covers and swirled her tongue around the head of his cock, licking up and down and flicking the head with her tongue as he squirmed and moaned. She continued teasing his cock with her tongue until he couldn't take it anymore and reached down and grabbed her by the hair, forcing his cock down her throat. She loved it when he did that. Josh wasn't a rough lover. He was sweet and loving, preferring to make love even when she was in the mood for a good hard fuck. But she had her ways of awakening the beast in him.

Josh aggressively fucked her throat and Sarah tried her best to ignore it whenever he felt like he'd shoved his cock too far down her throat and paused to ask if she was okay. Sometimes he was so nice it almost killed the mood. Josh may have had a huge cock but no man had made her gag since she was a teenager. It was no secret that she hadn't exactly been a virgin when they met, but Josh still treated her like she was made of china. It was usually pretty sweet but right now it was annoying. She grabbed his ass cheeks and forced his cock all the way down her throat past her tonsils; then she squirmed a finger up his ass to massage his prostate.

Sarah heard him gasp and felt his entire body tense. Right then she felt like the most powerful woman in the world. She was in complete control. He was completely helpless. A devilish part of her wanted to bite him a little just to let him know how helpless he really was, but Josh wasn't the type of man who needed to be reminded of that type of thing. He was the type who saved women from those types of men. Instead, she swirled her tongue around his cock while it was still buried in her throat. Back in high school, she and her girlfriends had practiced giving head on carrots and bananas, until she could swallow an entire banana with no problem. They'd read in a book on sexual positions, which her friend Ellie had taken from her mother's nightstand, that women were supposed to practice. It had paid off.

"Oh my God!" Josh cried out and his legs shot out straight and began to tremble.

He began fucking her throat harder and more urgently. His entire body quivered and he ejaculated down her throat. He was still coming as she slid her mouth back up to the end of his cock.

Josh came like a porn star too. He could shoot a fly off the wall across the room. Sarah's mouth was completely filled with his warm semen when she rose from the covers. She gargled his seed, making bubbles and letting some dribble out of the corners of her mouth. Then she swallowed and licked her lips, scooping up the semen that had dribbled down her chin and licking it from her fingertips. She smiled, watching Josh's jaw drop. She'd learned long ago that one of the keys to a successful marriage was throwing something new into the mix every now and again. Internet porn was a great source of new bedroom tricks. And Sarah had a lot of time on her hands to learn new things.

"That was incredible! Wh-where did you learn to do that?" Josh was still breathing hard and little spasms continued to wrack his body intermittently.

"My turn."

She crawled up Josh's body and straddled his face. He went to work immediately, flicking her swollen clitoris with his tongue and stabbing it up inside of her, then dragging his tongue down to her anus and giving the rose-colored bud of her asshole the same attention, alternating back and forth between clitoris and anus while Sarah scratched at the headboard and cried out in ecstasy.

"Oh, fuck! Oh, fuck! Oh, my fucking God! Yes! Yes! Oh, fuck, YES!"

When she came, it was like the world was ending.

Her body began to spasm and convulse as orgasms tore through her.

Suddenly, images of the neighbor began flashing through her mind. Images of him fucking her from behind, forcing her to look at him in the mirror over the vanity as he raped her ass, bent over Josh's lifeless corpse, then slit her throat from ear to ear. Another orgasm ripped through her as she screamed. She climbed off Josh and sat with her back against the headboard, still reliving the rape.

Josh smiled, unaware.

"Wow. I can't remember the last time you came like that. You definitely are not on your period."

Sarah began to cry.

"What? What did I do?"

"I was raped. I was raped, Josh! The neighbor, Dale, he raped me!"

"Are you sure? You sure this wasn't a dream?"

"He raped me!"

Josh jumped up from the bed and snatched up his clothes. He walked into the closet and came out with a semiautomatic handgun that Sarah never even knew he had. He pulled on his jeans, moving fast, and Sarah was afraid he was going to zip up his cock in his zipper. She had never seen him look so angry.

"Where'd you get that? What are you going to do?"

"I bought it a few weeks ago when one of the guys at work got beaten up in the parking lot by a bunch of teenagers, some sort of gang. It's a Glock nine-millimeter. I'm going to put a couple of hollow points in Dale's head. You stay here. Just call the police and tell them what happened."

Josh walked out of the room and started down the stairs. Sarah was so confused. She didn't know what to do, what was real, or what was in her head. She looked around the room, searching for something that would make the whole thing make some kind of sense. She looked across the street and could see Dale cutting the small six-by-eight-foot patch of lawn in his front yard with one of those old manual lawnmowers. He was sweating profusely and the muscles in his skinny little arms were quivering as he struggled to push the lawn-mower. He looked so weak and helpless. The whole thing was just so ridiculous. Dale looked like anything but a rapist and murderer. It couldn't have been real.

"Josh, no! Wait!"

Sarah ran out of the room and dashed down the stairs to catch him.

"Wait, Josh! It was a dream. It was just a dream."

Josh was still moving toward the front door. He cocked the nine-millimeter, jacking a round into the chamber.

"Josh, no!"

Sarah raced past him to block the front door.

"It was just a dream! Don't kill him. I was just dreaming. I don't know what's wrong with me."

"Are you sure?"

"I'm sure. I don't know why I keep having them. I don't know what it is about that guy that freaks me out so much, but it was just a dream. I promise I'll go get help. I'll go see someone."

Josh relaxed and gathered Sarah into his arms.

"Okay, baby. I'll make sure we get you some help. But get dressed first. We're going to buy you a gun."

CHAPTER TEN

On the way to American Marksman they stopped at the hotel to get Josh's paycheck. A white F-350 pickup truck cut them off as they drove up the ramp to the second-floor parking level and Josh had to slam on the brakes to avoid hitting them. Josh leaned on the horn and the three rednecks in the car glared at him and the driver flipped him off. Sarah winced. That was one thing you didn't do to Josh. He was not the most even-tempered guy to begin with and disrespecting him when you were in the wrong brought out his violent side. Josh was out of the car before Sarah could restrain him.

"You could have fucking killed us!"

"Fuck you! You should have been watching where you were going."

Josh walked right up to the car and put his foot into the driver's-side door, leaving a huge dent. The three occupants of the car leaped out. The driver was the closest to Josh and the minute he stepped out of the car Josh launched a fist into the man's temple, knocking him cold. The passenger door closest to him had opened at the same time but the tall skinny guy in the backseat had been a little slower getting out, giving him an extra thirty seconds before Josh smeared his nose all over his face in an explosion of blood that gushed down his face, turning his white T-shirt crimson. The passenger door on the other side of the truck had opened at the same time but the overweight guy in the black and blue NASCAR hat and the multicolored Hawaiian shirt with topless hula dancers on it was in no hurry to join his friends. He held up his hands as he walked around the truck as if Josh were aiming a gun at him.

"It's cool, man. It's cool."

Sarah knew that he wanted to hit the guy anyway. Josh turned reluctantly and walked back to the car. It was this side of Josh that made people certain that he abused her until they saw them together. As big and mean as her husband was, he was a teddy bear with her.

They parked in front of the hotel valet and Josh let one of the attendants know that he was just picking up his check and would be leaving in minutes, then jogged into the casino while Sarah waited for him in the car. Sarah thought about Josh beating up those two guys and began to laugh. This wasn't the first time she'd seen him beat the crap out of someone. It had been a regular part of Saturday nights back in college. If he wasn't getting into fights on the ice during one of his hockey games he was fighting someone in a bar or a movie theater or just walking down the street. The funny thing was that he never set out to start the fights. Guys just liked fucking with him. They felt they had to prove their manhood by challenging the biggest guy in the room, which was usually Josh. Something about Sarah's husband apparently threatened most men. It was even worse when the guys were drunk and feeling ten feet tall and bulletproof. Josh never hesitated to rip the *S* off a guy's chest and remind him of his mortality. Sarah suspected that he secretly delighted in it. Still, guys were always trying to test him, which drove him crazy.

It was hard for Sarah to rectify the softhearted gentleman she knew with the guy who had just minutes ago knocked out two guys in the parking garage. But Sarah loved the fact that he had that in him. It made her feel safe and, truth be told, it turned her on more than a little bit.

Josh returned to the car and after tipping the valet for letting him leave his car there, he drove out of the garage and back onto Las Vegas Boulevard. The 215 expressway was only a couple blocks away and soon they were headed southwest at seventy miles per hour. It took them less than twenty minutes to make it across town and soon they were exiting the freeway on Eastern Avenue.

American Marksman was a big store that looked like a supermarket from the outside; located in a strip mall on Eastern Avenue, it was by far the biggest store on the block. Sarah was surprised by how many people were packed into the store shopping with their families. Apparently, small-town folks weren't the only people who clung to guns when the economy went bad.

Some of them had infants in strollers as if they were just out bargain hunting at Wal-Mart. She was even more surprised by the number of single women, young and old, shopping for handguns, rifles, and shotguns. There were the typical rednecks, cops, and wannabe gangsters too. She wondered how often criminals were in here shopping for guns right alongside the cops who would later arrest them?

Josh and Sarah walked over to one of the many display cases. A salesman with a thick Alabama accent walked over to them.

"Good morning. What can I do ya fer?"

"I'm looking for a handgun for my wife."

"Something little?"

"No. Something big," Sarah said.

Both Josh and the salesman looked at her, surprised.

"Well, okay then little lady. You ever handled a weapon before?"

"My father was a lifetime NRA member. He taught all of us how to shoot. It's been about fifteen or twenty years though, so I'm sure I'm rusty."

"You wantin' this for home protection or to carry around witcha?"

Sarah looked at Josh, who shrugged in response.

"Home, I guess."

"Then how about a .38 Special? Smith and Wesson makes a nice one and it's relatively cheap."

"I don't want a revolver."

"Okay. Well, the customer's always right." He reached under the counter and took out a small semiautomatic. "How about a .380? It has about the same stopping power as a .38."

"Too small. I want to put a big-ass hole in whatever I shoot at."

Sarah didn't smile when she spoke.

"Then you want a .40. It has more stopping power than the nine-millimeter but it doesn't have the extra kick of a .44. Glock and Sig Sauer make nice ones but they're pretty pricey. We do have a used Sig on sale for five hundred dollars."

"That's a sale? How much is it regular price?"

"Nine hundred dollars."

"Wow. I guess that is a sale then." She turned to Josh. "Can we afford it?"

"Well, the mortgage is paid and we don't have a car payment. We'll have to tighten the belts a bit but, yeah, we can afford it."

"Then that's what I want."

"How many bullets you want?"

"I want two or three boxes so I can practice."

"How about two boxes of target ammo and then a box of hollow points for that stopping power ya want? How's that sound?"

"That sounds about right."

"You want to try it out first? We got an indoor range here in the back."

"Sounds like a great idea to me. What do you say?" Josh said.

Sarah shrugged.

"Then let's go for it. I guess."

The salesman handed them both a pair of plastic goggles, headphones, and a couple of paper targets with a bull's-eye in the center.

"Do you have any of those targets that look like people?"

The salesman cocked an eyebrow at her, then looked at Josh as if to say, "Are you sure you know what you're doin' here, buddy?"

Josh held up his hands in surrender.

"Yeah. They's two dollars a piece."

"I'll take five."

The salesman shook his head and took five targets out of a cabinet behind the counter. The targets had pictures of men in ski masks holding guns. They looked like the type of criminals Batman beat up in between fighting supervillains in the comic books Sarah had read as a child. The salesman handed the targets to Sarah, then opened the door and led the way into the shooting range.

"My name's Mike by the way."

He held out a big, meaty hand with hairy knuckles. Josh shook his hand first and then Sarah did the same.

"Josh and Sarah Lincoln."

"Pleased to meet you both. Go ahead and put the goggles and headphones on before we get in there."

He put on his own, then waited while Sarah and Josh donned their own protective equipment.

The range was full of people lined up putting holes in paper targets. There were couples like Josh and Sarah, fathers with their sons, and single men and women. The sound of the gunshots was deafening. They walked up to an empty booth and the salesman put the gun on the table along with two boxes of ammo and ejected the clip, laying the gun and the clip side by side.

"Now you load the clip like this."

The salesman shook out eight bullets into his hand, picked up the clip, and began pushing the bullets into it one at a time with his thumb. Then he took them all back out and handed the clip to Sarah.

"You try it."

Sarah loaded the clip, pushing the bullets in with her thumb just as Mike had done.

"Then you slide the clip into the gun like this, click the safety off. See that red dot? When you see that dot that means the safety's off. You just pull the slide back like this and that puts a round in the chamber there. Now you're ready to go. Just line up the sights, like this. Take a deep breath. Hold it. And squeeze the trigger."

Sarah went through a hundred rounds of ammo. By the time they were done she felt like an old pro. She was almost eager for someone to come walking into her bedroom uninvited. She wanted to see what those hollow points would do to human flesh.

"Why didn't we ever do this before? This is fun. We should go shooting every weekend," Sarah said.

"So, I guess we're buying the gun then?" Josh asked.

"Hell yeah we are!"

They walked back into the store area with Mike.

"Do you have a blue card?"

"I do. I just bought a gun here a few weeks ago."

"Then you should register it in your name. Otherwise you're going to have to go through a two-week waiting period while we do a background check on her. If it's just going to be in the house and she won't be carryin' it around, then it won't matter whose name it's in. Eventually, you're probably gonna want to get one registered in her name though."

Sarah watched Josh hand the salesman his gun permit and his driver's license. She felt amazingly relieved. If anything happened now, at least she'd be able to defend herself. The salesman copied down the information and took a Xerox of it along with Josh's driver's license. He handed both the license and the permit back to Josh and Josh handed him the credit card. Minutes later, Sarah and Josh were walking out of the store with her new gun.

"We need to make one more stop."

"Where at?"

"I want to get you something to hide that in where you can get to it fast if something happens. Just in case."

Sarah leaned closer to him and kissed him.

"Thank you, Josh. I know you think I'm losing my

mind but I appreciate you doing all of this to make me feel safe. You could have just taken me to the psych ward to get my head examined."

"Don't worry. I'm going to do that too."

Sarah punched him in the arm, then kissed him again.

When they pulled up at The Spy Shop, Sarah looked confused.

"Trust me. This place is cool. You're going to love it."

He looked like a little kid in a toy store as Josh rushed through the door, nearly forgetting to hold the door for Sarah, then catching it just before it swung back and almost smacked her in the face.

"Sorry, my fault. But just wait until you see the stuff they have in here."

Sarah followed her husband to the back of the store where deceptively innocuous clothing hung on racks. She could not wait to see what kind of weird stuff they'd built into these garments. She felt like James Bond preparing for a mission. There were leather jackets with built-in bulletproof vests and holsters, purses with a slit in them for storing a gun for easy access. There were kitchen aprons with gun pouches, negligees and garters with built-in holsters, a Kevlar baseball cap, a pair of gloves with a built-in Taser gun, Kevlar pillowcases with hidden gun pouches.

"Okay, this place is pretty cool."

They ended up buying the Kevlar pillow with the hideaway pouch for a gun. On the way out of the store, Sarah stopped to look at the surveillance equipment.

"I think maybe we should get a burglar alarm."

"I don't know if the house is prewired."

"I think it is. We just need to hire a company to set it up and monitor it."

"I'll look into it tomorrow. It sounds expensive."

She picked up a teddy bear with a camera in it.

"What's this? He's cute."

The man behind the counter perked up, sensing a sale. Sarah guessed that he was probably on commission.

"That's our nanny cam. It attaches to a VCR. You just turn it on and it'll record everything that goes on in the room. Then you just play it back when you get home."

"That's pretty cool."

Josh took the bear out of her hands and handed it back to the salesman.

"Maybe next time. We're going broke here."

"Oh, I'm sorry. We can take the pillow back if you want. We don't need it."

"No, I want you to have it. I don't work as hard as I do for nothing. We can afford it. Let's just leave before we buy anything else."

"There is one more thing that I want."

"What?"

"Let's stop by The Linen Store and buy some new sheets."

Josh didn't ask her why and Sarah didn't volunteer the information. She knew he'd figure it had something to do with some type of rape-trauma recovery, a ritual like cutting your hair or buying new clothes. Maybe he'd figure the sheets reminded her too much of the dream.

When they arrived at the store, Sarah began looking at sheets that she knew Josh thought were hideous. She didn't care. The more hideous they were the better the chance he would remember them and that's all she wanted. She picked up a set of green sheets with polka dots, flowers, and stripes.

"No way in hell. I'm sorry but those things are so loud they'd keep me awake all night."

Sarah laughed.

"Okay, how about these?"

She held up a set of paisley sheets with big lotus flowers all over it.

"Didn't Jerry Garcia die in those? They look like they should come with a bong and a nickel bag."

Sarah covered her mouth and giggled. She always loved Josh's sense of humor.

"It's either these or the green ones."

"Okay, but if I start having acid flashbacks in the middle of the night, you're going to have to talk me down."

When they got home, Josh went straight to bed, but not before Sarah stripped the bed and put on their new paisley sheets. There were still those disturbing bloodstains on the mattress. They had dried now but they were unmistakable.

"Jesus! You did bleed a lot."

"I never started my period though."

"Maybe you bled it all out in one night."

"That doesn't happen."

"It could have been a miscarriage."

Sarah stopped making up the bed and looked over at Josh. That was a possibility she hadn't considered. She and Josh had stopped using birth control so it was entirely possible. Sarah finished putting the sheets on the bed and then stared at the sheets thinking about the possibility that her body had rejected an embryo or a fetus and Josh was about to take a nap in the blood.

Why the hell did you have to say that, Josh? she thought. It was time to buy a new mattress. Out of the corner of her eye she saw Josh staring at her while she stared at the sheets.

"Those sheets trippin' you out? I'm suddenly in the mood to hear some Jimi Hendrix."

Sarah forced a smile and tried to snap herself out of it.

"I've got some Jim Morrison and The Doors on my iPod."

"I'll pass."

"Sleep tight, lover."

Sarah closed the door quietly as Josh slipped into bed. She walked back downstairs, leaving Josh to sleep. They had been out all day and now he had only a couple of hours before he needed to leave for work, just enough time for a quick power-nap. Sarah sat on the couch, pointing the Sig Sauer across the street at the neighbor's house and dry-firing it.

CHAPTER ELEVEN

Sarah got dressed for a late-afternoon run. The summer was nearly over but the temperature was still in the low nineties. A stark white sun blazed directly overhead. The air was hot and dusty and there was no shade to be found. Sarah imagined that she were running directly beneath the hole in the ozone layer. She could feel her skin tightening as the Vegas sun baked all the moisture from her pores. Next time, she'd have to remember to put on sunscreen. Sarah hated women who fried their skin to darken it and thought tan lines were absolutely hideous. Living in Vegas, she'd seen the aftermath of one too many tans, premature wrinkles and dark spots, skin the texture of leather, and eventually the big C. It was idiotic to do that to yourself on purpose just to look beautiful. Sarah thought her own milky white skin was beautiful as it was. Yet here she was risking melanoma under the hot September sun.

She decided to cut her run short. The idea of getting tan lines was freaking her out. Sweat stung her eyes and a crust of salt covered her forehead and cheeks. Her black dry-fit top had big white stains on it that resembled efflorescence from all the sodium and potassium she'd perspired. By the time she made it back to the house, Josh was already up and getting ready for work. Despite the new gun sitting on the kitchen counter where she'd left it before her run, Sarah experienced a moment of dread at the thought of being left alone.

"You sure you can't take the night off?" she asked as she hugged him from behind.

"Not after all the money we just spent. Tips have been slow lately, that's why I've been working so much. The days when I made five hundred dollars in tips on a regular eight-hour shift are pretty much over until the economy recovers. I was thinking about doing a double tonight if the pit boss will let me."

Sarah frowned.

"Just remember that I've got a gun now. If I find out that you're fucking around on me I'm going to give you a .40-caliber castration or, better yet, an enema!"

Josh kissed her on the forehead, then licked her salty sweat from his lips.

"You don't leave enough when you're done with me to share with any other woman. If you're still too freaked out to be alone, then I'll stay."

"No, you're right, we need the money. But don't do a double tonight. You can do it tomorrow but I need you tonight."

"Okay, I'll be home by one."

"Be home by twelve thirty."

"Yes, ma'am."

Josh smiled wide and kissed her on the nose, once more getting a mouthful of salty perspiration.

"When are they going to start giving you regular hours? You've been extra-board for over a year. One day you're working eight to five and then the next day it's four to twelve, then twelve to eight. And then with the overtime? This is getting ridiculous."

"Yeah, but that's why our house isn't in foreclosure."

Sarah smiled weakly, then made a pouty face.

"We could fuck just as well in an apartment. Probably better because I'd see you more."

"All you think about is fucking. I guess I should be flattered."

"What else is there to think about? I'm bored half to death!"

"You could work on your dissertation."

"But if I finish my degree I'll have to get a real job; then I'd have even less time to drive you crazy."

Josh kissed her again and wrinkled his nose at her musky smell.

"I hope you're going to shower before I get home."

"You know you like me when I'm dirty."

She winked at him as she pulled her shirt over her head. She was pleased to see his eyes zero in on her breasts. It meant that he was still attracted to her. He knelt down to slip on his shoes and Sarah wondered what he would have done if she'd dropped her shorts and told him to lick her pussy—sweat, funk, and all. Knowing him, he would have probably done it just to please her. He may have even enjoyed it. The thought of it began to turn her on. One day she'd have to try it.

"Good-bye, beautiful." Josh walked out the door.

Almost immediately the silence became deafening. Sarah walked into the kitchen to get her gun and then walked upstairs, leaving all the lights on downstairs. This was not the time to worry about the electric bill. The last thing she wanted was to be in a dark house alone.

Sitting on the edge of the bed, on her ugly new sheets, cradling the gun in her lap, Sarah wished she had talked Josh into buying her a pit bull. As much as the notion of pooper-scooping repulsed her, it would have been nice to have something big and mean in the house that was on her side. She'd have to talk to Josh about that when he got home.

The forty-two-inch plasma-screen TV protruded from the wall opposite the bed, flicking from one channel to another as Sarah hunted for something to preoccupy her. Her bedroom was painted a light tan with a cola-colored accent wall behind the king-size four-poster bed and the light from the TV cast flickering shadows across the dark wall. She loved this room. But tonight it was filled with bad memories, memories she wasn't even certain were real.

There was nothing on TV and Sarah didn't feel like cleaning. She felt exhausted, as if she'd just run twelve miles instead of four, but she was afraid to fall asleep. Dark, violent dreams still echoed in her mind.

Sarah began flicking through pay-per-view channels, growing increasingly frustrated. She'd already seen all of the new releases and she had no appetite for soft porn. Sarah clicked off the television, tossed the cable remote across the room onto her love seat, and grabbed her laptop.

She went onto eBay and surfed through the ads for iPods, laptops, designer purses and shoes, and various collectibles before logging on to a local runners' message board and checking the forum threads for any interesting discussions. This was her ritual. It was what she did to convince herself that she hadn't logged on just to look at porn. But the truth was that surfing the porn sites was her favorite pastime. It wasn't something she did for titillation so much as morbid curiosity. The bizarre fetishes she ran across amused her to no end. She kept telling herself that she was going to write a book someday and that this was simple research.

Sarah clicked through all the usual bukkake, farm sex, amputee, and midget porn sites until she got to the weird stuff. She stopped at a "sleepy sex" website for men who liked to make love to women who just lie there like corpses and then a necro-sex site for men who liked to make love to actual corpses. Josh would have lost his mind if he knew about the type of websites she went on. The necro-sex sites were all geared toward the goth crowd and featured women lying in coffins wearing pale makeup with black eye shadow. Sarah laughed and clicked on another link. For some reason, even the goth freaks who fucked fake corpses were making her uncomfortable.

She found a site for blood-play that showed men and women making love while cutting each other with razor blades and another site showing nude women hanging from nooses. Sarah shuddered and clicked off the website. It was just too much for her tonight.

"What the fuck is wrong with people?"

But Sarah knew that normally she would have found even the most violent and perverse porn sites fascinating. That was before she dreamed about being murdered, then woke up the next morning on a blood-soaked mattress. Now she wanted something more vanilla. She clicked on a lesbian site and tried to amuse herself with pictures of women who looked like anything but lesbians fucking for the camera. She closed her laptop and lay back on the bed with the gun on her chest. There was no fighting it. She was tired as hell and, for once, she wasn't the least bit horny. She felt like she'd never be horny again.

Sarah closed her eyes and clicked the safety off the pistol.

CHAPTER TWELVE

Sarah woke up as Josh walked into the room.

"Sorry, baby. I didn't mean to wake you."

Sarah wiped her eyes with the backs of her hands, then sat up straight in bed. She looked around the room in a panic.

"Turn on the lights."

"Go on back to sleep," Josh whispered.

"Turn on the lights!"

The room filled with light and Sarah immediately looked down at the sheets. Her heart began a drum roll in her chest. The sheets were white. No flowers. No paisleys. No psychedelic colors. Just plain white. Sweat broke out on her brow and she began to hyperventilate.

"Oh shit. Oh shit. Oh shit."

Josh's forehead wrinkled and he held his hands out helplessly. The gesture annoyed the hell out of Sarah and made her feel completely alone. He eyes began to tear up.

"Oh God. Oh shit."

"What? What is it?"

"Where are the sheets? Where are the sheets, Josh?"

Josh shrugged.

"What sheets?"

"The ugly ones we bought from The Linen Store.

The hippie sheets with the paisleys and the big ugly fucking flowers? I put them on the bed before I went to sleep. Where are they? Where the fuck are they, Josh?"

Josh looked down at the bed.

"Are you sure you put them on?"

"Of course I'm sure! That's why I bought them. So I wouldn't forget them. I know I put them on the bed."

Sarah sprang from the bed and stomped into the closet. She rummaged through the laundry basket, tossing jeans, T-shirts, skirts, and bras onto the floor. She ran out of the closet and downstairs to the laundry room with Josh following close behind her. She opened up the laundry machine and there were her sheets, clean, wet, balled up at the bottom of the washer. A pair of her underwear were in there too. They were the same ones she'd been wearing when she'd fallen asleep. She looked at Josh. He stared back at her wide-eyed. Slowly he shook his head.

"I didn't wash them." Then she added, "Where's my gun?"

Josh stared at her blankly.

"Where's the fucking gun? I had it with me when I went to bed. Where is it? Where's the fucking gun?"

"Um, I think I saw it upstairs."

Sarah dashed back up the stairs. She found the Sig Sauer sitting on the dresser. Her hand shook as she reached for it. She paused, her hand hovering over the pistol as if she was afraid to touch it. She turned and looked at Josh who was watching her, holding his breath, as if she were about to pick up a poisonous snake. They were both breathing hard.

"Did you put this here, Josh?"

"No. It was there when I walked in."

"It was lying on my chest when I went to sleep. I was holding it with both hands."

She picked up the gun and ejected the clip. It was empty. She pulled the slide back. The bullet she'd placed in the chamber was gone. Josh sucked in a quick breath and began looking around the room for bullets.

Sarah knew that this must be hard on Josh, suddenly being forced to be the calm, steady one while she fell apart. It was a complete reversal from their normal roles. She could tell that he was having a hard time holding it together. Seeing the panic on her face was unnerving him but he was trying to remain calm for her sake. Staying calm was not one of his strong suits and the strain was showing on his face. She loved him for the effort he was making.

"Do you smell that?"

Josh's expression was beginning to look as panicked as her own.

"What?" Sarah asked.

Josh took the gun from her and sniffed the barrel. He held it out to her. Sarah sniffed it as well. There was the unmistakable smell of burned carbon.

"It's been fired."

Sarah began looking around the room for bullet holes while Josh checked the floor for spent casings. It didn't take her long to find one. There was a hole in the bedroom door. Josh closed the door and behind it was a nice, neat round hole in the drywall.

"You shot at something, someone maybe? The neighbor? Did you have another one of those dreams?"

"I don't think they're dreams, Josh. Do you think I changed the sheets and did a load of laundry in my dreams? I think someone was in here. I'm scared, Josh."

"Should I go over to the neighbor's house?"

"And do what? We have no proof he did anything. If you kill him or kick his ass, then you'll just go to jail and I'll be all alone."

Sarah reached out and pulled her husband close. She wrapped herself in his big, thick arms, leaning her head on his muscular chest, searching desperately for some sense of security, wanting to believe that her husband could protect her from whatever this was.

"Well, then what happened? Do you really think he came in here and attacked you? Then stripped the sheets off the bed and washed them? That just sounds so crazy. This . . . this can't be happening."

"I don't know. I don't remember. I laid down with the gun on my chest and then I woke up when you came in the room."

"Well, something happened. I'm calling the cops."

"And telling them what?"

"I don't know. But I'm calling them. Something is definitely going on."

"B-but what if it's just me? What if I'm going crazy or something? I don't want them to put me away somewhere."

"They won't put you away. I don't think it works that way. They don't just lock you up for saying crazy shit. Half of Las Vegas would be in the loony bin if that's how it was. But maybe they can test the place, see if someone has been in here?"

Sarah was confused, uncertain, but she was scared to death. Maybe she would feel better if the cops came. Josh stood next to the bed holding his cell phone, looking at her, waiting.

"Okay. Call them."

Sarah looked around the room as Josh dialed the phone number for police emergencies. The more she looked the more things she noticed out of place. The light on the nightstand and the radio alarm clock had switched places. There was a big red stuffed bear that Josh had bought her for Valentine's Day the year they got married. She always kept it next to the bed and there it was, next to the bed. Only it was on Josh's side of the bed. Even her laptop was unplugged and sitting on top of the dresser instead of plugged in on the floor by the bed. And there were clean spots on the floor again. Places where the carpet was lighter, where it had obviously been scrubbed. Sarah knelt down and rubbed her hand over one large spot beside the bed that was almost three shades lighter than the rest of the carpet as if someone had used bleach on it. The carpet was wet.

"Yes. My name is Josh . . . Josh Lincoln. Someone has been in our house. I think they may have attacked my wife. Okay. Okay. How long before they get here? Okay. Thank you."

"Josh."

"They're on their way."

"The carpet is wet. It's been cleaned."

Sarah stood back as Josh knelt down and inspected the carpet. She already knew what he was going to say. There was just no denying the fact that the carpet had been cleaned. It looked as if all the color had been bleached out of it in spots. There was a cream-colored spot on the tan carpet that was nearly four feet wide. As they looked around they began to notice spots on the walls behind the bed that looked as if they had been cleaned or freshly painted.

"And, before you ask, no, I didn't decide to get up and clean the carpet in the middle of the night."

Josh just shook his head and rubbed his face with

his palms. He was trying to figure out what to say, obviously wracking his brain for the right words, visibly distressed by his inability to explain what he was seeing. Sarah was almost hoping that Josh would have had some rational explanation for it all, even if the answer was that she was crazy. But fear and confusion was written clearly across his face.

"Do you really think someone's been in the house? How could they sneak in here without waking you up? You think maybe somebody drugged you? Some sort of date-rape drug like rufinol?"

Sarah thought about it. If she had been drugged, then the gaps in her memory, the hazy dreamlike images that came back to her in brief flashes, would make a lot more sense. Even her memories of being murdered could be dismissed as drug-induced hallucinations.

But how could someone have gotten in here to drug me in the first place? How would they have slipped me the drugs? Sarah wondered. The idea created as many questions as it answered. And if it was true, that would mean that her dreams about being raped by the neighbor were real. Sarah hugged herself and shuddered.

"I don't know. But maybe I should go to the hospital to get checked out."

"Before the cops get here . . ." Josh paused. Sarah looked at him quizzically.

"What, Josh? What?"

"This is fucked up, but I have to ask you . . ."

"Ask me what?"

"The drugs . . . um . . . they aren't going to find . . . I mean . . . someone drugged you, right? You're not using . . ."

Sarah realized what he was getting at and something dark and mean spread inside of her, wanting to lash out at Josh and tear his face off his skull or at the least, slap the shit out of him. She knew that, given the circumstances, it was a perfectly reasonable question to ask. The whole thing looked and sounded insane. And if she wasn't schizophrenic, then the only other possibility, besides someone breaking in and raping and drugging her without her being able to remember it, was that she was using drugs herself and doing all of this in some kind of drug-induced delirium. Given the choices, it was far more likely from his perspective that she had started using drugs. She had also confessed to Josh once that she had used methamphetamines in high school as a weight-loss aid, "The Meth Diet" she and her friends had jokingly called it. She'd started using it again in college to help her stay up late to study just before she and Josh had met. He had every right to be suspicious. But right now she needed him to be on her side and this question, right at this moment, felt like a horrible betrayal.

"No, Josh. I'm not a fucking drug addict. I'm not snorting meth or smoking crack while you're at work."

Sarah turned her back on Josh as the tears began to flow. She started to throw herself down onto the bed but just the sight of those clean white sheets halted her. She didn't want to touch them. Whoever had broken in here and done things to her had also touched those sheets. Sarah stood in the middle of the room, with tears racing down her cheeks, and screamed.

CHAPTER THIRTEEN

"So, you're saying that your neighbor has been breaking into your house and drugging you and raping you?"

The cop looked like he'd just gotten out of high school but he already had that disinterested look of someone who was used to seeing the worst of humanity. He had that look of one who had grown bored with anything short of gunfights and fatal car accidents, that superior cop swagger as if everyone without a badge owed their existence to him. His prematurely thinning copse of blond hair, acne scars on his cheeks and forehead, and bulbous Adam's apple were clear indications that he had probably been on the wrong end of many insults and ass-kickings during his school years.

"We're not sure. That's why we called you. Someone has been in the house though."

"Someone came in and scrubbed your floors and walls and did the laundry but didn't take anything?"

"Someone raped my wife and cleaned up to hide the evidence. I mean . . . someone might have. She just keeps having these dreams and then all this stuff in the house that's out of place."

"And why do you think it's your neighbor?"

"My wife saw him. I mean . . . she thinks she did.

She has these dreams and in them it's him. He's there and he's raping her and killing her."

The police officer, who looked like a young blond Anthony Perkins, stared at Josh. He was obviously suppressing a laugh. Sarah felt terrible for putting Josh through this.

"Look, I know this all sounds crazy. Can you just check the house and see if there's any sign that someone has broken in?"

The cop sighed deeply.

"Okay, I'll check the doors and windows."

Sarah and Josh looked at each other. Sarah felt so foolish, she couldn't hide her embarrassment. She was blushing and fidgeting. She wished they hadn't called the police but she wanted to know. She had to know if someone had been breaking into their house.

The police officer checked the windows in the living room, the kitchen, and the den. He checked the front door and the rear sliding door.

"Sir? Ma'am?"

"Yes?" Josh walked over to the sliding-glass door where the cop was standing. Sarah came with him.

"How do you lock this door?"

"You just flip this latch at the bottom of the door."

"Up or down?"

"You just push it down with your foot."

"Uh huh. Go ahead. Flip the lock."

Josh stepped on the latch.

"Now, open the door."

Josh pulled on the sliding-door handle and the door slid open easily on its track.

"Try it again."

This time Sarah pushed past her husband and stepped

down firmly on the latch. She grabbed the door handle and once again the door slid easily open.

"You should get yourself a security bar for this door. With all these empty houses around it might not be a bad idea to get a security alarm too. Gangs and drug addicts sometimes squat in these abandoned houses. It's a real problem. These foreclosures send the crime rate through the roof."

"So, do you think someone has been breaking in here?" Sarah asked a little too anxiously.

"There's no sign of forced entry but then an intruder wouldn't really need to break anything to get in when he can just slide the door open."

"We'll get it fixed."

"Get that security system installed too."

"We will."

"Is that it?" Sarah asked. Her voice rose higher than she had intended it to, giving a panicky edge to it.

"That's all I can do with the evidence we have right now. If you remember anything more, then you can come down to the station and file a report. But I can't go across the street and arrest some guy because you had a bad dream."

"But you can question him?"

"Do you really want me to do that? I can. You're right. I could go across the street and ask him if he's been breaking into your house and attacking you when you're sleeping. But if he didn't do anything and all you had was a really scary realistic dream, then you might just piss him off and start a war between you."

"He's right," Josh said, and Sarah knew he was too, but that's not what she wanted to hear. She wanted the neighbor fingerprinted. She wanted her entire house dusted for fingerprints, checked for blood and semen and hair fibers and whatever the hell else they could find. She wanted him locked up and interrogated until he admitted the things he'd been doing to her.

"What about fingerprints? Can't you check the house for prints?"

"We would need to get his prints to compare them to and that would require a warrant. Unless you can tell me right now that you know for a fact that he attacked you, I can't get that warrant. If you tell me it wasn't a dream and you remember him breaking in here and raping you, I'll have that warrant in minutes and we'll get fingerprints and semen samples from him, run a rape kit at the hospital and dust the entire house for prints and blood and any other body fluids. Without that, there's nothing we can do. I can't get a warrant or call in for a CSU team based on a dream and some clean sheets."

"Could you run a rape kit on me anyway? Just to make sure it was only a dream? I haven't showered yet so if something happened there might still be . . ." Sarah paused. The words did not want to come out. A shudder went through her body once more and she grimaced as if she had tasted something foul, as if she could still taste *him*. ". . . evidence." She turned away in embarrassment, then turned back and forced herself to meet the cop's eyes, not wanting him to know that she was embarrassed, trying not to appear weak. She had no idea why that was so important to her. But she hated the idea of appearing weak in front of anyone except Josh and not even him most of the time.

The cop took a deep breath and let it out slowly. He tapped his pen against his notepad, upon which he had written absolutely nothing. He hadn't taken a single note about anything she had said.

It was apparent to Sarah that he wasn't planning on doing a single thing about her intruder and was just humoring her. She was almost tempted to tell him that they weren't dreams and that she knew for a fact that she had been raped but she didn't. She was still not sure how much of what she remembered was a dream and how much was real. She couldn't remember a thing from last night. Not being attacked. Not firing the gun. Nothing.

If this was all in her head and she was going crazy she'd be putting the neighbor through hell for nothing and causing him all kinds of problems. People only tended to remember when someone was accused of a crime not when they were exonerated. A rape charge might get him fired or chased right out of the neighborhood. He might even retaliate by suing them or calling the homeowner's association on them every time they were late bringing in their trash can on trash day or when they parked on the driveway instead of in the garage or if they didn't trim their shrubs or calling the Nevada Water Authority when they didn't change their sprinkler clocks on drought days or calling the police whenever their stereo was too loud or any of those other petty things neighbors did to one another to make their lives hell. It might even wind up with him and Josh in a fight or worse. She thought about Josh storming out of the house with a gun in his hand. What if Dale had a gun? That could get really ugly. She definitely did not want to start a feud with the new neighbor.

"What if she's been drugged, and that's why she can't remember anything? You could do a urinalysis while she's at the hospital."

"Still no way to prove the neighbor did it or that she didn't take the drugs herself."

"But if they find that she's been raped and they find some kind of date-rape drug in her system, that should be enough for a warrant then, right?"

The policeman looked down at his patent leather cop shoes and shook his head, raising his arms in surrender.

"All right. I'll take you down to the hospital."

"I'll get my purse."

Sarah walked into the living room and snatched her purse off the couch. She walked past Josh without looking at him. She was still angry that he'd doubted her about the drugs. As she walked out the door she hoped that if Dale had really drugged her, he hadn't used meth.

The ride to the hospital was loaded with tension as the police officer attempted to talk them out of it during the entire ride.

"You sure you want to do this, right? These examinations can be pretty invasive. I'll have to call a rape counselor. That's just procedure. And she's going to ask you some pretty tough questions."

"I'll tell her everything I can remember."

"They might have to ask you about your marriage. You know, to rule your husband out as the rapist."

"My husband didn't rape me."

"I'm not saying that. I'm just trying to prepare you for some of the questions they might ask you."

"It sounds to me like you're trying to talk me out of it."

"I'm taking you, aren't I?"

They fell silent for the rest of the ride. Sarah was

grateful for the break. She needed to think. She wanted to try to remember as much as she could.

Sarah still could not remember much of the previous night. She remembered changing the sheets. She remembered surfing the Internet and then putting the laptop down beside the bed and grabbing her gun. She remembered falling asleep with the gun clenched in both hands and held tight to her chest. And she remembered waking up when Josh walked in. Everything in between was completely gone. But she could remember the previous night clearly.

She remembered waking up and reaching out for her husband, only to feel that warm wetness and hearing him wheezing and gurgling as he drowned on his own blood. She remembered looking up and seeing Dale stab Josh again and again. And she remembered what he had done to her. She could not forget the image of his tiny penis thrusting between her blood-soaked breasts. The problem was that she could also remember waking up unmarred with no visible wounds or scars and seeing her husband . . . alive. It had to have been a dream. But then she'd started finding things, things that didn't add up, things that supported her memories. The only thing that didn't make sense was the fact that she and Josh were alive.

They arrived at the hospital with the police officer still visibly annoyed at being inconvenienced. There was a nurse waiting for him along with a victim advocate from the LVPD.

"We'll take it from here," the female detective said, and the young officer looked like he could just barely contain the urge to jump for joy.

"Have fun, guys," the officer said, and saluted them

with a flip of his hand as he turned and walked out the hospital's sliding doors, weaving around a gurney that was being rushed in by some paramedics with a man on it screaming his head off and bleeding from a huge wound in his leg. The officer gave the bleeding man the same flippant salute as he strode out into the parking lot.

"Asshole," Sarah and Josh said in unison as they watched him leave.

The female detective smiled at Sarah as she ushered them into a small examination room.

The victim's advocate from the police department was a tall black woman in her late thirties with thick curves. She had a kind face with a scar in the corner of her mouth that ran from the right corner of her lip up to her nose.

"My name is Detective Trina Lassiter."

"Sarah Lincoln."

"Okay, Mrs. Lincoln, tell me what happened," she said as she and the nurse pulled on a pair of latex gloves.

"I'm not really sure. I remember being attacked but I'm not sure it wasn't a dream."

The nurse just nodded without looking up.

"That's normal. Your mind sometimes suppresses unpleasant memories," the nurse, a Latino woman in her fifties, said.

The detective opened a big plastic bag and withdrew cotton swabs, Q-tips, and little plastic jars.

"When do you think this happened?" Lassiter asked.

"The memories are from two nights ago but I think something may have happened last night as well."

The nurse finally looked up. She looked at Detective Lassiter and then they both looked back at Sarah.

"You think you've been raped twice?" Lassiter asked.

"At least. I think the neighbor is doing it. I think he might be drugging me."

Detective Lassiter turned to the nurse who was still staring with her mouth open.

"Let's get blood and urine samples. Check her for GHB and rufinol."

She turned back to Sarah.

"Okay, let's get your clothes off. Is this what you were wearing during the attacks?"

"No. They happened at night when I was sleeping. I was just wearing my underwear but somebody washed them."

She related the entire incident, as much as she could remember including being stabbed and then waking up the next morning without a mark on her. She told the detective about the bloody sheets and then the missing sheets the next day. The tall black woman listened patiently.

"Okay. Okay, let's just get you undressed."

Sarah took off her clothes and slipped into the hospital gown. She put her legs into the stirrups and closed her eyes as the nurse swabbed the inside of her vagina and anus and then swabbed beneath her tongue and inside her cheeks, bagging each Q-tip and labeling it before placing them back into the plastic envelope. She winced as the nurse slid a syringe into the vein on the inside of her elbow and withdrew three vials of blood. Then she gave Sarah a cup and helped her into the bathroom to take a urine sample.

When she came out of the bathroom she could tell by the demeanor of the two women that something had changed.

"What did you find?"

"Nothing. We'll send the samples to the lab but there's no sign of vaginal bruising or tearing. No sign of rectal trauma either. It doesn't look like you've been raped."

Sarah just stared at them, trying to figure out what it all meant.

"But . . . ? But those memories? Those fucked-up horrible memories? Am I going crazy?"

"I'm not saying that nothing happened. If you were drugged your muscles may have relaxed, making it easier for him to penetrate. You may have even had an involuntary reaction and been lubricated enough that he didn't tear any tissue the way he would have if you weren't lubricated. That's normal and it doesn't mean you enjoyed it or anything. The body just acts funny sometimes and there's nothing we can do about it. You also said his penis was small. All of that may have contributed to the lack of evidence. A lubricated condom on a small penis could leave very little evidence of bruising or tearing."

Sarah nodded in agreement, barely listening. She kept thinking about what the detective had said about her being lubricated. Had she subconsciously enjoyed it? Maybe all the porn she watched had fucked up her head. How could she have enjoyed being raped by that perverted little freak? The woman had said that it happens all the time and it didn't mean that she was enjoying it or that the sex was voluntary but Sarah still questioned herself. She could only guess what Josh would say. He already thought she was a nymphomaniac. But there was, of course, another possibility. It might have all been in her head. She might have never been raped at all.

"Like I said, we'll test the samples. It might be a

good idea to get a semen sample from your husband too so we can exclude his semen."

Sarah nodded. She didn't want to talk anymore. She just wanted to go home.

CHAPTER FOURTEEN

Sarah didn't say anything to Josh when they left the hospital. She didn't know what to say that wouldn't make her sound insane.

"Let's call an alarm company when we get home. We'll see if we can get someone to install it tonight."

Sarah shook her head slowly, still staring ahead, eyes glazed, looking out the windshield at nothing.

"No. We don't need to spend any more money on this. But I can't take another night in that house. Not tonight. Let's just go home and get some clothes and I'll go with you to work. See if you can get us a hotel room."

"Okay. Okay. That shouldn't be a problem. I'll speak to the hotel manager. I should be able to get us a few nights for free. That will give me enough time to get that door fixed. I think I'm going to get an alarm installed anyway. I should make some good tips tonight and that cop was right. The neighborhood is changing."

Sarah nodded again, still staring out the windshield at the desert rushing by. The mountains surrounding the valley were still an odd sight to her. In Indianapolis there was nothing to see but trees and more buildings. Though, the mountains were the *only* things about the town that Sarah thought of as beautiful. This was a town that destroys its own history. Any building older than thirty years was threatened with demolition leaving only row after row of cookie-cutter stucco tract homes, most less than ten years old. More and more Sarah was coming to despise this city.

The collapse of the economy had devastated the town, leaving brand-new houses standing empty, vacant strip malls, and towering office buildings standing unfinished, little more than steel frames without the bank funding to complete them. And the crime rate had been steadily increasing year after year. There were more red and blue bandanas hanging from the back pockets of sagging jeans than she had ever seen before.

Their car pulled into the driveway and Sarah turned to look at the house across the street. She thought she saw the blinds close as she turned. A sudden fury rose inside her and she stormed down the driveway and started across the street toward the neighbor's house.

"Fuck this bullshit! I'm not going to let anyone terrorize me and scare me out of my own damn house!"

"Sarah!"

Josh came running after her, catching up to her in the street. Sarah did not slow her stride.

"Sarah? Sarah? What are you going to do?"

"I'm going to let this bastard know that I know what he's been up to. I want him to know that I'm not afraid."

Sarah walked up the neighbor's steps and pounded on his front door. It felt good to be doing something, to be taking control again instead of just sitting back waiting for him to break in and attack her again. Even if the entire attack was all in her head and the neighbor didn't know what the hell she was talking about, it would still feel good to be doing something. After being probed and examined and being told by those fucking nurses that she might have gotten wet when she was being raped, it felt great to go on the offensive. She waited. There was no answer. She pounded on the door again.

"Open this goddamned door! I know you're there. I saw you looking at me through the blinds!"

The door swung open and Dale stood there in a robe that was too big for him and made him look even smaller, weaker, and emaciated.

"Yes?"

"I know what you've been up to and if I ever catch you sneaking into my house again I will kill you. Do you hear me? I will blow your fucking head off!"

Dale looked terrified. His eyes shifted nervously from Josh to Sarah.

"I-I-I haven't been in your house. What are you talking about? I wouldn't do anything like that."

Josh tried to step in front of Sarah.

"My wife has been under a lot of stress lately."

Sarah whirled on him, pushing him back and jabbing a finger in his face.

"Don't! Don't you fucking dare!"

Josh fell silent and dropped his head. Sarah turned back to Dale.

"I don't know how you're doing it, but we are going to catch you and then your ass won't go to jail. I won't call the cops. I'm going to send your scrawny ass to the fucking morgue!"

Dale smiled. It was quick. He suppressed it almost immediately and resumed his look of fear and confusion. But Sarah saw it. He had smiled. Before she could think, question herself, talk herself out of it, she drew her hand back and slapped him. She turned her shoulders into the blow, giving it her all. He fell against the doorjamb and a big, angry red welt in the shape of four fingers rose on his left cheek. The expression on his face was one of stunned outrage but then she saw it again, that quick smile. Sarah balled up her fist and pulled back and Josh grabbed her, dragged her off the steps and into the street.

"I'll fucking kill you! Do you hear me, you fucking pervert! I'll kill you!"

Up and down the block, doors and windows opened as the few remaining curious neighbors looked out to see what was going on. Sarah knew she ought to feel embarrassed but she didn't. She felt great!

"Why did you hit me? You're crazy! I'm calling the cops! You're crazy!"

But for the first time in days she didn't feel crazy. She felt strong again. She felt in control again. And even if she was imagining everything else, she had not imagined that smile. She was certain about that.

She turned and shook free of Josh, then walked into the house, stomping her feet with her hands balled into tight fists. Josh walked in right behind her.

"I can't believe you slapped him."

"He fucking smiled at me. That slimy, nasty little bastard was grinning at me."

"I think we need to get you someone to talk to."

"What?"

"Maybe . . . I don't know . . . Maybe you need some help."

There it was, out in the open. He thought she was crazy.

"Do you think maybe we should at least wait for the lab results?"

"That policewoman told me they found no physical signs of rape."

"She told you?"

"I'm your husband. I was concerned."

"Did she tell you that it could have looked that way because he used lubrication and had a small dick? Or because the drugs relaxed my damned vaginal muscles?"

"Well, drugs or lubricant would show up in the lab results."

"That's why maybe you should wait before you try shipping me off to the fucking loony bin! Wait to see if maybe I'm fucking right!"

Josh was keeping his distance. He appeared to be afraid that she would attack him too the way she had attacked the neighbor. He held his hands out palms up as if he were trying to negotiate with a gunman. Sarah really did want to hit him. Josh knew her well.

"But what if nothing happened? You just slapped that guy. He could press charges. You were about to beat the hell out of him. Can you seriously imagine that little guy attacking anybody?"

"Maybe that's why he uses the drugs? So we can't fight him."

"We don't know that he uses anything! We don't know that anything happened! This could all be in your head. You could have sleepwalked and shot off that gun and changed the sheets and scrubbed the carpet and then crawled right back into bed and went back to sleep. That sounds a whole fucking lot more likely than some sheepish little guy who lives across the street has been breaking in at night and raping and killing you but you can't remember it and, did I forget to mention, you aren't fucking dead!"

Sarah was stunned. Now it was all out in the open. Everything she had felt before, all the power and confidence, was now gone. Now, she felt crazy again.

"Wow. I-I really didn't know you felt that way."

Josh deflated, collapsing on the couch.

"Look, I'm sorry. I just don't know what to think. This is just so fucking confusing and scary as hell . . . either way. I mean, if this guy has been drugging both of us and then breaking in and raping you, that's fucking terrifying. And if you're, you know, losing it, that's almost worst. You-you're my rock. You're supposed to keep *me* from losing it."

There was a hitch in Josh's voice. When he looked up at her there were tears in his eyes. It broke Sarah's heart. She felt like she had let him down, as if she had failed him in some way.

Sarah hadn't thought much about how this must have been impacting Josh. She knew that Josh was not built for stress or surprises. He was a middle-of-the-road business-as-usual type of guy and this was as far from that as could be. This was the other side of the moon.

A silence fell between them, heavy and uncomfortable. Sarah walked over and plopped down beside Josh. She leaned over and put her head in his lap.

"I'm not crazy, Josh. But I can't expect you to believe that. I mean, crazy people don't know they're crazy right? If I'm sleepwalking or something, I guess I wouldn't really know. Let's just get away for a few days. It might make things a little clearer We could both probably use a little break from all this."

Once again, in the midst of her own trauma, it was her taking care of Josh. Sarah didn't mind. It felt normal. She hated that she had been leaning on Josh so much lately.

"Let's just grab a few things and go. We'll treat it like a honeymoon."

Josh nodded and slowly rose from the couch. He still looked shaken, scared, uncertain. Sarah cupped his face in her hands and forced him to look her in the eyes.

"I'm not crazy, Josh. Don't worry. I'm not crazy."

Josh smiled weakly and hugged her. She could tell that he was still not certain. Neither was she. She would have to change that.

CHAPTER FIFTEEN

Once she had settled into the hotel room, the first thing Sarah did was plug in her laptop and get online. She looked up The Spy Store and began scouring through their surveillance equipment. Most of it was prohibitively expensive. She settled on the nanny-cam teddy bear. Both attacks had taken place in her bedroom. If she could catch it on film, then she could prove to Josh and herself that she wasn't crazy. Then she'd have that fucker arrested and her life would go back to normal . . . after a few years of therapy.

Sarah wrote down the model number and the address to the store. Then she opened her documents and began working on her dissertation. She had no desire to surf through porn sites. She'd already seen enough violent and deviant sex acts to support her theory that human sexuality on a whole was growing more nihilistic as overpopulation increased. She didn't need to see any more pictures of women being brutally fist-fucked and gang-raped. Her sex drive had already crashed and burned. She wasn't certain she'd ever have the desire for sex again. That alone made her want to murder Dale.

Sarah took a digital voice recorder out of her overnight bag and slipped it under her pillow. If anything happened tonight, she would at least have a recording of it. She began to write about the increased popularity of what she called "nonreproductive sex" such as sadomasochism, anal and oral sex, the use of sex toys, and ejaculation outside the vagina, on the face, breast, buttocks, etc., following the start of the AIDS epidemic.

Human sexuality had been a major focus of her study ever since she was an undergraduate. She had grown up in a very religious household where sexuality was never discussed. Sexually explicit books, movies, or TV shows were not allowed in her home when she was young. Even music with explicit lyrics was banned. She had first learned about sex from her friends in high school. It was a wonder she hadn't gotten pregnant at fifteen like most of them had.

In college she'd finally had the freedom to explore her sexuality and divide the facts from the fiction. She had become fascinated with both the lore and the science of sexuality and had switched her major from psychology to social anthropology. She was hoping to someday write a groundbreaking book that would shed new light on human sexuality and show the necessary social function of so-called deviancy. She believed that the evolution of sexuality followed a Darwinian trajectory where acts like sexual violence would have long been eliminated from the human gene pool if they did not serve some purpose. In this case, she theorized, that the purpose was to harness sexual energy into nonreproductive activities that would not further contribute to overpopulation or exposure to disease.

Of course, by that logic, she should have found greater sexual diversity in the more overpopulated cities and countries than her research had so far uncovered. There should, in fact, have been an exponential increase in sexual deviancy in cities with populations over five million as compared to those of a million or less. But she could not find any significant differences.

Sarah closed the laptop in frustration and picked up the room service menu. She was beginning to doubt if she would ever finish her dissertation and was starting to lose her drive. She kept finding new holes in her theory that needed to be filled and each time she plugged one hole it created another. She was also worried that all of this research might be the cause of her violent sexual dreams. And if they were real than she didn't want to rationalize the things that monster had done to her, which is what it felt like she was doing with her research.

Sarah scanned down the menu straight to the deserts. She needed some comfort food. She found some chocolate cake and vanilla fudge ice cream. It was just what she needed. She picked up the remote and turned on the TV. She pushed the menu button and clicked on pay-per-view movies. She needed a good romantic comedy, something silly with Ben Affleck or Hugh Grant. That, along with the ice cream and the cake, was guaranteed to take her mind off her troubles. And if that didn't work there was always the hotel gym, though she hated running on treadmills. The wind in her face and watching the scenery rush by were part of the thrill of running. But she didn't feel like battling crowds trying to jog up the Las Vegas strip. Even with the decrease in tourism due to the recession, the strip was still packed like a nightclub on Saturday night.

There were no movies on that Sarah either hadn't seen or could stomach. As much as she wanted to feel girly and feminine and lose herself in something mindless, she just could not stomach another girl-from-the-wrong-side-of-the-tracks-meets-perfect-rich-gentleman movie. She had her limits. Finally, she settled on a nature documentary about the migration of gray whales. Not what she had in mind but the sound of the ocean and the whale calls were strangely soothing.

She had almost fallen asleep when there was a knock at the door. Sarah's pulse rate shot up and it suddenly became difficult to breath. She scrambled off the bed, groping for her purse and the loaded .40-caliber pistol inside it.

Sarah's hands shook as she removed the semiautomatic pistol from her bag, jacked a round into the chamber, cocking it as she walked toward the door.

"Who is it?"

"Room service."

"Just leave it outside the door."

"Um . . . I need you to sign for it."

Sarah let out a low moan. There was no peephole in the door. She would have to open it to see who was on the other side. She put the chain on the door and put the barrel of the gun against the door as she slid it open, prepared to pull the trigger if it was Dale. She could hear her own heart hammering in her ears.

A young Latino man stood on the other side of the door wearing a red jacket and pushing a cart with a silver tray on it that held her ice cream and cake. She flipped the chain off the door and hid the pistol behind her back.

"Sorry, come on in."

She opened the door and stepped aside so the waiter could wheel in her dessert.

"Anything else, ma'am?" the waiter asked as he handed her the bill.

Sarah paused and placed her gun on the nightstand, then walked over and took the bill from the waiter. She signed for it and scribbled a generous tip at the bottom, then handed it back. The waiter stole a quick glance at the gun, smiled, then began backing out of the room.

"Thank you. You have a nice night, ma'am."

Sarah smiled back and followed him to the door, closing it behind him and reengaging the chain lock. After pushing the cart up to the bed, she plopped back down on the bed to eat cake and ice cream and watch gray whales migrate.

Less than an hour went by before she'd had enough. Sarah was bored. She decided to go downstairs to the casino and gamble a bit. She loved playing slot machines but usually resisted the urge. Gambling was a bad hobby to get into when you lived in Las Vegas. She had known more than one friend who'd moved to the city and then had to move back home after a few months of losing their entire paychecks to slot machines and video poker. Maybe she'd play blackjack instead. She wondered if Josh would be surprised or embarrassed or both if she was to sit down at his table to play. She wasn't sure whether it was legal to play at her husband's table. It might break some sort of federal gaming laws. She decided not to risk it. She could always play at the table next to him. That might even be more fun, she thought. It would drive him crazy to see her there.

Sarah stood up and started getting dressed. She considered wearing a miniskirt with no panties but was just not in the mood to call sexual attention to herself. She had the irrational fear that even there in the casino Dale might still be watching her. She couldn't stand the idea of him staring at her from across the casino and getting aroused. Right now, the idea of anyone getting aroused by her felt creepy, scary.

Instead of the miniskirt she picked up a pair of sweatpants and slid on some flip-flops. She pulled Josh's favorite college T-shirt on over her head. She looked about as unsexy as could be. She decided to at least do her hair and makeup.

She grabbed her makeup bag and pulled out lipstick, blush, mascara, and eye shadow. She sprayed a little too much perfume on her neck, then wiped it off with her hand and rubbed it between her breasts and onto her thighs. Sarah laughed at herself. For someone with no interest in having sex she was acting like she were getting ready for a booty call.

Her lipstick was a light pink from M-A-C Cosmetics called "Barely Legal." She rubbed it on her lips, then puckered in the mirror. She brushed out her long eyelashes until they were fluffy and thick and gave her eyes a sultry sleepy look. She added a dark shimmering plum eye shadow and outlined her eyes with a thick eyeliner that further darkened her eyes.

Sarah smiled. Even in sweatpants and a T-shirt she still looked fuckable. Her smile faltered as she once again thought about Dale. For a second she even considered wiping off all the makeup. She shook it off.

I'm not going to let that son of a bitch turn me into some homely spinster.

The gun still sat on the nightstand and Sarah looked at it for a long moment, trying to decide before she picked it up and popped it into her Coach purse. She grabbed her hotel key and walked out the door, making sure she closed it firmly behind her before she walked off toward the elevator.

As Sarah made her way down the hall to the elevator a man stepped out of his room just as she passed his door and Sarah jumped and groped for her purse, trying to open it and get at her gun. Just as she realized that he was no threat, just a guy heading down to the casino, she also realized that, had he been Dale or some other rapist, he would have been all over her before she could have gotten to her pistol. It made her feel a lot less secure and made the ride down to the elevator a lot more tense and terrifying. Sarah had her hand in her purse the entire time with her finger lightly touching the trigger guard. When the man smiled at her she almost pulled the trigger.

The Hollywood Galaxy Casino was one of the newest hotel/casinos on the strip. It had pictures and memorabilia of famous Hollywood and recording stars all over the walls and in glass cases placed strategically throughout the casino. There were statues dressed in clothes almost as famous as the stars who had originally worn them. Clark Gable's clothes from *Gone With the Wind*, Jim Carrey's clothes from *The Mask*, Wesley Snipe's costume from the *Blade* movies, the original Batman costume, a few outfits from Madonna, Cher, Michael Jackson, Prince, LL Cool J, Run DMC, Metallica, Nirvana, Kiss, The Doors, and countless others.

Sarah hadn't been in the casino for months and she found herself walking around like a tourist, staring wide-eyed at the photos of old Motown stars and eighties heavy-metal hair bands. The casino wasn't as full as she remembered from the last time she'd been there. There were almost as many locals as tourists, which was a bad sign for a casino on Las Vegas Boulevard whose main trade were the steady tide of out-of-town guests who came here to blow off steam, get drunk, gamble, patronize the many strip clubs on Industrial Avenue just one block over from Las Vegas Boulevard and the even more numerous call girls and prostitutes who lined the hotel bars after midnight. Sarah wondered how the prostitution trade was faring during the recession. Had they likewise discounted their services like every other retail industry? Were they now giving two-for-one hand jobs and blow jobs? Fifty percent off on anal with a free golden shower?

Sarah chuckled as she wound her way through the casino. The idea of discount pussy was just hilarious to her. She wondered why anyone would have bothered raping her when they could have had a professional willing to do whatever they wanted for a negotiable fee.

She glanced over at the bar where a few prostitutes had already begun to congregate in their skintight party dresses cut down to their navels. A couple of middle-aged conventioneers were already mingling among them. The girls cast angry glances at her as she passed, which caused her to laugh harder. Of all the companies going bankrupt, the world's oldest profession would definitely not be one of them. Business was slow but steady, at least in this casino.

There were blackjack dealers standing at empty tables and row after row of empty slot machines. Empty craps tables, poker tables, and roulette wheels gave the casino an almost abandoned look despite the fact that there were still a couple hundred gamblers on the casino floor. It was just a few hundred fewer than one would have expected.

It didn't take Sarah long to spot her husband. He was standing alone at one of the empty tables. Next to him a withered and wrinkled Asian woman who looked nearly a century old sat alone playing cards, just her and the dealer, a tall blonde in her early to midforties who looked like she had probably been stunning in her youth. She looked like an aging showgirl. Sarah decided to join them at the table.

As she walked up to the dealer's pit, Josh turned to her and smiled wide, obviously happy to see her. His smile widened further when he noticed that she was wearing his T-shirt. Sarah smiled back politely, then took a seat at the table adjacent to his, next to the old Asian woman.

"Hello, mind if I play?"

Josh's smile widened and he almost laughed as she pretended not to know him. The man Sarah had ridden the elevator down with took a seat at Josh's table. Sarah had an irrational moment of fear where she suspected he might have been following her. Then she saw Josh greet him with obvious recognition and realized that he must have been a regular.

Sarah reached into her purse and took out the money Josh had left her with. Two hundred dollars. Josh had intended it to be her spending money for the next three days or so. She hoped that she wouldn't lose it all on the first night.

"Uh . . . I need to buy some chips."

A cashier arrived within moments to relieve her of her cash in exchange for little hard circular pieces of plastic in three different colors stamped with the Hollywood Galaxy Casino logo.

"Thank you."

Sarah pulled out a yellow chip and tossed it on the table. She was ashamed to admit that even being the wife of a dealer she knew very little about the game.

She preferred slot machines. She wasn't even sure how much the yellow chips were worth. She hoped that she hadn't just bet fifty bucks on the first hand.

Sarah barely paid attention to the game. She preferred to watch Josh work. He and the man from the elevator were laughing and joking as the man played one hand after another, then lost it all, then won again, then lost again. Occasionally, Josh would stare over at Sarah and Sarah would stare back at him as if they were strangers flirting across a crowded room, trying to gain the courage to approach each other.

The man at Josh's table was tipping heavily whenever he won and Sarah found herself wishing he'd keep winning and keep tipping but inevitably he'd lose all his money to the house. They all did. No one built a multimillion-dollar casino to make other people rich. She'd heard a statistic once that 85 percent of the people who gambled in casinos won but only 13 percent actually left the casino with their winnings. The rest gambled it all away, giving it right back to the casino and usually with interest. The casinos knew this and that's why they made sure to keep you there as long as possible.

There were no clocks and no windows in the casinos. Nothing to give customers any indication of how long they had been sitting at the poker tables or blackjack tables or slot machines. As long as you were playing the drinks were free. And cocktail waitresses came by three or four times an hour to make sure you had everything you needed, making sure that there was never any need for you to leave the casino. The waitress had already come by her table three times and she was starting to feel a bit of a buzz from her third glass of chardonnay. They were not supposed to let you gamble if you were drunk but, as long as a customer didn't actually pass out at the table and as long as you continued to gamble, the drinks usually kept flowing. There was even a famous rumor that the casinos pumped pure oxygen into the casino to keep you awake. As far as she knew it was just a rumor but she wouldn't have been surprised.

You could cash your paycheck at the casino and they would even give you a free roll of quarters if you did as a sort of incentive, not just to cash your check there but to stay and gamble. You could even take a loan out against your house right there at the cashier's window inside the casino. Sarah wondered if perhaps the psychology of the compulsive gambler might have made a better subject for her dissertation. At least gamblers didn't freak her out the way porn and just about anything sexual had begun to disturb her.

Sarah was starting to lose too much money and she was drinking a bit more than usual, feeling quite good but aware of how easily it could turn bad with just a few more drinks. She stood up and gathered what chips she had left. Smiling at the Asian woman, and leaving a twenty-dollar chip for the dealer as a tip, she walked over to the cashier's booth to cash in her chips.

She'd started with $200. After a dizzying series of wins and losses that she had just barely paid attention to, she'd come away from the table more than a hundred dollars short. She hoped that the man from the elevator started to win again soon. In addition to the gun and the alarm system, Josh would now have to make an extra hundred dollars to cover the money she'd lost. But Josh had always forgiven her recklessness. Her daring was a quality he lacked and had always admired her for. From the beginning of their relationship he'd always said that he found her wild spirit to be one of her most attractive features second only to her breasts. But with all the money she'd been spending lately, her breasts were going to have to pick up some of the slack.

Sarah took the eighty-two dollars she had left after playing blackjack and cashed them in for quarters. She took her bucket of quarters and sat down at a row of slot machines. She sat down at the machine at the very end so that she was still in sight of Josh. As she pumped quarters into the machine, she watched the other patrons. Most of them were elderly retirees gambling their life savings, their social security checks, the equity in their homes, all in hopes of hitting it big. There was a smattering of young couples and young singles but they were few and far between.

A young Mexican woman sat on her boyfriend's lap feeding quarters into the machine and pulling the lever. The hopeful expression on her face each time she plopped in a quarter was as if she expected each one to hit the jackpot. She was barely old enough to be in the casino. Her breasts were even larger and more perfect than Sarah's. She had long, thin, muscular legs sticking out from beneath a tight plaid miniskirt. Thin, muscular arms like a dancer. A gorgeous body except for a stomach that bugled out over the top of her skirt, giving her a muffin top.

Her boyfriend looked to be almost twice her age. He was in his early thirties and wore a clean white polo shirt, plaid Carhartt pants, and black leather loafers with white socks. He had tattoos on his hands, arms, and neck. His eyes were completely dead. He showed no interest at all in either the slot machine or the woman on his lap. When he turned and looked at Sarah, no doubt wondering why she was staring at him, she felt as if she were looking into the cold black eyes of a great white shark. Sarah smiled weakly and turned back to her own machine.

Sarah was nearly down to her last ten dollars when the lights went crazy on her machine and a siren went off. She had hit the jackpot. More than $2,000 in quarters poured out of the machine. Sarah started clapping and jumping up and down, screaming as silver coins rained from the machine. She collected herself just in time to shove a bucket under the tray. One of the cocktail waitresses came and brought her more buckets. The Mexican couple sitting just a few machines away were staring at her now. The young woman looked happy and excited. Her boyfriend was just staring with those dead eyes. Sarah was happy she would not have to leave the casino. She would have been terrified that the man might have followed her out into the parking lot. She scolded herself for stereotyping but the tattoos on his neck certainly looked like gang tattoos to her, not that she was an expert on such things.

The waitress helped Sarah carry her buckets over to the cashier. Sarah could not get the grin off her face as she watched the cashier dump her quarters into a counter and then slowly count out $2,500 in hundred-dollar bills. When Sarah turned around, stuffing her cash into her purse, Josh was standing behind her.

"It looks like you made out better than I did tonight. I only had about half a dozen customers during my whole shift. I made about a hundred and twenty bucks."

Sarah opened her purse and showed Josh the fat wad of hundreds.

"Well, I made enough for both of us."

"That's beautiful. I guess that pays for the Sig Sauer."

"And the alarm system!" Sarah beamed.

"And a few drinks at the martini bar?"

"Oh, definitely."

Sarah was smiling from ear to ear. It was the happiest she'd been in days and after a few drinks she was going to feel a whole lot happier.

Josh ordered something called a macho martini, which contained Red Bull. Sarah sat next to him on a plush blue velvet couch sipping a pomegranate martini. There was a band playing jazz versions of R&B songs. Sarah sat back and relaxed to a slow sax-driven cover of Smokey Robinson's "Tears of a Clown," letting the music and alcohol slowly take her away. She could feel her muscles unwinding, the tendons in her neck and shoulders unknotting, all of her tension and fear slipping away. Even when the saxophonist attempted a sloppy, amateurish cover of a Miles Davis tune and then an even worse John Coltrane cover, it didn't bother Sarah at all.

"He should be shot for that," Josh whispered.

"Shhhh," Sarah replied with her eyes still closed. She threaded her arm through Josh's and pulled him close, snuggling up against him.

Sarah ordered a watermelon martini and then a sour apple martini and then something called a love martini, which had strawberries cut into the shape of hearts. Josh was still sipping his first martini when Sarah gulped down her fourth and began nibbling on the strawberries at the bottom of the glass.

"I guess you needed that, huh?"

Josh kissed her on the neck and his warm breath traveled up behind her ear sending a pleasant tingle down her spine. Sarah giggled, then turned and kissed him, tasting the bizarre combination of vodka, vermouth, and

Red Bull on his tongue. It really wasn't as bad as it sounded. She scooped a strawberry out of her glass and slid it into his mouth. She was going through all the motions, just as she normally would, but she felt none of the usual stirrings, none of the usual desire. She felt the love for her husband. But instead of wanting to break bedsprings, all she wanted was to be held and kissed and told how beautiful she was. She wondered if she was becoming like all the other wives whose sex drives were murdered by those two magical words: I do. Only hers was destroyed by a knife and an oily little uncircumcised penis. She shook the memory from her mind and hugged Josh tighter. She was enjoying herself too much to let those disturbing images invade her mind and ruin her night.

"You hungry?"

Sarah tried to remember when she had eaten last. It had been ice cream and cake back in the room hours ago.

"I certainly am."

"They have the best chicken fingers ever here."

"Chicken fingers? Are you serious?"

"Trust me. They use strips of fresh chicken, not processed, so it isn't dry and rubbery. Then they roll them in Cap'n Crunch, fry 'em up, and cover them in hot buffalo sauce. They taste amazing."

Sarah was still frowning.

"Okay, I'll try it."

"You will not be disappointed."

Sarah ordered another martini while Josh ordered the fingers. She knew she had already had too many. She was afraid of what would happen if she stood. She didn't think her legs would hold her. Luckily, Josh could easily carry her if it came to that. It wouldn't have been the first time.

The band was breaking down and a new band began setting up. They made the transition in minutes and the next band was playing by the time the chicken fingers arrived. They were a Prince cover band and when they started off their set with a really good version of Prince's classic "Sexy Motherfucker," Sarah attempted to drag Josh out onto the dance floor. She had been in middle school the last time she'd heard the song. Back then she'd considered Prince the sexiest man on earth.

The lead singer of the cover band could have been Prince's twin. Except for the fact that it was a woman, which Sarah would have never guessed if Josh hadn't told her. The Princess drew her mustache on with eyeliner. She had all of Prince's moves and sounded exactly like him, easily imitating His Royal Badness's ear-splitting falsetto on the high notes.

Josh was not a dancer, however, and he did all he could to resist her efforts to make him shake his groove thang. His strategy was brilliant. He shoved a chicken finger into Sarah's mouth. She was just about to protest when she tasted it. It was tender and juicy. Josh was right. This wasn't the usual processed meat. This tasted as if it was fresh off the bone and the sauce was amazing, hot and sweet. The sweet was obviously from the Cap'n Crunch. It was a combination that worked amazingly well.

"Oh, my God. That is incredible!"

"I told you so."

Content now to simply listen to the band while she licked buffalo sauce off her fingers, Sarah picked up another chicken finger and slowly tore it apart, savoring each moist, delicious bite. The band switched to "Baby I'm A Star!" and were only halfway through the next song, "Erotic City," when she cleaned her plate, shoveling the last piece into her mouth as if it were her last meal on earth. Then she turned to look at Josh's plate. There was just one more piece on his as well.

"If you loved me you'd share."

Sarah batted her eyelashes at him and stuck out her bottom lip in the most adorable pout she could manage.

"Uh, uh. No way. You already ate all of yours."

"Pleeeeeease?"

She looked too adorable to resist. Josh ripped the last chicken finger in half, gobbling up his half and feeding the other half to her.

"See, I knew you loved me."

"I'm just a sucker for a pretty face."

"Awww. He thinks I'm pretty. He wants to kiss me." She teased in a mocking singsong voice. She puckered up and gave him a big, wet, sloppy, drunken, clumsy, sexy kiss that almost knocked both of them off the couch and onto the floor. They began to laugh uncontrollably.

"You ready to dance now, sexy man?"

Josh turned up the last of his macho martini, emptying the glass in a few quick gulps. He stood up from the couch, bowing slightly and holding out his hand for her.

"Fuck it. Let's dance."

Luckily for Josh, the band had just slowed things down. Lucky for Sarah too since the martinis had taken away a great deal of her motor coordination and just walking to the dance floor was a challenge. She had to lean on Josh for support, enduring his frown of disapproval. He hated to see her this drunk but he was giving her a pass because of all the stress he knew she was under.

The band began playing "The Beautiful Ones" as Josh wrapped his big, meaty arms around her and began to sway. They danced through a long drawn-out version of "Purple Rain" that began with the entire instrumental version before beginning the song. By that time enough of the alcohol had worn off that Sarah felt a bit more confident with trying to dance. When the band began playing "Diamonds and Pearls," Sarah twirled on the dance floor like a ballerina and then, taking Josh's hand, she guided him through an awkward drunken waltz that left them both giggling hysterically and took away enough of Josh's inhibitions that he stayed on the dance floor, working up a sweat as they danced their way through "Kiss" and "Get Off." They were both exhausted when they finally left the dance floor and returned to their couch. They even received a smattering of applause from some of the other bar patrons.

"You know, I've been thinking about it . . ." Sarah began as they both got comfortable back on the velvet couch.

"Thinking about what?"

"What if, instead of an alarm system, we bought a dog?"

"A dog? I don't think a little puppy is going to do much."

"I don't mean a puppy. I mean a full-grown big-ass

dog. Like a Rottweiler or a Doberman? We could get one that was already trained. I heard that you can adopt retired police dogs."

"Do they use Rottweilers as police dogs?"

"Well, it doesn't have to be a Rottweiler. A German shepherd would do."

"I'm good with that. Let's look into it."

Sarah smiled.

"Thanks for tonight. I needed this. Even with everything that's going on. I'm having a great time. I think we both needed this."

Josh smiled back at her, then leaned in and kissed her on her forehead and then on the tip of her nose.

"I think I needed this too. I know I haven't really been handling this whole thing well. I-I haven't really said anything . . . you know . . . because I don't really like to talk about it but part of the reason I've been freaking out is because this thing just brings back my own memories."

"I know. I figured. And you've been great. I know it's been hard on you too. Do you want to talk about it at all?"

Josh shook his head

"I'm having too good a time to fuck it up now. Let's just listen to the band some more."

Sarah wondered if even listening to this old music might have been reminding him of his youth. She laughed when the band made a major goof. Josh looked at her. He had caught it too.

"That's not Prince. Is it?"

"That's Michael Jackson."

The band had launched into an energetic version of M.J.'s classic "P.Y.T."

"I'm getting tired anyway."

"Okay. Let's go up to the room."

They staggered toward the elevator, with the Prince band wailing out "Pretty Young Thing" in the background. For some reason, the absurdity of it brought them to another fit of laughter as they waited for the elevator.

An hour later they were back in the hotel room snoring soundly. For the first time all week, Sarah had no dreams.

CHAPTER SIXTEEN

Sarah woke feeling rested and warm and cozy, wrapped in a goose-down comforter that smelled like lavender and jasmine. She reached beneath her pillow and took out her digital recorder. It had recorded nothing but hours and hours of snoring and the sound of rustling pillows and sheets. Sarah sighed, relieved. She stretched, reaching up toward the padded headboard and flexing her toes, smiling, feeling wonderful. She leaned over and kissed Josh on the lips. His breath reeked of alcohol but Sarah didn't mind. She slid her tongue between his lips and kissed him deeply, teasing and tickling his lips and tongue with the tip of hers, then sucking on his tongue and twirling her tongue around it like she were giving him head. She knew she was a fabulous kisser and sure enough he responded.

She could see the outline of his erection through the sheets. She reached down and stroked it a little as his eyes fluttered open.

"Good morning, lover."

"Well, you're in a good mood."

"Let's order room service."

Josh nodded toward the tent that was rising in the sheets.

"Do you want to play first?"

Sarah couldn't remember the last time Josh had initiated sex. It figures that he would choose this time to do it. She was still feeling weird about sex, still feeling somehow violated. She didn't think she was ready to open herself up to anyone right now, not even her husband. She wasn't ready to feel anyone inside of her.

"I'm sorry. I'm just not ready yet."

Josh visibly deflated, even down to the root of him where he had been swollen and throbbing just moments before. He looked disappointed. I guess it took her denying him sex before he showed any interest in it. Though, truth be told, she had never before given him an opportunity to miss it. He never had to ask for it because she was usually all over him before he had the chance to.

Maybe a little break would be good for both of us, she thought.

"That's okay. When you're ready."

"How about we spend the day riding roller coasters and shopping and acting like tourists? We haven't done that since we moved here. We could even hit the buffet or go to one of those new four-star restaurants with the superstar chefs?"

"Now, *that* sounds excellent."

"Have you ever had caviar?"

Josh wrinkled up his nose and shook his head.

"Well, we're going to have to educate that palate of yours."

"I thought you did that on our first date?" Josh joked.

"Second date. And I don't recall you needing much instruction. You were already quite the cunnilingus connoisseur if I remember correctly."

Josh turned and looked deeply into Sarah's eyes.

Sarah could feel her body melt under the heat of his gaze. She could feel all of his love and desire boiling from his eyes. It had been far too long since he'd looked at her that way.

"Actually, you were the first and only woman I'd ever done that to."

"Really?"

"Really."

"Wow. I'm flattered. What made me so special?"

Josh shrugged. "You did me first."

"Don't tell me that I was the first woman who ever gave you a blow job?"

Sarah saw Josh's eyes gloss over and she knew she had gone too far.

"Yeah, you were the first woman."

The air between them suddenly went flat and stale. Silence fell like a curtain. Once again Sarah felt like she needed to do something to comfort him even in the middle of her own crisis.

"Ever ride the Big Shot?"

Josh's eyes refocused and he looked at her as if she were speaking a foreign language.

"The what?"

"The Big Shot. At the top of the Stratosphere?"

A smile spread across his face. A love of thrill rides was one of their mutual vices.

"Are you serious?"

"Oh yeah. Are you game?"

"Hell yeah! But first, let's order that breakfast."

Sarah grabbed the room service menu as Josh reached for the phone.

"Oooooh! They have bagels with lox and cream cheese. And they have French toast!"

"I just want steak and eggs."

"Okay, go ahead and order it. I'm going to take a shower."

Sarah climbed out of the bed. She saw Josh look at her as she scrambled up from beneath the sheets and then saw the look of disappointment when he noticed that she was wearing pajamas, long flannel pajamas. She had never worn pajamas in their entire marriage. She had complained and protested vehemently when Josh had worn them, calling them his armor, an attempt to put a barrier between them. She'd even gone so far as to cut holes in all of his pajamas forcing him to go to bed nude, the way she preferred him. Now, she was the one wearing armor.

Just feeling Josh's disappointment again, twice in the space of two minutes, was overwhelming. Still, she walked into the bathroom and closed the door before she disrobed.

The shower had twin heads that shot two forceful sprays of water. Sarah had the temperature turned up as hot as she could stand it and the two powerful multijet sprayers felt like a deep tissue massage, blasting away the last vestiges of tension and stress from her muscles. This was all she had needed, a good night's sleep and a hot shower to scrub the filth and sweat from her dreams off her skin. Her complexion was turning red as the scalding water scoured her pale flesh. It felt as if her soul were being cleansed and purged. Unexpectedly, she began to cry.

Her body hitched and jerked as the tears burst up from deep within her as if she had tapped some deep underground reservoir of sorrow. Everything had been so perfect. Her life had been flawless. Her biggest

complaint until less than a week ago had been bore-
dom. Now she was either being raped, probably drugged,
and possibly murdered every night and somehow resurrected each morning or she was crazy or some combination of the two. Somehow, in the span of a few
days, her perfect, flawless life had turned into a nightmare, literally.

The tears continued to come with increasing force
and for once she made no attempt to rein them in. She
allowed them to come unrestrained, emptying her soul,
and letting the water from the shower wash them
away. She had cried more this week than she could
ever remember crying in her adult life. But this time,
it felt good.

When she finally stepped from the shower, all the
tears were gone. She had expected to feel exhausted
after crying so hard and long but instead, she felt re-
freshed. She looked in the mirror at her eyes. They
looked puffy and swollen. She opened up her cosmetic
case and withdrew some eye shadow and cover-up. By
the time she stepped out of the bathroom her face held
no evidence of her crying jag even though she was
certain Josh had heard her.

This time she didn't bother to cover herself when
she stepped naked into the bedroom. The quick intake
of Josh's breath made her smile and almost brought the
tears back. She still took his breath away. He still found
her beautiful and desirable. But the last thing she wanted,
the last thing she would have been able to stand, would
have been for him to touch her. She turned away from
him and began getting dressed.

Someone knocked on the door and Sarah reached
for her purse even as she heard the man on the other
side call out, "Room service."

Sarah looked at Josh who stood up and walked to the door. Not a single part of him was worried that it might be Dale on the other side with a knife, ready to plunge it into his chest and then rape and murder her, and that let her know loudly and clearly that he didn't believe her at all. He had already made up his mind that it was all in her head. Sarah kept her hand on the gun in her purse and tried her best not to feel resentful.

It was the same waiter from the night before. He smiled politely and then looked down at her hand, which had slipped inside her purse and was clutching the Sig Sauer. Her finger was a fraction of an inch from the trigger. The butt of the gun had been sticking out of the purse and she slid it back in when she saw him looking. He looked up at her eyes and then managed a weak smile. Josh followed the waiter's eyes down to her purse and then he let out a sigh, scribbling a tip and a signature on the receipt and ushering the waiter out the door. Sarah could tell that Josh wanted to say something about the gun but with it still clutched in her hand he obviously thought better of it. Sarah let go of the Sig Sauer and joined Josh by the bed. The silence was back and it coated them like a blanket all through breakfast. Sarah didn't mind it though. The food was too good for her to even think about having a conversation unless it was about what she was putting into her mouth at that moment.

The French toast was fluffy and covered in powdered sugar, cinnamon, nutmeg, butter, syrup, and whipped cream. Truly decadent. Sarah began shoveling the toast into her mouth like she were a fat kid at a pie-eating contest. Like it or not, she was going to have to hit the treadmill tonight after Josh left to start his shift. It was either that or get curves in places she didn't want them.

The bagels were covered in cream cheese that had been whipped until it was as light as Cool Whip. They were piled with smoked salmon, slices of beefsteak tomatoes, red onions, and capers. Sarah showed them no more mercy than she had shown the French toast.

She looked over at Josh who was patiently cutting his steak into little cubes and dipping each individual piece in A1 sauce before putting it in his mouth. He'd eaten his eggs and hash browns first, everything in order, and had just begun on his steak. Sometimes she even had a bigger appetite than he did and she had to remind herself of the number of calories she burned doing cardio to keep from feeling like an absolute cow. Making love to her was about all the cardio Josh ever got. Still, she was going to have to start cutting back. Her metabolism was bound to slow down and when it did she'd be 300 pounds if she continued to eat like this. But that was something she would hopefully not have to worry about for a long time and in the meantime there was so much good food to eat in Vegas. She was happiest of all that Las Vegas had given up on trying to be a family destination and had begun going after the high-end crowd with fancy restaurants and designer boutiques. Today, she intended to sample her fair share of both. She had already decided on Spago for lunch at Caesars and then dinner at Fleur de Lis at the Mandalay Bay where she was going to force Josh to try caviar for the first time. After that, they'd go to Joël Robuchon at the MGM Grand for dessert. It was a good thing she'd won all that money playing the slot machines. If she had it her way, she was going to need it.

Sarah finished eating, then slipped into a pair of jeans and a baby T-shirt as she waited for Josh to finish eating his steak.

"Hurry up. I want to hit every roller coaster on the strip before lunchtime."

CHAPTER SEVENTEEN

Dale was afraid that he was going to be discovered. Ever since the woman across the street had shot at him he'd been waiting for the police to come and arrest him. He had been certain that one of the neighbors must have heard the gunshot and called the police but, after he'd stabbed her and left her bleeding on the floor, he could not stand the idea of wasting the opportunity. If he was going to go to prison, he wanted this to be his last memory of the outside world. He wanted to fuck that beautiful whore one last time.

He'd pulled off her clothes and raped her there on the floor. Then he'd dragged her onto the bed and sodomized her while her body continued to exsanguinate, cumming inside her sweet little ass as she'd bled to death. The very next day, she'd knocked on his door and he'd been certain that one of the neighbors had seen him fleeing the house. As he'd opened the door he had begun going through the details of the previous evening, trying to remember if he'd done anything to give himself away, left any evidence that might lead back to him, and simultaneously composing lies to explain them away.

But Dale had been careful. He was sure of it. He was always careful. He had scrubbed the blood out of the carpet using bleach and detergent. He'd stripped the bed and changed the sheets, then washed the sheets in the laundry. He'd even dragged her body into the bathroom and washed the blood from her skin before putting her back into bed. There should have been no evidence that he'd ever been there. So why was she standing outside his door?

Her husband had been with her and the look in his eyes, embarrassed, uncertain, rather than vengeful and enraged, let him know that whatever they thought they'd found was not conclusive. Her husband was still not convinced. Her eyes, on the other hand, were full of fury. Even still, he'd been surprised when she had slapped him. It was something new, something different. None of the others had slapped him. None of the others, as far as Dale knew or cared, had the slightest clue that anything had ever happened to them, except maybe for Dorothy Madigan. He'd heard that she'd killed herself just like his mother had, burned herself alive. But this woman knew, or thought she knew something. She had slapped him. She had been ready to beat the hell out of him when her husband had dragged her away, apologizing for her behavior . . . and now she was gone. She had not been home all night. It was driving Dale crazy.

He'd broken into her house again last night and it had been empty. Her toothbrush and makeup case were gone along with some clothes. They had packed in a hurry and fled. That left Dale without a playmate.

He imagined that she was at the police station giving a statement and that soon the police would come and take him away or else her gigantic ape of a husband would beat him to death. Dale paced the floor nervously, wondering what to do. He needed something to calm his nerves. Usually, that meant raping and killing someone but the only person he wanted to fuck, the most beautiful woman he'd ever seen let alone actually had sex with, was missing and he didn't know where she was or what to do about it.

It wasn't fair. He wasn't hurting anyone. There was no way she could remember what he'd done to her and besides, he always brought her back. He'd always brought them back. *Thou Shalt Not Kill.* All except Grandma, but that hadn't been his fault. She'd died of natural causes. And his mother had still blamed him for her death. She'd punched and slapped him because he wouldn't bring her back. But he had never liked Grandma and without her around he had his mother all to himself. Right up until she'd set herself on fire and tried to take him with her.

Why? Why didn't she love me? Why doesn't anyone understand me?

Dale knew he was not an attractive man. He had never filled out. He looked like he were on chemotherapy. His childhood acne had never fully gone away and had left his complexion scarred and pitted. His posture was bowed with narrow shoulders that rolled inward making him look almost hunchbacked. He looked like Gollum from *The Hobbit.* No way he could have ever gotten a real girlfriend. No way he could have ever gotten anyone as beautiful as Sarah Lincoln. She belonged to her idiot husband with his big chest and thick, hairy arms. He got to fuck Sarah every night and what was he? A fucking blackjack dealer! What made him so much better than Dale? That's why Dale had taken so much joy in killing him.

Sarah's husband was the same type of guy who'd teased Dale all of his life, the high school jock who got to fuck the homecoming queen in the back of his daddy's car. Dale could never have gotten a woman like that to give him the time of day. That's why God had given him this gift. It evened everything out. It allowed him to have things he wouldn't normally be able to touch, things like Sarah Lincoln.

Where the fuck was she?

CHAPTER EIGHTEEN

Sarah and Josh were at the top of the Stratosphere hotel, the tallest building in the city, strapped into a thrill ride a hundred stories, 1,081 feet, above the strip, prepared to be rocketed to the very top of the tower at forty-five miles per hour and then dropped 160 feet. She could see all the way up Las Vegas Boulevard from Sahara to St. Rose.

"I am scared to fucking death!" Sarah called out to Josh.

"Me too!"

The air jets went off, propelling Sarah and her husband straight up, the sky rushing toward her, the wind whipping tears from her eyes and splaying them across her face. Sarah screamed, then laughed when she realized that Josh was screaming too. The ride paused at the top. Weightlessness. Then it began a vertical free fall almost more terrifying than the ascent. It felt as if they were falling all 1,081 feet rather than 160. The street below rushed up toward them and Sarah felt as if they would just keep falling all the way down to Las Vegas Boulevard.

She could imagine herself and her husband shattered on the concrete and asphalt, their bones and organs spilling out from the broken sacks of flesh that had contained them and intermingling in a bloody collage of mangled meat. The ride slowed and when it neared the bottom it bounced back up. Then weight-lessness again, then another bounce before it came to a halt.

Her heart felt as if it had risen into her throat and then collapsed down into her stomach. Josh looked like he was going to throw up.

"Oh shit."

It was all either of them could say.

They left the Stratosphere and went to the Sahara to ride Speed, another air-propulsion ride that traveled at incredibly fast speeds and left her feeling as if her stomach had leaped up into her chest. From there they walked up the strip to Circus Circus. Las Vegas Boule-vard was packed. Tourists were walking by staring at the hotels and not paying attention to where they were going. One of them bumped into her and Josh started to go after him. The guy began stammering out a hur-ried apology as Josh lunged for him.

"It's okay. He said he was sorry."

Josh relaxed slightly and they continued walking again but this time Josh walked slightly ahead of her, holding Sarah's hand and pushing anyone out of the way who looked like they were about to bump into her. He almost knocked one kid into the street and Sarah had to restrain Josh again when the guy called him a dick.

"Well, you were being a dick. Now, relax. I can take care of myself. It's so crowded down here that you can't really expect no one to bump into me and you can't kick everyone's ass. I don't want you to get shot over something stupid." Josh considered it and tried to relax. He still walked the rest of the way with one arm around Sarah's waist and the other hand in front of them, deflecting pedestrians.

They finally made it to Circus Circus and Sarah headed straight for the Canyon Blaster, an indoor roller coaster that was just a bit of a disappointment after riding the Big Shot and Speed but was fun nonetheless. Then they went on to ride the big roller coaster at New York–New York. Sarah's pulse felt as if she'd just run a 10k at full sprint.

"You ready for lunch now?"

Sarah nodded.

"I guess it's a good thing we didn't eat first."

"Where do you want to go?"

"It's either Spago or Little Buddha's."

"Mmmm! Sushi."

"Little Buddha's it is."

They made their way to the parking garage. Sarah felt so happy she was almost giddy. The past few nights had been so terrible, so unbelievably horrific, that riding roller coasters and heading over to the Palms hotel to eat sushi in a four-star restaurant felt surreal. This day felt far more dreamlike than the nightmares she'd been having.

Little Buddha's was a Japanese restaurant that had one of the most romantic atmospheres of any restaurant in Las Vegas. The décor was black and red with a twenty-foot bronze Buddha overlooking the dining area. Sarah and Josh were seated at a booth opposite the bar, which was already crammed with yuppies, models, and young club-hopping tourists as well as a few high-end call girls. Even among this gathering of Las Vegas's most beautiful, Sarah stood out.

Wearing only a T-shirt and jeans and with her hair

pulled back in an unruly ponytail, she easily shamed the heavily made-up, surgically enhanced twentysome-things in their designer dresses and their hundred-dollar hairdos. Josh was staring at her with those love-struck puppy-dog eyes that made her melt inside. He reached out and took her hand. Sarah smiled and the candlelight twinkled off the tears in her eyes.

"I love you, Sarah."

"I love you too, Josh."

The waiter came by and took their wine order, then whisked away and came back almost instantly with a bottle of Riesling. Josh loved sweet wines and, though she loved to tease him about it, secretly, so did Sarah. They went down the sushi menu, ordering only the fanciest rolls. Josh was allergic to shellfish but in these small quantities it was relatively harmless. Between the two of them they ordered seven rolls.

"You should have brought Benadryl with you. I ordered a bunch of rolls that have shrimp in them."

"Mmmm. I love tempura shrimp rolls. Besides, I have an early warning system. My lips will swell long before my throat does. As soon as I feel my lips start tingling I just back off the shrimp and start drinking a bunch of water."

"Well that sounds sexy. I always wanted to kiss Dizzy Gillespie."

"What if I told you that I looked more like Steven Tyler when I go anaphylactic?"

"Steven Tyler in the seventies or now?"

"Hmmm? I'm not sure. You'll just have to let me know."

The first few rolls arrived and Josh went straight for the tempura shrimp roll wrapped in eel.

As fast as the rolls came Sarah and Josh cleaned

them from their plates. When they were finished they both felt as if they would burst. Sarah's tongue still burned from the wasabi. She doused her taste buds with the last of the wine, reducing the fire in her mouth to a pleasant sting.

The rest of the day was spent sightseeing, window-shopping, and eating. They wandered through the Forum shops at Caesar's Palace, pausing to watch the talking Greek statues do their once-an-hour show, before wandering through Hugo Boss, Versace, and Calvin Klein. They crossed the street to the Bellagio and wandered through the Prada store and Sarah almost succeeded in talking Josh into a $900 handbag. Hours later, hungry again, they wound up at Fleur de Lis where, just as she'd promised, Sarah got Josh to try caviar for the first time.

She ordered a two-ounce tin of beluga caviar that came with chopped shallots, egg whites, and sour cream.

"Oh, my God. This is amazing."

"It's eighty-five dollars an ounce so don't fall in love."

"Too late." Sarah smiled and winked at Josh.

Josh chuckled and shook his head. "I guess I need to start making more money."

"Just stick with me, kid. I'll take you places and show you things."

After dinner they drove back up the strip to The Venetian.

"You know what I've always wanted to do?" Sarah asked.

"What?"

"Ride the gondolas. I know it's corny but I think it would be fun."

"I'm down for it."

"I know it's not exactly Venice but it's the next best thing."

"Actually, the French Riviera is the next best thing or maybe Paris. These guys don't even have real mustaches. I bet they don't even speak Italian."

"Don't ruin it. Let's go. It'll be fun."

"*Buon giorno! Benvenuto, signore! Benvenuto, signora!*"

The gondolier welcomed them aboard. Sarah turned and winked at Josh as if to say: "See, he does speak Italian."

They pushed off from the little dock and began rowing toward a small walk bridge where another gondola had just passed. As they drifted out across the artificial lake, the gondolier began singing "Caro Mio Ben," an old Italian love song.

"Isn't this cool? He's got a pretty good voice, huh?"

"Ask him if he knows any Prince."

"You're funny." Sarah smacked him on the arm, then snuggled up against him again.

Night had fallen and the lights of the strip outshined the moon and stars. It felt like a perfect honeymoon. It was easy for Sarah to imagine that they were actually in Venice, that they weren't in the same town they lived in every day. Sarah pulled Josh closer as she realized that the night was almost over. Tomorrow they would be going back home, back to their normal lives. Sarah hoped the nightmare was over now.

Back at the hotel, Josh and Sarah ordered a bottle of champagne from room service and crawled into bed. They clicked through channels on the TV and then settled on a prime-time special about Barack Obama. They watched it for a while, then changed the channel to *Big Love* on HBO when the president began talking about the economy. They didn't need any more bad news.

They sipped wine and cuddled, enjoying the warmth of each other's body. Occasionally, they kissed. Before she fell asleep, she turned on the digital recorder and slid it under the pillow.

CHAPTER NINETEEN

Once again, Sarah woke up and reached under the pillow for the recorder. Josh was still sleeping, snoring a low, rumbling lion's purr that was somehow not the least bit unpleasant. Sarah rewound the recorder and pressed play. She sat for a long moment listening to nothing but the occasional moan and snort and the sound of rustling pillows. She was just about to turn off the recorder when she heard herself scream.

"No! No! Noooo! Oh my God! Don't. Don't! Helllllllp!"

All the hairs stood up on Sarah's skin and she sat up bolt straight in bed. Her jaw dropped and the saliva in her mouth dried up. She began to tremble all over. Her teeth chattered as a chill crawled over her. She could not move, couldn't think.

"AAAAAaaaaaaaarghhhhhhh! NOOOooooooooooo!"

It sounded like she was being murdered. Sarah rolled over and shook Josh awake.

"Josh! Josh! Oh, my God. Listen! Listen. I'm not crazy!"

Sarah shook him until his eyelids flew open and he rubbed the sleep from his eyes, trying to orient himself and give her his full attention. She held the recorder out to him, pressing it up against his ear as he struggled up from sleep. Just then she heard the unmistakable sound of Josh's voice come over the recorder.

"Shhhhh. Baby, you're having a dream. Go back to sleep."

Sarah wilted.

"A dream?"

"You woke up screaming in the middle of the night. You said you were being attacked."

"A dream?"

It should have been a relief but somehow it made her feel like an idiot. She tossed the covers aside, ran into the bathroom, and shut the door. This time, she didn't make it into the shower before the tears came.

Sarah sat in the bottom of the tub letting the water strike the top of her head and run down her face. She didn't know how long she'd been sitting there when she slowly began to feel another emotion come over her, relief. If it was all a dream, then that meant she had not been raped. It also meant she owed the neighbor an apology. Her relief was short-lived however.

Through the sound of the shower, Sarah heard Josh knocking on the door. They were gentle, cautious knocks, Josh checking to see if she was okay.

"I'm all right. I just feel a little silly. I'll be out in a minute," Sarah called out.

Josh knocked again.

Sarah turned off the shower and stepped out of the tub.

"I'll be out in a minute."

"I think you need to come out now. You've got a call. It's the detective."

Sarah wrapped a towel around her head and another around her waist. She stepped out of the bathroom and the moment she opened the door and saw her husband's face, she knew there was something wrong.

"They found semen," he said.

Sarah's expression asked the question that froze on her lips.

Josh shook his head and dropped the phone into her hand.

"It's not mine."

Sarah couldn't believe what she was hearing. She lifted the phone to her ear, still staring at Josh.

"Hello?"

"Mrs. Lincoln?"

"Yes?"

"This is Detective Trina Lassiter. I met you at the hospital on Friday."

"Yes?"

"I wanted to let you know that we got the lab results back. They tested positive for seminal fluid."

"Wh-where? Where did they find it?"

"Everywhere."

"Wh-what do you mean everywhere?"

"Mrs. Lincoln, we found traces of semen in your rectum, in your vagina, in your mouth. It was everywhere."

Sarah shook her head in disbelief, her mouth still hanging open in shock, stupefied by what she was hearing.

"D-did they test it against my husband's?"

"Yes, we did. Unfortunately, your husband's semen was a negative match."

Sarah felt her stomach drop as if she were back on one of the roller coasters. Her vision narrowed to a pinpoint. She dropped to her knees and began regurgitating violently.

"How is that possible? Th-they said there were no signs of rape. How is it possible? It was him! It was Dale. I know it was him."

Sarah picked up the phone again.

"What about the drugs? Did they find anything in my blood?"

"No signs of any barbiturates or narcotics. No sign of hallucinogenics either."

"Did they check for roofies? What about GHB or ketamine?"

"They ran a full toxicology screen. There was nothing but estrogen and alcohol. Look, the mind is a funny thing. You might be blocking it out. That could be why you don't remember."

"I want him arrested. I want my neighbor put in jail."

"Are you sure it was him?"

"I remember him. I can see his face as clear as day."

"When I spoke to you before you weren't certain you'd actually been raped."

"But now we know. We have his semen."

"I'm still not certain that I can get a warrant to compel him to give us a DNA sample. Not with the evidence we have. I don't know if your statement would convince a judge."

"Wh-what? Well, what am I supposed to do?"

"I'll come to your house, we'll go over your statement again, and I'll talk with your neighbor. Are you at home now?"

"No, we've been sleeping in a hotel room. I couldn't stand to stay in that house."

"I could meet you at your hotel. Where are you staying?"

"Hollywood Galaxy. Room 1912."

"I'm going to question your neighbor first. I want to see if he'd be willing to give us a DNA sample voluntarily. Will you be staying at the hotel a few more days or will you be returning home?"

"I'm not sure. I'll have to ask my husband."

Sarah hung up the phone and stared out the hotel window. *They found semen. Everywhere.*

Josh was on his knees scrubbing the floor where she'd vomited with a bath towel. He didn't look up when he spoke to her. He just kept scrubbing.

"How is that possible, Sarah? They didn't find any drugs in your system. They didn't find any bruising. Anywhere!"

"I don't know."

"How can you not remember someone cumming in your ass? How the hell do you expect me to believe that? How do you think that makes me feel?"

A sudden rage came rushing through Sarah and it was all she could do to control it. She didn't want to let this thing, whatever it was, tear her and Josh apart. But she couldn't stand the thought of Josh questioning her about something like this. *How fucking dare he?*

"How it makes *you* feel? Are you fucking kidding me? Do you know how selfish, how fucking insensitive that sounds? I was fucking raped! It wasn't you who they found a stranger's semen in, Josh. It's me getting violated every night by Lord knows who!"

Josh shook his head and let out a sharp exhalation of breath that almost sounded like a chuckle.

"I'm sorry. I am. I just don't know what you expect from me. I mean, look at it through my eyes. You can't even explain what the hell is going on. All I know for a fact is that someone else's semen was inside my wife."

Josh threw the towel on the floor and wiped his eyes with the back of his hand. He looked away from Sarah,

still refusing to make eye contact. Sarah knelt down
and put an arm around him. She was still angry but her
instinct was still to comfort him, to try to make everything okay.

"I don't know. I don't know what's happening to
me."

Josh picked up the towel and started scrubbing the
carpet again.

"So what happens next? What happens if Dale's
DNA is a match with the semen they found? Are they
going to arrest him? I mean, you'll get ripped apart on
a stand. They'll say it was consensual. It'll be your word
against his and you don't have a shred of proof. He'll
say you two were having an affair or something."

"Is that what you think?"

Josh was still not looking at her. He had soiled three
towels and was reaching for a fourth. He squirted shower
gel onto the floor and continued rubbing the carpet
with the fresh towel.

Sarah took her arm from around his shoulders and
stood up, both hands on her hips, feeling that rage boiling inside her again, wanting to explode. She felt the
urge to kick Josh in the back of his head. Instead, she
took a deep breath and knelt back down beside him.

"Look at me, Josh. Is that what you think?"

Josh still did not turn his head toward her when
he spoke. She put a hand on his cheek to try to turn
his head to face her but he jerked his head away and
continued staring at the vomit stain on the floor.

"I don't know what to think. I don't know. I mean,
you don't remember, and I have heard of people getting raped and blocking it out. I know it happens. And
with the sliding-door lock busted I suppose someone
could have come in the house. But I was home. I was

home, Sarah! It's just not possible that we're both blocking it out. It's not possible that someone broke in while I was asleep, fucked you and ejaculated in you, then got it up again and fucked you in your ass, ejaculated again, then got it up a third time and came in your mouth, all while I was snoring beside you. How could that be possible?"

Sarah shook her head. Her rage turned to a deep sadness. Josh was right. There was no reason for him to believe her. She wouldn't have believed him if the tables were turned. Whatever was happening to her was about to destroy her marriage. It was rapidly eroding the trust she shared with her husband and she knew that once the trust went the love was next. Tears were streaming down her face. She began to dry heave.

"I don't know!"

Josh punched his fist into the floor and Sarah jumped. For a moment she was afraid he was going to hit her. It was the first time she'd ever found herself afraid of her husband and she immediately felt guilty for it. Josh was big but he'd never been a bully. He was usually gentle and sensitive. This, however, was uncharted territory. She'd never before given him a reason to question her loyalty. Still, Josh was mild and nonconfrontational by nature unless he felt like he was being deliberately provoked. Attacking a woman just wasn't in him. Sarah thought about Josh storming out of the house with a gun in his hand when she'd first told him that she thought she had been raped. He had been fully planning on killing their neighbor. Sarah wondered if she really knew her husband as well as she thought she did.

"It's not possible, Sarah! It's just not fucking possible!"

"So you think I cheated on you?"

"Maybe it was a date rape or something and you felt

guilty about it and so you invented this whole thing. Maybe you blocked that out and you really believe that this whole fantasy is true. Maybe you sleepwalked across the street and fucked the neighbor in your sleep. I don't fucking know, Sarah, but you're a sex addict, a goddamn nymphomaniac or something! I know I can't satisfy you. So why wouldn't you be getting it somewhere else?"

Sarah reached out for him and Josh pulled away. He was sobbing but he wouldn't let her see his face. It was some type of pride thing.

"Josh, I didn't cheat on you. I'm not a sex addict. You satisfy me completely. We have a great sex life. I'm sorry if I made you feel like I wasn't satisfied. You always make me cum. I don't need anybody else but you. I love you and I think you're sexy as hell."

Josh finally turned to look at Sarah. Tears were streaming down his face. Sarah felt her heart break.

"Then explain this to me. Tell me what the hell happened."

"I don't know. I'm not lying to you and I'm not trying to hide anything."

This was so natural for Sarah, comforting Josh when she ought to have been losing her mind, when she ought to have been screaming at him, punching him, and crying hysterically. But flipping out like that wasn't like her. She had not been herself since this thing started; it felt good to be calm again. This was normal to her.

Sarah had just gone from vomiting on the carpet to kneeling down to take the soapy rag from his hand and wrapping her arms around him, laying his head on her chest and rocking him like a baby. Surprisingly, the transition felt effortless to her. Comforting him helped take away some of the terror she was feeling. She had to be strong for Josh. He needed her.

"I'm sorry, Sarah. I know you wouldn't cheat on me. I'm just so fucking confused. None of this makes any sense. I just don't know what to do."

"Let's try to figure this out together then. Okay? Look, let's go over what we know."

"Okay. I'll try."

Trying to solve this puzzle would make them both feel like they were doing something. It would make them feel less powerless, more in control of the situation like Sarah felt after they had purchased the gun. Sarah knew that Josh needed this. He immediately became more alert, less depressed.

"Okay," he said, turning to face her, "what do we know?"

Sarah took a death breath and hesitated for a long moment before she spoke.

"First, I saw you getting murdered by the neighbor. I remember him raping me and slitting my throat. When I woke up the next morning, you and I were alive but the bed was saturated with blood. The dreams or memories or whatever they are seem to come and go. Sometimes they're vivid and I can remember just about every detail and sometimes I can't remember anything. I woke up three nights ago and found that the sheets had been changed, the walls and the rug had been cleaned, my gun had been fired and all the bullets had been removed from the clip. But since we've been in the hotel there hasn't been any strange things happening."

"Except you did have a nightmare."

"Yeah, true, I had a nightmare. But that was it. Nothing in the room had been changed. There wasn't any sign that anything abnormal had happened at all. No bloody mattress and no missing sheets. And the digital recorder didn't record anything unusual."

"But we know that someone other than me had sex with you on the night before we got here because they found another man's semen inside you."

Josh was staring at Sarah, studying her face, trying to gauge her reaction. It pissed her off. He still doubted her.

Sarah wanted to tell him to shut the fuck up about the semen. Just hearing him say it made her feel as if there were a cold draft wafting beneath her skin. It made her want to stab him to death just to keep him from repeating it again. She wanted to forget about it, she wanted to pretend that the detective had never called. But she needed to figure out what was happening to her. This wasn't something she could just ignore.

"Yeah, okay. They found semen, but no signs of vaginal or rectal bruising or tearing and no drugs in my system."

Josh stood up and began to pace the floor.

"It doesn't add up."

"No. It *doesn't* make sense. But we know something is going on. So, what are the possibilities?"

"You could be sleepwalking and washing the sheets in your sleep."

"But then where did the blood in the mattress and the semen come from?"

"You could be having sleep sex."

"I don't see me being able to leave the house without waking you up."

"Well, they didn't test me for drugs. Someone could

still be drugging me and then sneaking in and having sex with you and you could just be blocking it out."

"That's possible. Or I could be drugging you and then sneaking out and having sex with other men and making up all the rest of this."

Josh looked at her. Shocked.

"Somebody had to say it. I know you've been thinking it. You've damned near said as much. We have to address every possibility. Then we can exclude them one by one. So, is it possible that I could be cheating on you and just making up all of this?"

Josh blushed, then shook his head, dismissing the notion.

"It wouldn't make sense. You were the one who insisted on the rape kit and they would have never found the semen if you hadn't. Why would you do that if you were cheating on me? I mean really, I wouldn't even know about any of this if you hadn't told me about it. It wouldn't make sense for you to bring all this up if you were fucking around on me."

Sarah was relieved. She slapped Josh on the arm.

"Then why the fuck did you say all that shit about me being a nympho and not being satisfied with you? Why'd you make me think you didn't trust me?"

Josh shrugged.

"I'm sorry. That was just my insecurities talking. The thought of another man having sex with you is just driving me crazy. I want to fucking kill somebody."

Josh was pacing the floor, clenching and unclenching his fingers, looking for something to break that he wouldn't have to pay for. He settled on punching the pillow.

"Someone could still be drugging us both. They

could be using something rare that they don't test for. We can't rule that out."

"A new date-rape drug?"

Sarah nodded.

"Could be, I mean it's possible. I still think we're missing something though. We need to think waaaaay outside the box."

"Okay, let's do it. Let's not rule anything out yet even what we know is impossible. What if everything you remember is true?"

"You mean that I've been raped and murdered two or three nights in a row? That you were murdered too? How would that be possible?"

"We're not thinking about what's possible yet. We're just laying everything out right now. We can start ruling things out later."

"Okay, so then we've both been murdered."

"But we both woke up, alive."

"So somehow we healed. Either we healed on our own or someone healed us."

Sarah shivered.

"Okay, that's just fucking creepy. What else?"

"Hypnotism? Some sort of subliminal suggestion or mind control of some sort? Someone could be attacking you and maybe knocking me unconscious somehow and then hypnotizing us both so we don't remember, maybe making you think you've been murdered just to freak you out more."

"Even weirder. What else?"

"I don't know. Can you think of anything?"

"Well, we've covered sleep fucking, infidelity, drugs, spontaneous regeneration, and hypnotism. I think that about covers it. So what do we do now?"

"We need to prove that you're being attacked. Catch the fucker red-handed."

"Well, we could always go back to The Spy Shop and buy that nanny cam. If we can get him on camera, then we'll have our proof."

"You're right, that's probably the only way. Do you have any money left from the slot machine?"

Sarah picked up her purse and began shuffling through a stack of bills. They were mostly twenties and fifties with only a few hundreds left.

"About nine hundred dollars."

"We spent sixteen hundred dollars last night?"

"Well, we spent about four hundred on food and then I bought you that shirt from Armani Exchange and those pants from Hugo Boss and then I bought a skirt from Calvin Klein . . ."

Josh shook his head and laughed.

"Okay, it doesn't matter. It was your money. I guess that means we can either buy the camera or the alarm but with the money we already spent on the gun, we can't do both. I haven't put anything in the bank for next month's mortgage yet."

Sarah didn't hesitate.

"Let's get the camera."

"Are you sure? What if we see something . . . terrible?"

Sarah thought for a moment. An alarm would just chase the rapist away. Then she'd never know what was happening, who was causing all of this, or if she was crazy. She had to see it to believe it. But even more, she wanted Josh to see it. She wanted him to see with his own eyes that she wasn't crazy, wasn't lying, wasn't cheating. It made her skin crawl to imagine watching herself getting raped on camera. Her stomach did a little flip as she tried to picture it in her mind. She shuddered and turned back to Josh.

"We need to catch this fucker. We need evidence."

"If we set up a silent alarm and link it to an armed security response, then we might still catch him red-handed."

"Might. He might still get away before security could get there. They might get there too soon before he can do anything and he could get off with simple breaking and entering. If I had it my way we'd have both. Catch him on camera and then apprehend his ass coming out the front door. But we can't afford that. Given our options, the camera makes the most sense."

Josh nodded.

"Okay. We'll get the camera. When is that detective coming?"

"She said she was going to talk to the neighbor first. See if he'd give a voluntary DNA sample."

Josh turned to look at her.

"You think he will?"

"I don't know. Would you? I mean, after I slapped him and threatened to kick his ass?"

Josh shook his head.

"I'd tell you to screw yourself."

"Yeah, that's what I thought."

"It would make him look guilty though."

"Yeah, but that's not the same as actually being guilty."

Sarah looked around. Her mind was working overtime. She wanted an answer now. The idea of going back to that house without knowing if she was still in danger was starting to make her panic.

"Maybe we could steal a DNA sample from him somehow."

Josh shook his head.

"And where would we get it tested? Do you have a DNA lab I don't know about? We don't even have the sample they took at the hospital to compare it to and the police won't test it because it would be inadmissible."

"Maybe we could ask that detective to give us the sample she took from me and we could take it to one of those paternity-testing places?"

"We could certainly ask but she'd be crazy to give it to us."

Sarah's brow furrowed.

"Why do you say that? Why shouldn't she give it to us?"

"Because she knows we'd need to get a sample from him in order to compare it to, which means we'd have to either steal a sample or coerce one out of him and probably by force. And then what happens if it's a match and I kill the guy? She'd be an accessory to murder."

Sarah looked at Josh, shocked.

"Would you? Would you kill him? I mean . . . if it turns out that he is the guy doing all of this?"

"I don't know. I don't know what I'd do."

Sarah rushed into his arms and hugged him tight.

"I don't want you to go to jail. I don't want to be without you. Promise me you'll let the police handle it no matter what we find."

Josh turned his head. His body tensed.

"I can't promise you that."

CHAPTER TWENTY

The knock on Dale's door was hardly a shock. He had been expecting to hear from his neighbor again. He knew he should stay away from her but he couldn't help himself. She was just so beautiful—and she remembered. He was sure of it, could see it in her eyes. She remembered, and yet she wasn't afraid. She had even come over to confront him. Had even *threatened* him. It was something new and exciting to Dale, a murder victim who remembered her own murder, and actually had the nerve to confront the man who had raped and mutilated her. Dale had an erection just thinking about it. He was having a hard time keeping himself from masturbating, but didn't want to waste his potency on his hand. He wanted to save every ounce of it for Sarah.

Someone knocked again. Dale took his time walking to the door, trying to think of things to relax his erection so whoever was on the other side wouldn't see that his cock was hard. Dale looked through the peephole and was surprised to see a black woman standing outside his door with a young Mexican police detective at her side, his gold shield clipped to his belt next to his holster. He was in shirtsleeves despite the weather, which had turned unusually cold for September. Dale didn't recognize the woman. She wasn't bad looking despite her obvious age, but Dale couldn't remember doing any black chicks lately. He hadn't done anyone but the neighbor since he'd moved in. Since meeting Sarah, Dale had discovered the joys of monogamy. Besides, the black chick wasn't his type. Her hips and thighs were too big and her breasts would have smothered him.

On closer look, the black woman was obviously a detective as well. She wore a gray blouse, gray pleated pants, and ugly black loafers. Definitely a cop. Dale began to sweat. *What were the cops doing here?* Had he left behind some evidence? Were they about to put him in jail? Dale knew he was too frail for prison. Those big, angry convicts would rape him every night and there'd be nothing he could do about it. The detective banged on the door again while Dale's eye was pressed to the peephole, startling him.

"Shit! What do you want?"

"Mr. McCarthy? Dale McCarthy?"

"Yes?" Dale had a moment were he considered running. He looked at the back door and then calculated his chances of reaching it before the two detectives kicked in the front door. He wondered if he could elude the cops long enough to make it out of town and then maybe out of the country.

"I'm Detective Trina Lassiter and this is my partner, Detective Michael Torres. We need to speak to you a moment."

"About what?"

"You know what it's about."

Dale felt as if his entire world had just imploded. They knew. They'd come to arrest him. His face would be on television. Everyone would call him a pervert, a sadist, a murderer.

But how can I be a murderer when I haven't killed anybody? Sarah and her husband are both still alive.

"You here about that crazy bitch across the street? She assaulted me!"

"Just open the door and we'll talk about it. You can tell us all about how she attacked you."

Dale could see the detective beside her chuckle.

Fuck them both, he thought. But he opened the door.

"Do you mind if we ask you a few questions? Can we come in?"

Dale didn't answer. He stepped aside and gave them room to enter. The two detectives filed past him and immediately began looking around the room, no doubt searching for clues, as if they expected to find a bloody knife and a pair of Sarah's torn underwear on the living room floor.

"So what's this about?"

"Your neighbor across the street claims you broke into her house and raped her while she was sleeping."

Dale smirked.

"She'd have to be an awfully light sleeper."

The two detectives looked at each other. Dale caught the look between them and tried to wipe the smirk from his face.

"She thinks she may have been drugged. Do you mind if we look around your house?"

"Yup. I certainly do mind."

Lassiter stepped closer to Dale, purposely invading his space. She was a large woman, physically intimidating. Dale knew she was trying to unravel him. Unfortunately, it was working. Dale looked away from her, at the floor, the walls, the other detective, back at the floor, anywhere but at the woman with her enormous breasts almost poking him in the chest.

"See now, Mr. McCarthy, being uncooperative like that makes you sound guilty. What would we find in here if we were to look around? A collection of Mrs. Lincoln's underwear? Your porn collection? Maybe pictures of the neighbor you took peeking through her windows when she wasn't looking?"

Detective Torres started wandering around the living room looking at Dale's books, his DVDs, peeking under his couch cushions.

"Hey! I said you couldn't search my house!"

"Oh, I'm not searching. I'm just looking at what's in plain sight. You're kind of a boring dude, ain't ya?"

The detective was holding up a DVD of *Splash* with Daryl Hannah that Dale had bought from Wal-Mart.

"When was the last time you updated your DVD collection?"

Dale felt his blood pressure escalate. He knew that the detectives were trying hard to anger him and that losing his temper would only further amuse them or give them the probable cause they needed to arrest him. He tried his best to keep his voice calm and steady, but he could feel the heat in his cheeks and forehead, knew his face was probably the color of a particularly livid sunburn.

"Please, do not touch my things."

Dale gently removed the DVD from the detective's hands and replaced it in his DVD stand.

"Afraid we'll find that porn collection?"

"I'm going to have to ask you to leave my house right now."

Lassiter stepped up close to Dale again, once more invading his space.

"I can tell you don't like us, Dale." She pulled out a plastic ziploc bag with a Q-tip and a specimen slide inside it. "How about you let us take a swab of the inside of your cheek. Then we can test it against some DNA we took from Mrs. Lincoln and exclude you as a suspect. Then you never have to see us again."

Dale's face lit up. He tried his best to hide his smile, dropping his head to stare at the floor. But as quickly as he would suppress the self-satisfied grin spreading across his face, it would come bursting back wider and more exuberant than ever.

"W-where did you find the DNA?"

The detectives exchanged quick looks. Torres shook his head and rubbed the back of his neck with his hand.

"Now why would you want to know where we found the DNA?" Torres asked.

Dale looked from one detective to the other. He felt his smile returning so he averted his eyes back to the floor.

"Just curious. Did they find it inside her?"

Lassiter turned pale and Dale could tell that Detective Torres wanted to hit him.

"Excuse me?" Lassiter said.

"Where'd they find it? It must have been inside of her. It's semen isn't it? Someone came inside her. That's why you want my DNA. Was it in her ass? In her mouth? Or was it all over her tits?"

"That's enough, Mr. McCarthy."

"Have you seen her tits? It looks like she's had a boob job but she hasn't. They're real. I can tell by the way they jiggle when she walks. They're real and fucking perfect. Not all big and flabby like yours. Hers are firm and perky. I bet that's where they found the semen. Because if it was me, that's what I would have done. I'd have fucked her right between those perfect tits. Now, since I'm not going to let you swab my cheeks for DNA so you can try to frame me for something I didn't do"—Dale turned to the female detective, no longer bothering to hide either his smile or his erection—"no matter how much I would love to have been the one who fucked that sweet cunt, you can go on and get the fuck out of my house."

The detectives looked shocked. That made Dale's smile widen even more. They had been trying to make him uncomfortable. But they were amateurs. Dale was a master of psychological warfare. He watched them turn and walk toward the door. The big black woman turned toward Dale one last time before she left.

"You know we're going to catch you, right?"

Dale chuckled.

"You mean you're going to catch the rapist, right? The one that you say attacked her in her sleep, as incredulous as that seems? But since that isn't me, I guess I won't be seeing you again."

Torres stopped this time and grabbed Dale by his T-shirt, balling the front of the shirt up into his fist.

"You'll be seeing us again, motherfucker. Believe that."

Dale began to shiver.

"Do-don't-don't manhandle me! Let me go!"

The detective let him go and walked out the front door, slamming it behind him. "Fuck you very much, Detectives," Dale muttered at their backs.

CHAPTER TWENTY-ONE

Sarah was just about to call downstairs for room service when the phone rang. She picked it up on the first ring.

"Hello?"

"Hello, Mrs. Lincoln?"

"Detective Lassiter?"

"My partner and I are in the lobby. Do you mind if we come up?"

"No. Come on up."

Sarah didn't like the sound of the detective's voice. She sounded too serious, almost angry.

"That was Detective Lassiter. She's on her way up."

Josh looked anxious and excited but there was definitely worry on his face.

"Did she say anything?"

"No. But she didn't sound too happy."

Sarah and Josh sat on the bed waiting. It took a long time before the detectives finally knocked on the door. Sarah fidgeted the entire time. She kept looking from the bedside clock to the door and biting her nails. It felt like time had slowed to a limp.

"Mr. and Mrs. Lincoln?"

Josh got up and opened the door while Sarah remained on the bed, anxiously gnawing at her fingernails.

Josh opened the door and Detective Lassiter rushed into the room followed by a short Mexican detective.

"That guy is an asshole!"

"Who?" Sarah asked.

"Your neighbor. Dale. He's a fucking dick! Excuse my language."

"That's quite all right. What did he say?"

The detective paused. She looked over at the other detective beside her.

"This is my partner, Detective Michael Torres."

"Uh . . . hi. What did he say?"

The two detectives looked at each other. Sarah could tell something was wrong. Josh looked agitated as well. He could obviously sense that something wasn't right.

"He asked us where we found the DNA. He wanted to know if whoever raped you had ejaculated on your breasts. Then he indicated that that's what he would have done."

"I'll fucking kill him!"

The way Josh said it, no one in the room doubted his seriousness.

"Look, I talk to a lot of insensitive assholes and not all of them are guilty. Not every pervert is a rapist. Some people just have a twisted sense of humor."

"You think he was just kidding? You told him that my wife had been raped and he said that he wished that he could have cum on her tits and you think that was just some kind of fucking joke?"

"What I'm saying is that I can't prove he did it. Yeah, I think the guy is fucking weird, disgusting, and probably guilty of something. I just can't say that he's guilty of raping your wife. I can't say it for sure because she can't."

"But what do you think?" Sarah asked. "Do you think he did it?"

The detective opened her mouth, then hesitated. Sarah knew that the woman had been about to give the automatic response, the one she'd been trained to give, something safe and legal. The detective looked at her partner and then back at Sarah. She let out a sigh, then sat on the bed next to Sarah.

"He seems guilty to me. All of my instincts tell me that he's a fucking creep who belongs behind bars. It's just that my hands are tied without an eyewitness. I can't compel him to give us a DNA sample. No one's going to give us a warrant on what we've got. I can dust your house for fingerprints and then see if he has any on record to compare them to but I can't arrest him."

Sarah nodded, acknowledging the detective while at the same time wondering why she bothered. She certainly wasn't agreeing with her. She was getting sick of these cops telling her that they couldn't do shit to help her.

She smirked and wiped a tear from her eye, then picked up her suitcase and began balling up her clothes and shoving them in without folding them.

"Thank you, Detectives. We're going home now. I guess we just have to do this ourselves."

"Don't do something you'll regret. I'd hate to have to arrest either of you."

"Don't worry, I won't let Josh kill that piece of shit. Not unless we catch him in our house. Then all bets are off. But one way or the other I'm going to get that evidence. I'll make sure you have enough to arrest him."

Detective Lassiter stood in the middle of the room not saying a thing. Sarah could feel the woman's eyes on her back as she packed. Josh began packing as well, leaving the two detectives to just stand there and watch.

Finally, Detective Torres spoke up.

"I'll speak to the lieutenant and see if we can get a patrol car to cruise by your place a few times at night. You know, just to check for anything suspicious. But like Detective Lassiter said, we don't want you two doing anything that's going to make us have to arrest you. Just stay cool and let us do our thing. If this guy's really been breaking into your house, we'll catch him. Believe that."

"Thank you," Sarah said without turning around, still hurriedly packing her suitcase.

"Are you going straight home?" asked Detective Lassiter.

"No. We have one stop to make," Josh said. He had already thrown a pair of jeans and a T-shirt, along with his work uniform, deodorant, shaving cream, razor, and toothbrush into a duffel bag and was ready to go.

"Do you mind if we stop by later on today?" Lassiter asked. "We'll dust your house for prints and see what we find. We'll need to get your prints as well to compare them against any that we find."

"That's fine. We should be home in a couple of hours."

"Okay. We'll come by this afternoon."

The two detectives turned to leave. Sarah had just zipped her suitcase shut. Detective Lassiter turned back to face Sarah. The two women made eye contact and Sarah saw the woman mouth the words, "I believe you." Reflexively, Sarah reached out and hugged her.

"Thank you, Detective. You don't know how much that means to me."

"Call me Trina. I'll see you this afternoon."

Sarah fought back tears as she let the detective go and watched the two of them leave the hotel room. Now she and Josh would have to leave as well. It was time for them to go back to the house.

"If you want, I could take the night off."

"You're working tonight?"

"Yeah, I was called in to work the high-limit table."

"That's more money isn't it?"

"Yeah. Much bigger tips."

"Then you've got to go. We need the money. All of this is just costing a fortune. I've got a gun, we're buying a security camera, and there'll be a patrol car cruising by the house a few times a night. I'll be fine."

"I'm just working ten to six. I'll be home by seven. We can take a nap when we get back to the house until I have to leave and then you can stay up until I get home if you're nervous."

"That's fine. I'll just load up on coffee. I'm thinking about changing my dissertation topic anyway so this'll be a perfect excuse to get some work done."

"You're changing it again? What to this time?"

Sarah picked up her suitcase and handed it to Josh, who took it automatically and carried it out the door. That was the best thing about being married to a guy as big as Josh. She felt no need to try to prove to anyone that she was his physical equal. He was a big man so he moved all the furniture and lifted all the heavy stuff. Fuck women's lib. Sarah waited for Josh to hold the door for her before she walked out of the hotel room.

"I have no idea what I'm going to write about. I was thinking about doing something on the psychological effects of the housing crisis and the recession on marriages. Losing your dream house to foreclosure must be devastating to a relationship. And a lot of marriages are going through a total change of dynamics since most of the jobs lost are in male-dominated industries like banking and construction. Women are taking over as breadwinners. That has to fuck with a guy's ego, and that in turn must wreak havoc on the marital bedroom and would probably even cause an increase in domestic violence and divorce."

What didn't need to be said was that she was changing it this time because she just couldn't write about sexual deviancy while she was going through her own sex-crime drama.

"That sounds pretty damn interesting. If you can write that one fast enough you could probably sell that as a book. It's timely enough."

"We'll see."

"You sure you're going to be okay?"

"Yup. I'll be fine. I'm going to go for a long jog to burn off all that rich food we ate last night. I haven't worked out the entire time we've been in the hotel. And then I'm going to spend the rest of the night doing research until you get home. I'll keep the gun right beside the computer and put holes in anyone who steps foot in that door."

"Then we're stopping by the hardware store to get a security bar for that slider door. And we're leaving all the lights on in front of the house. If someone walks up to the house, I want everyone to be able to see him."

After checking out, they drove directly to The Spy Shop.

"I knew you two would be back. I could tell the way you were looking at that nanny cam, the one with the teddy bear, right? It's one of the most popular items we sell. But that's kind of old-school. I've got something a bit more state-of-the-art."

The clerk walked them over to a tiny round disk with a lens in it.

"This is the perfect camera for any type of light conditions and the lens is only one and a quarter inches. It's the smallest camera we make. The Night Observer Wireless B/W Camera System can 'see' in three times less light than the standard nanny cam, making it perfect for mounting in any darkened area around your home. Its small size makes it easily concealable. You could lay this sucker out in plain sight and no one would even notice it."

"How much is it?"

"I can let you have the camera and the remote VCR for just about a hundred and forty dollars."

"Why is it so much cheaper than the bear?"

"Because the bear is cuter."

The guy winked at Sarah and Sarah scowled back.

"Does it have a motion detector?"

"No. Once you turn it on it's just on."

"But the teddy bear has a motion detector and it's in color?" Josh asked.

"Yeah, and we've got it in a wireless version now."

"We want something that will record everything that happens in the room. Or something we could put really close to someone, close enough to see their face, without them knowing it's there," Sarah said.

"If you like the concealment possibilities of the teddy bear, and the color recording features, we have a few other hidden cameras you might be interested in."

The clerk walked them over to where the teddy bear camera sat amid a bunch of other seemingly innocuous household objects.

"We have a radio alarm clock with a camera in it.

This one has that motion sensor you asked about, and it comes in color."

Sarah looked over at her husband and smiled. This would be perfect if she was attacked in her bed again. The camera would record everything. But if he raped her on the floor as the stain on the carpet would indicate he did at least once, this camera might miss it. Josh looked over at her and Sarah shook her head.

"What else do you have?" she asked.

"We have stereo speakers with a camera in it. We have fake plants. We even have toasters and wall clocks and, of course, paintings and pictures. If you want to get the entire room, this smoke-alarm camera mounts to the ceiling and will capture everything in the room from an overhead perspective. I don't know how clear the details will be but it's at least as clear as those old surveillance cameras they used to put in liquor stores, and they caught criminals with those. It has a ninety-two-degree field of vision and a seven-hundred-foot line of sight. If you mount it over your door you should catch the entire room. It's wireless and can be hooked up to a wireless VCR to record everything it sees."

Sarah looked at Josh and they nodded in unison.

"How much?" she asked.

"This one is three hundred and fifty dollars plus another sixty for the VCR."

"Wow. That's a little more than we were planning on spending."

"But it's perfect," Josh said. "We'll take it."

Sarah couldn't help but feel a little foolish as they left the store. They had already spent over $2,000 trying to prove she wasn't crazy and protect her from her phantom rapist. As confident as she was that she was being raped by the neighbor, she had just as many doubts. She couldn't help but feel a little worried that she might turn on the VCR in the morning and see video of her leaving the bedroom in the middle of the night and then coming back and changing the sheets and scrubbing the walls and floor. She was even more terrified that the video would show her welcoming Dale into her bedroom while she was sleepwalking. If that happened, her marriage was over.

They drove to the hardware store and picked up the security bar and then drove straight home. The detectives were already at the house when they arrived, parked by the driveway in a black Crown Victoria. Their presence made Sarah even more confident. They were starting to take her seriously. They believed her. At least Detective Lassiter did.

Sarah stared hard at the closed blinds across the street. They did not move as she pulled up but she had little doubt that Dale was over there watching. His lawn was beginning to look unkempt, as if he had not mowed it since he moved in. Sarah couldn't remember ever seeing him outside since the day he moved in.

The detectives met them on the driveway as Sarah and Josh parked their car and began pulling their bags out of the trunk.

"Would you mind if we went in first? We'd like to try to get as many prints as we can and you might smudge them."

"Sure. We'll wait outside."

"You can come into the living room after we've dusted the front-door handle and the living room furniture, at least the surfaces that we can get prints from."

"Don't you have a team for this? A CSI unit? Like on TV?"

The detectives gave each other one of those looks, the kind people give each other when they're sharing a secret and weighing the pros and cons of letting someone else in on it.

"We're sort of doing this unofficially. That rules out the crime-scene unit," Lassiter said.

"In the movies cops can just call up their buddies in CSU and they'll do a job for them as a favor. In the real life there's a shitload of red-tape bureaucratic bullshit involved," Torres added.

"So, you're saying this whole case is unofficial?" Josh asked.

"It's not closed, if that's what you're asking. It's our case and we're keeping it open."

"But your superiors aren't committing any resources to it."

"No. The lieutenant thinks there's no crime or that we'd never be able to prove it if there was one because of your police statement. So it's just the two of us."

"Well, thanks. Thanks for believing us."

The detectives started at the front door, examining the handle set with a flashlight. Detective Torres was twirling a brush, fluffing its bristles. He dipped the tip of the brush into a can of black latent-print powder, then lightly dusted the powder onto the door handle. The detective knelt down and gently blew off some of the powder. Then he pressed some clear tape onto the door handle and began smoothing it down with his thumb. He then transferred the tape onto a card and labeled and initialed it.

"I'd better sign it too," Detective Lassiter said. "Chain of evidence."

Detective Torres passed the card to his partner while he scribbled in his notebook. He took four more prints from the handle, labeling each one.

"The rest of the prints are too smudged. I think that's all we're getting off this."

"I think that's good. Most of them are probably from the Lincolns anyway. Let's go inside."

The detectives entered the house, leaving Sarah and her husband on the front porch.

"Do you think they'll find anything?" Sarah asked her husband.

"I don't know. But remember what they said about getting a print match. If he's not already in the system, then the only way they can get a copy of his prints will be to arrest him."

"Do you think they would?"

"You mean arrest him?"

"Yeah, they could probably pick him up for something even if it isn't for rape. Maybe trespassing or something."

"I don't know if they would go that far," Josh said.

Sarah looked across the street.

"That fucker. If they find his prints in our house I might just kill that bastard myself."

"If they find his prints in the house they'll arrest him and that will be the end of it."

"Not really. I'd have to testify in court. Fuck, that would suck. Do you know what a terrible witness I would make? I don't even really remember what happened."

An hour went by before the detectives poked their heads out and told Sarah and her husband that they were okay to come inside.

"Sorry, I almost forgot about you. I'm going to fin-

gerprint both of you while Detective Torres goes upstairs and dusts your bedroom."

"Did you find anything?"

"Most of the prints are identical, from what I can tell.
Those probably belong to you two. But there were some
on the slider door handle and the dining room window
that didn't match the others. They may be from a houseguest or a visitor, a friend, the pest-control guy, just
about anyone but we'll run the prints anyway just to be
sure."

It took two more hours before Detective Torres
came back downstairs.

"We'll get back to you if we find anything."

"Thank you, Detectives," Sarah said.

Josh walked them to the door and then walked into
the living room and collapsed onto the couch.

"Tired?"

Sarah sat in Josh's lap and wrapped her arms around
him.

"Exhausted." Josh laid his head on her breasts.

"Let's go upstairs and take a nap. It's been a long
day."

"Let's set up the camera first."

Sarah carried the bags upstairs while Josh removed
a stepladder from the downstairs closet. Sarah was already unwrapping the box, sitting on the bed reading
the installation instructions when Josh returned.

It took them a moment to figure out how to sync the
camera with the VCR but soon they had it installed in
the ceiling where the smoke alarm had been.

"Well, let's just hope there's not a fire."

"The other alarms are still working. The house isn't
that big. We'd hear the one in the hallway if there was
a fire."

They stripped down to their underwear and crawled under the covers. Josh turned on the television and they lay in bed together watching *Oprah Winfrey* and *Dr. Phil*, falling asleep just before *Judge Judy*. Sarah kept waking up every ten minutes and reaching under her pillow for the gun, just to make sure it was still there, just wanting to feel the comfort of its weight. She stared at the front door, expecting it to creak open at any moment and for Dale to be standing there holding his stumpy little cock.

She felt her eyelids begin to close and her head droop forward. She forced her eyes open but the weight of the day lay heavily upon them, slamming them shut. Soon she was dreaming about roller coasters and caviar.

Minutes went by before she opened her eyes again, feeling a moment of panic before she reached once again for her gun and felt it there, tucked into the pocket of her Kevlar pillow. Beside her, Josh was sleeping soundly. His snores were comforting. He sounded like a purring lion. As Sarah stared at the door, she remembered that Josh had never put the lock on the new security bar on the sliding door. She reached under the pillow and began to remove the Sig Sauer.

Pulling it from beneath the pillow, Sarah rose from the bed and walked across the room, stepping around the clean spot on the carpet as she made her way to the bedroom door and opened it. Sarah had been prepared to scream. She had not been prepared to be struck over the head with a hammer. The gun tumbled from her hand and bounced across the plush carpeting with the upgraded padding. It barely made a sound. Sarah could still hear her husband snoring as Dale stepped over her limp body into the bedroom. Everything began to go black as she heard the hammer whack into bone and Josh grunt once, then fall silent.

It wasn't over when she woke up. Dale was still there. Josh was alive, bleeding from his head, one eye closed, the other one dilated, duct tape over his mouth, around his wrists and ankles. It was still light outside. *How did Dale know we would be sleeping? How was he watching us?* The questions came and went. There was too much going on to dwell long on them.

Seeing Josh helpless like that, big, strong Josh who had always been her protector, who had always made her feel safe, turned her world upside down. It was more terrifying than the realization that she too was bound and gagged and would soon be raped and murdered. Seeing that helpless, frustrated, terrified look in his eyes made her ache deep inside. It broke her heart. She knew that he would have helped her if he could and that not being able to was killing him. Being helpless in the face of this anemic little scarecrow of a man whom he would have murdered in a fair fight, if the guy hadn't caught them both by surprise. *And how is he doing it? How is he able to ambush us both and overpower us before we know he's here? How does he know when we are sleeping?*

Josh began to scream against the tape as Dale turned toward Sarah. Sarah winced as Dale smacked her husband with the butt of her gun, the gun she'd bought to defend herself.

"Okay, Mr. Big Man with your big muscles. Think you're so fucking tough? You come to my house and threaten me? You send the police to arrest me? Well, who's in control now? We'll see how tough you are after you watch me fuck your pretty little wife."

Sarah wept as she felt Dale's hands on her breasts. She closed her eyes when she felt the hands pry her legs apart and tried not to show her fear or her pain, for Josh's sake. She could still hear Josh screaming against the duct tape, roaring in impotent rage. When she felt Dale's lips and tongue slathering her nipples in saliva, felt him bite them and twist them as if he was trying to tear them right off her chest and then felt his tiny cock begin thrusting inside of her, she wished with everything she had that Josh had been strong enough to rip through the duct tape and save her. She wished that she could have watched Josh tear this pervert's head off his fucking shoulders with his bare hands. Part of her was disappointed when it didn't happen. Part of her hated Josh for not defending her. She tried to ignore the thoughts going through her head, telling her that Josh could have broken the tape if he really wanted to. It was just tape not rope or chains or something. She tried to ignore the thought that Josh was just too scared to help her, that he would have rather let her get raped than risk getting shot or stabbed or hit over the head with the hammer again. She hated herself for feeling that way. She felt guilty and ashamed but she couldn't help it. This skinny little bitch of a man was raping her while her big, strong husband sat helpless two feet away on the same bed and just watched.

Sarah moaned and wept as she endured the invasion of Dale's oily little cock, his mouth biting and slobbering all over her breasts, hand groping savagely, mauling her flesh. When he withdrew his cock from within her and pointed it in her face ejaculating on her forehead, eyelids, and cheeks. Sarah broke, weeping out loud. Dale continued fondling her breasts and twisting her nipples until they turned purple while stroking his limp cock back to full erection.

"My dick may not be as big as your husband's over there, but I've got stamina. I can fuck you all night."

Dale was grinning at her, still stroking his diminutive pink penis, and Sarah wished that she didn't have the gag over her mouth so she could have spit in his face. Sarah looked over at her husband. Dale's semen had dribbled down her forehead and into her eyes, burning them and blurring her vision. She blinked it from her eyelashes and tried to focus on Josh's face. There were tears streaming from his eyes. Sarah was both touched by his compassion and empathy and disgusted by his weakness. He could find the strength to beat up guys in bars and parking garages for insulting him but here was this piece of shit fucking her in front of him and Josh did nothing. Deep down she knew that it wasn't fair to blame him. He'd still been asleep when Dale had clubbed him over the head with the hammer. He'd had no chance to defend himself or her. But she couldn't help feeling like he should have been able to do something. Six hundred dollars' worth of weight equipment in the garage, Josh could bench-press over 500 pounds and squat more than 700, but he couldn't stop this waifish little geek from raping her.

"How does it feel, Big Man? How does it feel to watch another man fuck your pretty wife? I gotta hand it to you. You've got yourself one hell of a piece here. This is the best pussy I've ever had. Oh, but don't cry now. It ain't over yet. I'm going to give you something to cry about. You think it was bad watching your wife get raped while you just sat and watched? Well, now I'm going to let you know exactly how she felt." He turned back to look at Sarah. "And you'll get to know how he felt. You can sit there and watch while your big manly stud gets fucked in his ass."

Josh really began to struggle now, twisting and rolling around on the bed as if trying to escape, kicking out his taped feet in Dale's direction, trying to keep him away from him. Sarah couldn't help but notice how much harder he fought for his own ass than he had fought for hers. Dale easily rolled her husband onto his stomach, cracking him with the pistol once more and then digging the barrel of the gun into his check to keep him quiet as Dale spit in the crack of Josh's ass and then inserted his thumb. He fucked Josh in the ass with his thumb, then removed it and spit in his ass once more.

"You're going to like this. My cock may not be as big as yours, but as tight as your ass is it should be just perfect for you." Dale licked his palm and then used it to lubricate his cock. "Relax. You might enjoy it."

Sarah closed her eyes and turned away as Dale eased his cock into Josh's ass. She could hear Josh grunt and moan in pain and roar in outrage. Their eyes met and Sarah could see the shame and embarrassment in his eyes. She closed her eyes and tried to block out the sound of the rhythmic slap of Dale's balls against Josh's hairy, muscular ass and the squishing, wet burping sound of his cock plundering her husband's rectum. Sarah began to scream when she heard Dale laugh. No matter what it takes, she had to kill him. She forced her eyes open and tried to focus on everything that was happening, trying to will herself to remember.

When Dale began to shake and quiver, ejaculating in her husband's dilated rectum, Sarah forced herself to keep watching. She forced Dale's grinning face into her memory, Josh's agonized, shamed expression, the sound of flesh slapping flesh, the smells of sweat, blood, and feces. She didn't blink once even when Dale drew the knife across Josh's throat and cut him from one side of his jaw to the other. Even when Dale withdrew his stubby penis covered with blood, semen, and excrement from her husband's anus and came toward her baring the knife, still wet with Josh's blood, Sarah did not look away. She looked Dale right in his eyes as he drove the point of the knife down between her breasts.

"See you again soon," Dale whispered, grinning at her still as her heart stuttered in her chest and died.

CHAPTER TWENTY-TWO

Josh was already up, getting ready for work when Sarah awoke. It was dark outside. Sarah could see the full face of the moon beaming through her windows.

"I was gonna wake you before I left."

"Do you have to go?"

"I probably should. We need the money. Do you have Detective Lassiter's number with you?"

Sarah nodded toward the purse on the dresser.

"It's in my purse."

Josh began digging through her bag. He removed Sarah's cell phone and the detective's card.

"I'm going to program it into your phone. She's number eleven on your speed dial. If anything happens just hit eleven. What about your gun?"

Sarah reached beneath her pillow and felt for the pistol.

"Got it right here."

"Okay. Just stay awake with that gun where you can get to it and I'll be home soon."

"I can't believe I slept that long. I didn't even get to go for a run. Do you think we should check the camera?"

"We weren't asleep very long. I seriously doubt anyone broke in here in broad daylight. The sun had just set when I woke up an hour ago."

"Okay."

"We'll check it in the morning when we both wake up."

Josh kissed her on the cheek and walked out the door.

"Josh, wait!"

Josh walked back into the bedroom.

"Do you think you can install that security bar before you leave?"

Josh took a quick peek at his watch and Sarah knew that he was calculating how long it would take him to drill the four holes it would take to install the bar and screw it into the metal door frame versus the time it would take him to get to work.

"Sure. I'll take care of it."

Sarah rose up on her tiptoes and kissed Josh on the cheek. She followed him as he walked into the garage to get the screw gun, a level, and a hacksaw, and then back to the rear slider door. It didn't take Josh long to get the bar cut down to the right size and installed. Sarah felt a pang of guilt as she watched him work. They hadn't had sex in days. He hadn't mentioned it but she knew it must have been bothering him. Just a week ago she would have been begging him for a quickie before work rather than pestering him to install a lock on their door so no one could break in and rape and murder her. She couldn't wait until they finally caught that fucker. Sarah couldn't wait to get her life back.

She walked over to the cupboard and took down a tin of Colombian coffee. She pulled down the coffee filters and prepared a fresh pot. It was going to be a long night with Josh gone. There was no way she was going to allow herself to fall asleep without him.

"Okay, it's all done. I'll see you in a few hours."

Josh kissed her and headed swiftly for the door. Sarah knew that he was trying to leave before she asked him to do anything else or tried to get him to stay. As badly as she wanted to yell for him not to leave, she remained silent as he walked out the door. She peeked through the blinds and watched as Josh pulled the Saturn out of the garage. As he drove off down the block, Sarah turned her gaze toward the neighbor's house. The blinds in the front room facing the street were swaying again. Someone had been there just moments ago, watching her, watching Josh leave, she was sure of it.

"That son of a bitch!"

Sarah ran upstairs and retrieved her gun from beneath the pillow. She checked the chamber and the clip as she ran back down the stairs. She ejected the clip into the palm of her hand and froze. It was empty. Sarah was positive that she had loaded it.

"Oh shit."

She looked back down the stairs and then turned and looked back up the stairs at her open bedroom door. Sarah walked upstairs and back into the bedroom. She looked over at the VCR, then up at the smoke-alarm camera. Before she checked the tape she went into the closet and found the box of .40-caliber bullets and reloaded the clip. As she slid bullets into the gun, she checked the room for bullet holes. There were no holes except for the one in the door and the drywall from the week before.

Sarah's hand trembled as she reached for the universal remote and turned on the TV. She pressed PLAY and then REWIND and watched in horror as Dale cleaned her bedroom in reverse. Sarah rewound the tape past the murder and then paused it at a scene that made her stomach lurch and heave: Dale raping Josh. She fast-forwarded and rewound it several times to be sure what she was seeing.

"Oh God. Oh God."

She rewound the tape all the way to the end and then watched the entire thing at regular speed. She saw Dale ambush them both and club her and then Josh with the hammer. She watched him pull out a roll of duct tape and bind Josh's wrists and arms before he regained consciousness and then do the same to Sarah. Then she saw him rape her and then Josh. The next part turned her blood to ice water. She watched Dale murder them, both of them; then she watched him wrap them both loosely in plastic that he had brought with him as he went about tidying up, scrubbing the floor and the wall behind the bed, wiping blood spatter from the nightstand, and then changing the sheets and the pillowcases. Sarah hadn't even noticed that earlier when she had reached under the pillow for the gun. He had changed the pillowcases. The Kevlar pillowcase was gone. She watched him empty all the bullets from the gun and place it under the pillow and then he arranged Sarah and Josh next to each other in bed.

Seeing her own lifeless body bleeding out onto the plastic was surreal. How was this possible? How could she possibly be watching her own murder on video? It didn't make sense. She looked down at her chest and there was no evidence of a wound. Just one small freckle she'd had for as long as she could remember. Other than that, her skin was smooth and unblemished. She continued watching the rest of the video.

She watched him struggle to lift Josh back onto the bed without the plastic slipping and spilling more blood onto the freshly cleaned bed and floor. Then she saw him kneel over her. With the camera's overhead angle she couldn't see exactly what he was doing. It looked like he was kissing her. Then she saw him begin removing the plastic from around her, once again being careful not to get any blood on the new sheets. That's when she noticed that the wound in her chest was gone and she was breathing.

"What the fuck?"

Sarah rewound the tape. Sure enough there it was. One minute she's dead and bleeding and the next she's breathing. She let the tape play and watched as he did the same thing to Josh before gathering up the plastic and the duct tape and his knife and the hammer and slipping out the door. A few more minutes passed and she watched as Josh got up and began getting ready for work.

"This is impossible. This is fucking impossible!"

She had her evidence, the evidence she'd been waiting for, but evidence of what? Even looking at it on tape she couldn't believe it.

"Because it's not fucking possible!"

Sarah rewound the tape and watched it again, once again feeling nauseated and having to fast-forward past the video of Josh's rape.

"My poor husband." She wondered how she could ever let him see this. It would scar him for life. Then she watched the murders again, the cleanup, and then the resurrection. Dale had somehow brought them both back to life.

Sarah collapsed onto the floor and just sat there staring at the TV, not knowing what to do or whom to call. She knew she had to call Josh but she didn't want him to see what she had seen. She knew that it would have destroyed him. She had to call the cops. But what would they do with this? This didn't make sense. Sarah picked up her cell phone and dialed eleven. Detective Lassiter picked up on the second ring.

"Hello?"

"Detective Lassiter?"

"Yes. Who's this?"

"This is Sarah Lincoln."

"Mrs. Lincoln?"

"Yeah."

Sarah paused not knowing what to say.

"Is everything okay?"

"No. I mean . . . I don't know. I've got something you need to see. I got it on tape . . . on video."

"The rape?"

"Yes." Sarah paused again. "And more."

"I'll be right there."

Sarah hung up the phone and took a deep breath; then she dialed Josh's number. He didn't answer. After five rings his voice mail picked up. He must have already been on the casino floor.

"Uh . . . Josh. You need to call me back. It happened again. And . . . and I got in on video, all of it. It's terrible. That sick bastard. It's so terrible. And there's more. I know why we can't remember anything. I know why I thought he murdered me. He did. He murdered both of us. This is so crazy. Call me back. No. Just come home. Come home. I can't explain this over the phone. You have to see it. I have to show you."

Sarah hung up and sat down with the gun in her lap. She stared out the window at the house across the street trying hard to suppress the urge to walk over there and knock on Dale's door and blow his fucking head off. It was harder than she ever could have imagined.

When the black Crown Victoria pulled up outside, Sarah was still holding the gun. At some point she had cocked it. She was aiming it at the neighbor's door when the insistent ringing of the doorbell finally registered through her fugue. As she uncocked the pistol, Sarah had a moment to wonder what she would have done had Dale opened his front door and stepped outside. She imagined herself pulling the trigger again and again and watching tiny explosions of red blossom in his chest, abdomen, neck, and forehead as the tiny full-metal jackets tore holes in his flesh. The doorbell rang twice more accompanied by a fist pounding on the door before Sarah ran downstairs to let the detectives in.

"You okay? I was just about to kick the door down!" Detective Lassiter said as she stepped into the house and reholstered her weapon. Detective Torres still had his own Glock nine-millimeter clutched in his hands, eyeing her suspiciously before finally opening his sports jacket and slipping the gun back into its holster.

"I'm sorry. I was . . . distracted."

"So, you said you had some new evidence? A video?"

"Yes. It-it's upstairs. Maybe you can make some sense of it. Because I don't know what the fuck is going on."

The two detectives followed her upstairs and into her bedroom.

"Sit down."

Detective Lassiter took a seat on the bed across from the TV while Torres remained standing. Sarah turned on the television and then started the VCR.

"We installed a security camera this afternoon when we got home. It's in the smoke detector."

Sarah watched the detectives' expressions as the

tape played. She watched them wince and scowl and frown in discomfort as the rape and murder played out on-screen. Their jaws dropped and Detective Lassiter turned to look at her with a dozen questions on her face as, on the TV screen, Sarah's and Josh's corpses began to reanimate.

"What the hell?"

"What the fuck is this?" Detective Torres asked. "Is this some kind of CGI shit? This was all bullshit?"

"No! It's real. I don't understand it either."

"Mrs. Lincoln, this isn't going to work. If you faked some kind of murder scene to set up the neighbor we can't go along with it," Detective Torres said.

"I didn't fake anything!" Sarah shouted.

"I just saw your husband get up and go to work after having his throat slit! And here *you* are standing and talking to us after I watched the nerd next door stab you to death. How do you expect us to take this to a jury?" Torres was livid.

Sarah shook her head.

"How the fuck should I know? You're the cops. I have this piece of shit on tape raping and killing me and my husband and I expect you to do something about it!"

"But you're not dead!" Detective Torres shouted.

"But I was raped! Here's the fucking evidence. Now do your damn job!"

"Mrs. Lincoln—"

"Sarah. I told you, call me Sarah."

"Okay, Sarah. We can't do anything with this tape. A defense attorney would tear us apart. And what do you think would happen if a jury saw you pop up out of the bed after being stabbed in the chest? They'd think it was all special effects or CGI."

"Then don't show them the whole film. Just show them the rape and the murder until we figure out how he did whatever the hell he did to us."

Detective Torres shook his head.

"I don't know."

Detective Lassiter began to speak and then paused. She looked up at the ceiling and then around the room, then back at Sarah.

"We could. We could try to use it to get a confession. We could use it to get a warrant for his arrest and a search warrant for his home."

"Trina, we would be willfully tampering with evidence," Torres said.

"Not really. I'm not saying we erase the rest. We just don't show them the rest. We stop the tape right after the murders."

There was a long silence while everyone in the room considered the possibilities. Detective Lassiter spoke up first.

"You swear that this tape isn't a forgery? You didn't fabricate this or alter it in any way? You swear this is real?"

"I wouldn't even know how to fake something like this. I don't know who would outside of Hollywood."

Detective Lassiter held up her hand to silence her and Sarah stopped talking and tapped her foot impatiently. She felt like she were back in grade school being chastised by one of the Catholic school nuns.

"Fuck all of that. That's not what I asked you. I want to hear you swear it to me. Swear that the whole thing went down just like you said it did."

"I swear."

Detective Lassiter took a deep breath and then ran

her hand over her forehead. She looked at the floor and then up at the ceiling and then let out all the air in her lungs in one long, exhausted exhalation. Sarah was afraid the woman was going to call bullshit on the whole thing and just walk right out the door. Sarah had gotten visual proof of what she had been saying the whole time and still the story was no more believable. It still made no sense at all.

"Okay. Then we do it. I'll go talk to the judge. Torres, you get some black-and-whites across the street and arrest that piece of shit."

Detective Lassiter stood up from the bed and both Sarah and Torres gasped. Where the detective had been sitting, blood had soaked through the sheets leaving a perfect impression of both butt cheeks. The detective's entire backside was wet with blood.

"What the fuck?"

"I guess we have what we need to get the CSU over here now."

"Shit. These are my favorite pants."

Detective Torres smiled. "And now they're evidence."

"Shit," Detective Lassiter repeated.

Sarah was still staring at the bloodstain. Somehow, it was more real and terrifying than the video. Because that puddle of red made the images on the tape undeniable.

"Why don't you try calling your husband again. Have him meet us down at the station. We're going to need statements from both of you. I would suggest that you both try to remember as much as you can."

Sarah's hands trembled as she picked up the cell phone. She was still staring at that big red ass-print in the sheets. Her fingers were just about to punch in Josh's number when the phone began to vibrate, startling her and causing her to drop the phone. It continued to vibrate as Sarah stood above it just staring at it. Finally, she reached down and picked it up on its final ring.

"Josh?"

"What's going on? Are you all right?"

"The detectives are here. I'm fine. He was in the house again. While we were both sleeping. He broke in and he raped me again. It's all on tape."

There was a pause.

"Have the detectives seen the tape?"

She knew that he was looking for some sort of corroboration. He wanted them to verify her story for him.

"Yes. They've seen it. Josh?"

"Yes?"

"He did things to you too."

She hadn't intended on saying anything. She didn't want him thinking about it as he drove home. She didn't want him to be distracted and drive too fast and get into an accident. She didn't want him playing scenes over in his head, each one more terrible than the previous one, trying to imagine what "things" Dale had done to him. But she didn't want him discovering what had happened for the first time surrounded by cops, watching him getting raped by that fucking emaciated geek.

Josh's voice sounded weak and unnaturally soft and timid.

"What things? How could he have done anything to me without waking me up? How could he have done anything to either of us? Did he drug us like we thought."

"No. We were both awake."

"Awake? How is that possible."

"You need to see the tape. He killed us. Both of us. And then he . . . I don't know what he did. He brought us back somehow."

"Brought us back?"

"Just meet us at the station. I'm headed there with the detectives right now. They're going to need a statement from both of us."

"Let me speak to the detectives."

Sarah handed the phone to Detective Lassiter.

"Hello, Mr. Lincoln."

"What the hell is going on?"

"I have no clue. All I know is that I have a tape showing a multiple rape and murder and I am going across the street to arrest your neighbor and I need you to come down to the station to give a report."

"Did you say multiple rape?"

"Mr. Lincoln, just meet us down at the station. There's really nothing I can tell you right now. You're going to have to see it for yourself. None of this makes sense to me."

Detective Torres was on the radio calling for backup while Detective Lassiter was talking to the assistant DA trying to get a warrant for Dale's arrest.

"I'm going to arrest him on probable cause but it would be nice to have a warrant to back me up. We've got him on tape committing two rapes along with two counts of attempted murder."

Sarah was barely listening to the detective's heated exchange with the assistant district attorney. She was too busy trying to imagine what must be going through Josh's mind. She tried to imagine how he would react to seeing what Dale had done to him. All she could think about was Josh beating the hell out of those two guys in the parking garage and then him storming out of the bedroom with the nine-millimeter in his hands.

CHAPTER TWENTY-THREE

Sarah watched Dale through the two-way mirror. He looked so small as he sat at the metal table across from Detective Torres. The detective didn't say a word to him, he just sat there staring at him. Dale had asked for his lawyer immediately after being arrested so they couldn't talk to him until his lawyer arrived. What they could do is make him as uncomfortable as possible.

Detective Torres scowled at him and shook his head. Then he hissed and looked Dale over from head to toe, sneering in disapproval. He stood up and walked around the table glaring down at Dale, then stood behind him and lit a cigarette.

Dale's discomfort was written all over his face. He was twitching and fidgeting, clearly anxious to speak to the detective and explain himself or flee from the man's presence. He kept looking over his shoulder to try to catch sight of Torres as if he was afraid the man was preparing to attack him. When his lawyer stormed into the room, he let out a huge sigh of relief.

"Look at that piece of shit," Detective Lassiter said as she stood beside Sarah, watching through the two-way mirror as Dale began to smirk and grin. "Don't worry, we're going to break him."

Sarah nodded, still staring at Dale as he began to

look more and more arrogant and confident now that his lawyer was present. Sarah wasn't so sure that Dale was the type to break easy. There was something about him that appeared so deeply twisted and disturbed that it made it feel as if her skin were trying to crawl off her.

Dale's attorney was a portly Italian man in his mid-fifties with hair plugs, a dye job, and an expensive Italian suit that looked like Armani. The man looked like a mafioso, gold pinkie ring and all. His eyes were hard and aloof. He walked past Detective Torres and plopped down in the chair the detective had previously occupied and slammed his briefcase down on the table. He looked expensive. Sarah wondered how in the hell Dale could afford him.

"I'd better get in there. Are you going to be okay by yourself for a minute? You can wait at my desk."

"I-I want to see. Do you mind if I stay here? Until Josh gets here?"

The detective looked at her, then looked back into the room where Dale was leaning back in the metal chair, smiling confidently.

"Okay, but be quiet and don't leave this room. The assistant DA will be here soon."

She left Sarah and walked into the room to join Detective Torres. She walked over to Dale's lawyer and stuck out her hand.

"I'm Detective Lassiter."

"Raul Severino. So, what are we here for?"

"Your client here is being charged with rape and attempted murder. We've got him on tape assaulting the couple who lives across the street from him. He broke into their home, knocked them both unconscious with a hammer, raped the wife and sodomized her husband, then slit his throat and stabbed her in the chest."

Sarah watched the attorney's face for a reaction. He raised his eyebrow slightly and grimaced but that was it.

"You say you have all of this on tape?"

"All of it."

"So, let's see the tape."

Detective Lassiter turned to her partner, who left the room, then came back minutes later pushing a TV and VCR on a cart. He plugged them both into the wall directly across from the mirror and turned them on. Then he popped in the tape. Just as the tape began to play, Josh walked into the room with Sarah followed by a young Asian woman in a tan suit who Sarah guessed was the assistant DA. Josh looked miserable. He had obviously been thinking about what Sarah had told him was on that tape during his entire drive to the station.

"What's going on, Sarah?"

"They're about to play the tape."

"I'm Assistant District Attorney Patricia Yu."

"Hello, Ms. Yu." Sarah shook the woman's hand and then turned back to watch the TV in the other room.

Once again, Sarah watched as Dale struck her over the head with a hammer and then attacked her husband, clubbing him repeatedly with the hammer and cracking Josh's skull. She turned to look at Josh as the tape played. It was obvious that he was having a hard time watching it.

"How? How can I not remember this?"

Sarah took his hand.

"Just watch. It gets worse. Much worse."

Josh met Sarah's eyes and it was obvious he didn't want to look away from her, didn't want to see the rest of the tape.

The tape played, revealing Dale as he bound their wrists and ankles and then as he raped her and then Josh, and finally ending with him slitting Josh's throat and stabbing the knife into Sarah's chest.

"No."

Josh turned to Sarah with a look of shock and confusion. His face was pleading with Sarah for answers and she felt helpless and guilty because she had none to offer and somehow felt that she should have. Josh turned back to finish watching the tape.

"That sick fucking . . ." Josh's teeth were clenched tight and his jaw muscles bulged as if he were trying to bite through something particularly tough. His hands were balled into fists and his shoulders were hunched. Veins and cords bulged in his forearms and biceps.

Detective Torres turned off the tape. Josh had turned red and his body was literally vibrating with hatred flowing through his blood like an electrical current. Sarah could almost feel her husband's rage boiling in the room, raising the heat and humidity, a storm cloud crackling with fury. His lip had curled up into a snarl. His eyebrows were furrowed and his nostrils flared. She was concerned that he was going to have a nervous breakdown right there on the spot.

Josh continued staring at the TV long after the screen had gone black and Sarah continued staring at Josh. She put her arm around him and Josh pulled away, still staring at the screen. Gradually, his eyes drifted over to Dale and the rage that sparked in them was murderous. Sarah could see Josh breathing hard as he struggled to hold in his emotions like a drowning man trying to hold in his last gulps of oxygen before being sucked underwater. His eyes welled with tears even as he continued to bare his teeth in an angry grimace. Sarah was fairly certain that had Dale been in the same room with them there would not have been enough cops in the station to keep Josh off him. Even now, Sarah was worried that Josh was going to burst through the mirror and go after him.

"Josh? Are you okay? Josh?"

When Josh turned to look at her she barely recognized him. She had never seen that combination of emotions on his face before, anger, shame, revulsion, and fear all deforming his facial features into something hideous and frightening. Sarah knew that he was reliving the abuse he'd suffered as a child. It must have been terrible to see the same thing happening to him all over again, and this was so much worse. This was forcible rape. Despite his size and strength he had been victimized yet again. Sarah could not imagine what her husband was feeling. He looked at her as if she had just asked him to solve some impossibly complex mathematical equation.

"Are you okay?" Sarah repeated.

"No. I'm pretty fucking far from okay."

Sarah pulled him tight, pulling his head down into the crook of her neck, inviting him to cry but knowing that he wouldn't. His body was as tense and rigid as an iron bar. Sarah turned back to the interrogation room. She wanted to hear what Dale had to say after watching the tape. She wanted to hear his confession.

"The district attorney's office is willing to make a deal in exchange for your confession."

"I don't see anyone from the DA's office here. And why would they be willing to make a deal if they have this tape?" Mr. Severino asked.

"Ms. Yu from the DA's office is on the other side of that mirror. If your client is willing to sign a confession, then I'll bring her in here and we can make a deal. Otherwise, she stays right where she is."

"But why the hell would she want to make a deal?"

Sarah watched as Dale leaned over and whispered something in his attorney's ear. The triumphant grin never left his face. After Dale had finished whispering in his ear, his attorney nodded slightly, looking somewhat confused. Then he turned to the two detectives and smiled.

"My client wants you to play the rest of the tape. He also wants to see the hospital records from the couple he is accused of attacking, from the night of the alleged assault."

The two detectives looked at each other. Sarah felt herself deflate. The bastard had them. She saw the confusion in the lawyer's face turn to one of smug arrogance as he noted the hesitation in the two detectives. He was still not sure how or why but it was apparent that he now knew that the detectives were hiding something.

"I'm going to subpoena the tape anyway so you might as well show me now."

Detective Lassiter muttered, "Shit!" and then sneered at Dale who was now sitting back in the metal chair with both hands laced behind his head, grinning obscenely.

Detective Torres turned the VCR back on, starting it from right before Dale's murder. On the screen, Sarah watched the now-familiar scene of Dale slitting

Josh's throat, stabbing Sarah in the chest, rushing about, cleaning up the room, changing the sheets, moving the bodies, then kneeling over the bodies and bringing them both back to life.

Dale's attorney was even more surprised and animated than Sarah herself had been when she'd first seen the tape.

"Oh, you have got to be fucking kidding me! This is a fake? You faked this whole thing? I am going to have both of your badges. So, I think it's safe to assume that there's no emergency room report?"

"You know there isn't," Torres responded.

"Then, we're done here. You go near my client again and you're both going to wind up in front of an IAD review board."

Mr. Severino stood up and gestured for Dale to follow him. Dale reached across the room and held out his wrists. Detective Lassiter looked at her partner and then over her shoulder at the mirror. Somehow the woman's eyes found Sarah's through the mirrored glass. Sarah could read the apology in her eyes along with the frustration. The detective turned back around and removed the cuffs from Dale's wrists. Before Dale could pull away, she grabbed him by the wrist and pulled him close, whispering something into his ear. Dale's eyes hardened, narrowed, his eyebrows furrowed. When he spoke it was through clenched teeth.

"Go ahead, just fucking try it."

He turned and walked out the door with his lawyer, grinning all the way. Sarah watched the door close. Finally, she remembered Josh. He was still holding her but his body felt slack and loose.

"What the fuck was that? What the hell just happened? Was any of that real?"

"It was all real?"

"But he killed us. He killed both of us. Look!" Josh pulled his shirt collar down, revealing his smooth white throat. "There's no fucking wound! There's not even a scar! So what was that?"

"He killed us but he brought us back. He resurrected us both somehow."

"Resurrected us? You mean Christ on the cross? That kind of resurrection? You're kidding me, right?"

"That's why I couldn't remember anything. He's been doing this the whole time, ever since that first night. He rapes me, kills me, and then brings me back."

"Sarah? That's crazy. That's just crazy."

"Then explain it, Josh! Explain what's on that tape! Explain the bloody sheets. Explain his fingerprints in our house. Explain his semen inside of me!"

Josh began to calm down. He was staring at Sarah, still breathing hard, still looking confused. But he was convinced that she wasn't lying, she hadn't somehow manipulated the tape. She wasn't crazy.

The assistant DA had been silent the entire time. When Detectives Lassiter and Torres walked in she broke her silence.

"What in the hell were you two trying to pull with that stunt?"

"That wasn't a stunt, at least not on our part. This is the tape we took from the spy camera in their house. We didn't alter it in any way."

"Yes, but you knew what was on the tape. You knew it was a forgery."

"We knew what was on it but we still don't believe it's a forgery."

"So, you think maybe these two got stabbed to death and then just got up and walked away? Because if that's what you're saying, then I'm going to be speaking to your captain and recommending you both for a psych evaluation and an immediate suspension. So, which is it?"

"Well, how do you explain what you saw on that tape?"

"How about a fake knife, food coloring, and corn syrup? What are you both morons? You can see special effects like that in any freshman film-school class and you're willing to risk your badges for it?"

"Excuse me, but fuck you! We didn't fake that tape." Sarah spoke up.

The ADA stepped up to her. The woman's anger was plain and undisguised. She wagged her finger inches from the tip of Sarah's nose.

"I would say fuck you too but you've already fucked yourselves and this case with that bullshit tape. Now, it doesn't matter if you were raped or not because we can't touch him. You've managed to call into question every piece of evidence these two detectives have uncovered. The fingerprints, the DNA, the blood spatter, it's all useless now."

"But it's real!" Sarah shouted.

"Yeah? And so are Jesus and Santa Claus. Stay away from Dale McCarthy and feel lucky that I don't arrest you for filing a false police report." She stormed out of the room, leaving Sarah and Josh alone with the two detectives. Sarah winced when the door slammed behind her.

"We fucked up. We fucked up bad," Torres said.

"Okay, so I don't know what else we can do here."

"Are we on our own then?" Sarah asked.

"We're not going to let that guy keep attacking you. Our job is to protect and serve."

"But he's free. He's out there, right across the street from me. How are you going to protect us?"

"Maybe you should move. Start fresh somewhere new," Detective Lassiter added.

"Move? We can't afford to move. With the economy all fucked up we can't afford to sell our house. We've lost over a hundred thousand dollars in equity in our home. And we can't live out of a hotel until the damn market recovers. We can't afford to pay for a hotel and a mortgage. We're trapped. We're stuck there with that fucking psycho."

"We'll keep working on this. We still have his prints and the ones they found in your home. The CSU has been at your house and they've gone through Dale McCarthy's house as well. If he's been doing the things that we saw on the tape, then he's bound to have left evidence."

"But you heard what that prosecutor said. Dale's lawyer will get anything we find thrown out of court because of that tape."

Sarah shook her head. It would have been funny if it wasn't so damn infuriating. They had Dale on video committing rape, sodomizing her husband, and murdering both of them. It should have been enough to put him away for life, but instead it was the very thing that was keeping him out of prison.

"We'll find something. We're not giving up. In the meantime, don't do anything stupid."

This was addressed directly at Josh. No one could fail to notice the dark expression on his face. Sarah's husband was unusually quite. He listened to their exchange but his eyes were far away. Sarah knew where he was. She knew how his mind worked. He was trying to think of all the ways he might kill Dale and get away with it. Josh wasn't the type to just shoot the guy down in cold blood and spend the rest of his life in jail, not unless there was no other way. He would want to find a way to do it that would keep him out of jail. After everything that had happened today, he would be the number-one suspect if Dale were to disappear unexpectedly or if his body were to turn up riddled with bullet holes.

"I'm in no hurry to go to the penitentiary."

Josh's voice was low and without the slightest inflection. It sounded almost robotic. He turned and walked toward the door. His eyes were still glassy, staring off into space as if he were just peripherally aware of the existence of other people in the room.

"Make sure he doesn't go after him," Detective Lassiter said. "He's not thinking clearly right now. Who would be after seeing that? But that won't keep him out of prison if he goes after McCarthy."

"I'll make sure he doesn't do anything."

Sarah wondered if she would really be strong enough to keep him from killing Dale if he wanted to. It was not her physical strength she was concerned about. It was her will. She wondered if she'd want to stop him. Her only hesitation was the thought of Josh somehow failing to kill Dale and going to jail while Dale remained free.

It was after midnight by the time they left the police station. The drive home was tense and silent. Despite the lateness of the hour, the freeway was still full with drivers heading to and from the casinos and nightclubs. Sarah watched as Josh stared at the road. She wondered how much of the road he was seeing and how much of the videotape. Josh grimaced and punched the dashboard, tears began to race the crevices and lines in his face from his eyes to his chin.

"I'm so sorry."

"Did it happen? Did th-that— Did that really happen?"

Sarah nodded.

"That fuck! That little fuck! And I go to jail if I kill him? How is that right?"

"It isn't. It isn't right at all. But I can't live without you, Josh. I want us to have kids together and we can't do that if you're in prison."

"But what am I supposed to do? He raped you! He raped my wife and he . . . he . . . fuck! He raped me too! Why the fuck can't I remember it? How come you can and I can't?"

"I can't either. I don't think I'm supposed to remember. I don't think Dale expected me to. He looked surprised. I think he thought he would get away with it. I bet he's done this before. He was too sure of himself for this to be his first time."

"That fucking freak!" Josh punched the dash again.

"So what do we do?"

"We set a trap. We catch him sneaking into the house and we blow his fucking head off."

"But how does he keep getting in? How did he know we were sleeping?"

Sarah thought about it for a while. She thought about security cameras hidden in the house with Dale on the other end watching them as they slept. She shivered.

"Fuck."

"What?"

"I know how he's doing it."

"How he's getting in? How?"

"I know how he's getting in and how he knows when we're sleeping. He's already in the house."

"What?"

"I saw this news special about these teenage girls who would slip into houses after the owners would leave for work and sleep there during the day. Sometimes they would still be there, hiding in the attic or the closet when the owners would come home. They would share the house. The girls would live in it during the day, eating their food, sleeping in their beds, using their shower, and then they'd leave at night. Think about it. It's the only thing that makes sense. He probably has a key or something. He could have stolen one at any time while that slider door lock was broken and made a copy. He might have even broken the lock. He lets himself in and just hides in the house until we're asleep."

"Then he rapes and kills us both and sneaks back to his house. I can't fucking believe this guy!"

"I could be wrong."

"No, I think you're right. That piece of shit is living in our house with us and we don't even know he's there."

They took the exit off the 215 freeway onto Pecos Road. They were now only ten minutes from their house.

"So, how do we catch him? You want to put another camera in the house somewhere? In the hallway?"

"So we can just get more pictures of him fucking me in the ass? No, I want to catch this bastard in the act. No one gives a fuck about those videos." Josh sneered. "Maybe we just fake it. We pretend to be asleep and see what happens."

"But what if we fall asleep for real?"

"Then we're no worse off than we were. But we could always load up on NoDoz before we get in bed."

"But then what if he doesn't come? We can't keep staying awake night after night."

"We can for a few nights. I don't think it will take more than that. This guy is obsessed with you."

Sarah nodded her head. Chills had begun to climb up her back at the thought of Dale sitting across the street, or worse, in her own house, obsessing over her.

They turned into their small gated community and punched their access code into the keypad. Sarah laughed at the idea that this was supposed to somehow keep them secure. Cars regularly sat outside the gate waiting for someone to enter the right code and open the gates so they could follow them in and no one ever questioned them. Besides, the one person who scared Sarah the most was on the other side of the gate.

"Do we even have any NoDoz?" Sarah asked.

"We do. We've also got coffee. But let's not talk about it once we get in the house, in case he's in there somewhere."

"Why don't we just grab our guns and search the house before we go to sleep? If we find him in there somewhere we just blast his ass right then and there."

"I really like that idea. But even if we don't find him in there that doesn't mean he ain't there. We should still follow through with the rest of the plan."

"Agreed."

Josh pulled the car into the driveway and this time they both turned to look at the house across the street. The lights were on in the windows but other than that the house was still.

"I really hope he's in here. I can't wait to say hello."

"Josh, if nothing happens tonight, can I go to work with you in the morning? Or could you take a couple days off? I don't want to be in this house alone. I can't be."

"Don't worry. I'll think of something."

CHAPTER TWENTY-FOUR

Sarah took the gun out of her purse and cocked it while Josh opened the door and reached a hand inside to turn on the light. Sarah felt her heart thunder in her chest. Her hands trembled and the gun shook as she aimed it into the darkness. The light came on and the glare blinded Sarah for one panicky second during which she almost squeezed the trigger.

"Okay, it's all clear. I'll go upstairs and get the nine. Then we can check the house together."

"I'm going with you."

Sarah and Josh crossed the floor slowly, looking suspiciously at every dark corner of the room and turning on lights as they went. Sarah jerked open the closet door as they passed it on the way to the stairs. The light in the closet was on but it was empty inside with the exception of a few boxes filled with old clothes, books, and Christmas decorations. Sarah relaxed for a moment; then her heart began to pound again as she and Josh walked slowly up the stairs.

The hallway at the top of the stairs was dark. There was a light switch on the wall beside the stairs and Josh began to speed up to reach it. Sarah could feel his pulse pounding as she held his big, sweaty hand. He was just as scared as she was. They reached the light switch and illuminated the hallway; then they walked over to the master bedroom with Sarah still pointing the gun ahead of them. Josh pushed open the bedroom door and Sarah stuck the pistol into the dark room. She imagined Dale lunging at her out of the darkness and her squeezing the trigger again and again until his chest was filled with a profusion of bullet holes and he fell to the floor bleeding and convulsing. She found the image exhilarating and felt a moment of disappointment when Josh turned on the light and the bedroom was empty.

"Let me check the closet. My gun is in there," Josh said, and they both moved slowly toward the walk-in closet. Sarah doubted Dale would be hiding in there. It was too obvious and the chance of him being accidently discovered was too great. Still, her heartbeat began to ratchet up again as they crept across the carpet to the master closet. This time Josh opened the door and walked right in with Sarah aiming the gun at his back. If Dale had been in there, there would have been no way for her to get a shot off at him without hitting her husband.

Josh reached beneath the sweaters on one of the top shelves and pulled out the nine-millimeter that Sarah hadn't known he'd had until just over a week ago. He pulled out his car keys and used a tiny key that she'd never noticed before to unlock the trigger guard.

"How long have you had that gun anyway?"

"Since college. My apartment wasn't in the best neighborhood back then, if you recall."

"How come you never told me you had it and why did I have to buy a gun if you already had one?"

"You should have your own. I can't always be around and sometimes I have this one with me."

"You bring it to work with you?"

"Sometimes. People get attacked in the parking garage more frequently than they ever report on the news. And I have a permit. I got my CCW when we first moved here."

"And where the fuck was I?"

"Does it matter? Now we have two guns. Let's go ahead and check the house."

They looked under the bed first, Josh pointing the Smith and Wesson nine-millimeter under the bed from one side while Sarah stood on the other side pointing the Sig Sauer. It was only when Sarah saw the barrel of Josh's gun pointing at her face that she became aware of the very real possibility of a crossfire.

"Whoa! Don't point that thing over here! You could have killed me."

"Sorry. Why don't you stay behind me. I'll look first and you just watch my back. That way we don't kill each other."

They searched the other two rooms upstairs, looking in closets and under beds before they walked back downstairs to check the garage. Josh ran and checked the kitchen pantry while Sarah waited with her weapon aimed just over his shoulder. The pantry was empty as well. They peeked into the laundry room as they passed it on their way to the garage. There were clothes piled up on the floor and the laundry faucet had a slow drip but the room was empty. That just left the garage.

There were so many boxes of junk that Dale could have been hiding anywhere. Sarah paused outside the garage door. She squeezed Josh's hand and tried to think of all the places big enough to conceal a human being. There were too many. An old mattress leaning against the wall, broken furniture, an old foosball table with one broken leg, two barely used mountain bikes, stacks of old records and CDs. Sarah had a terrible feeling that she was about to walk into a death trap.

Josh opened the door and Sarah tried to squeeze through the door beside him in her eagerness to protect him. There was even more stuff in there than she had remembered. In addition to the king-size mattress on one side of the garage there were two old bookcases on the other side, three big moving boxes marked WINTER CLOTHES that stood four feet high were lined up in the center of the garage, the old foosball table was sitting alongside a broken air-hockey table. It was a junkyard maze with a dozen places for an intruder to hide. Sarah swallowed hard and gave Josh's hand a tight squeeze; then they began to search the garage.

They made their way over to the mattress and Josh peeked behind it while Sarah pointed her gun at it, terrified by the knowledge that she had her back turned to the rest of the room, leaving them completely exposed to an attack from the rear.

"Hurry up, Josh," Sarah said, looking around the room and bouncing from one foot to the other.

"No one there."

They checked the boxes next. Josh looked behind them and Sarah looked inside them. There was a large crash behind her. And Sarah felt something slam into her lower back and knock her forward. Sarah whirled around with her gun pointed in front of her and dropped down to one knee in a shooting stance, just like she'd seen the police do on TV. She squeezed the trigger and a shot went over Josh's head and penetrated the drywall. She heard it ricochet somewhere in the house.

"Shit!"

"Sorry, honey."

"You almost blew my head off!"

"I said I was sorry. I thought I was being attacked. Why are you over there knocking shit over anyway?"

Josh had accidently knocked over one of the boxes filled with clothes. Several pairs of winter boots spilled out, including a pair of black high-heeled patent-leather hip boots that Sarah hadn't seen since her club-hopping days.

"I tripped. We really need to clean this place out."

"Let's check behind the bookcases and then call it a night."

They hurried through the rest of the garage. Pointing the gun into dusty, cobwebbed shadows, pulse rate rising and falling again and again each time they searched behind or inside some aged and weathered keepsake only to find nothing.

There was no one in the garage.

"Let's fine those NoDoz. I'm exhausted."

Sarah and Josh walked back into the house and put their guns down on the coffee table. Just then the doorbell rang and someone knocked on the door so hard it rattled against the jamb. Sarah looked at her watch. It was two o'clock in the morning. Simultaneously, Sarah and her husband reached for their pistols.

"Mrs. Lincoln?"

Her hand paused. She looked at Josh and then back down at the guns.

"It might be the police. They probably heard the gunshot."

The doorbell rang again. A fist pounded on the door, this time even louder and more insistent.

"Mrs. Lincoln? It's Detective Malcovich from the police department. Are you okay? We had a report of shots fired at this address."

Sarah relaxed.

"Just a minute."

She handed both guns to her husband, who carried them into the kitchen and shoved them in a drawer. Sarah walked to the door and peeked through the peephole. She saw a big, grizzled middle-aged man with salt-and-pepper hair pulled back into a ponytail. He had an unkempt goatee with stray hairs of different lengths spiraling off in different directions. He was taller than Josh, well over six feet, though not as wide or as muscular. Even with his sports jacket buttoned his belly was still visible, bulging over his belt. He looked like an old hippie in a wrinkled brown business suit he'd picked up from the Salvation Army.

"Let me see your badge."

The man pulled out a gold shield and held it up to the peephole. Sarah had no idea how to determine if it was real or not. She didn't open the door.

"What do you want?"

"We had a report of some gunshots coming from your home. I stopped by to check on you."

"We're okay."

"I'm afraid I need to see for myself. I'm going to need you to open the door."

Josh was standing beside her now. Sarah unlocked the door but she let Josh step forward to speak to the detective.

"Can I come in?"

"Let me see your badge," Josh said.

The detective handed it to him along with his LVPD

identification. Josh studied the ID and then the man's face. He nodded his head and handed the badge and ID back to the detective.

"Harold Malcovich. You can call me Harry," the detective said, holding out his hand.

Josh shook his hand.

"My name is Josh and this is my wife Sarah."

"Can I come in now? It will only take a moment."

Josh stepped aside and Sarah stepped back, allowing the detective to enter.

"What can I do for you?"

"First, what were those gunshots?"

"Gunshot. It was just one. I startled Sarah when she was carrying her gun."

"Do you have a permit for it?"

"It's registered in my name and I have a license to conceal. Why would they send a police detective to investigate gunshots? They're supposed to have a patrol car checking on the house."

"I was on my way to your house when the call came in. Since I was already headed here I told the dispatcher that I would respond."

Josh narrowed his eyes in suspicion.

"By yourself? What if there really was something going on?"

The detective raised an eyebrow and shoved both hands into his pockets to pull his pants up.

"Well, I may look like Willie Nelson but I'm an old gunslinger. I can handle myself pretty well."

Harry winked at Sarah and scratched his scraggly facial hair. He nodded at them and then gestured to the couch in the living room.

"Do you mind if we sit? I think we have a lot to talk about."

Sarah looked at Josh and then back at Harry. Josh shrugged his shoulders as he always did and began walking into the living room, followed by the detective. The detective unbuttoned his sports jacket and sat down next to Josh on the sofa. His weight created a depression in the cushions that made Josh lean toward him. Josh scooted over, looking more than a little uncomfortable. Sarah joined them both on the sofa. Just a few weeks ago she would have found the image of Josh sitting on the couch looking painfully uncomfortable next to a big long-haired hippie in a wrinkled business suit hilarious. Now she had little humor left.

"So what's this about?" Sarah asked.

The detective looked Sarah directly in the eyes for an uncomfortably long time. He lowered his head and wrung out his hands; then he licked his chapped lips and brushed a long strand of gray hair back behind his ear.

"I saw the tape."

"It's not a fake," Sarah said before he could continue. The veins in her neck and forehead bulged and her hands clenched into fists.

The detective held up his hands palms out as if preparing to ward off a blow.

"I didn't say it was. I didn't think it was. In fact, what happened to you and your husband, I've seen it before. I mean, I heard about it. Once."

Sarah touched her forehead with her fingertips and closed her eyes. She was trembling. She opened her eyes and looked over at Josh. Josh's mouth hung open and his eyes had widened in surprise.

"You-you-you've seen this before?"

"Where?" Josh asked.

"Not on video. I heard an audiotape made by a

woman named Dorothy Madigan who was convinced
that she was being raped and murdered every night by
her coworker. She was having terrible dreams about
the guy in the next cubicle breaking into her house at
night and attacking her. She had hidden a cassette
recorder under her bed the night before and it had recorded everything. I heard her crying and begging and
pleading for her life. Then I heard that bastard laugh.
It was the most evil sound I'd ever heard. You could
hear the bed squeaking while he raped her. She was
weeping and praying and then I heard her scream and
that scream seemed to go on forever, getting louder
and more agonized. It really sounded like someone
being murdered. But there she was, standing in front
of me without a mark on her. We ran a rape kit on her.
We checked her for cuts and bruises. There was nothing. There was no sign, no evidence, that she had been
attacked except for that tape."

Sarah frowned.

"So let me guess. You didn't believe her?"

"She couldn't even remember what had happened.
She had gone to sleep and when she woke up she played
the tape and that's what was on it. But she couldn't remember anything. What could I do?"

Sarah wasn't sure what she was feeling. She was both
excited and scared. Anxious to hear what the detective
had to say but frightened because she thought she knew
what he had come here to tell her. The man who had
sat in the cubicle next to the woman who thought she
was being raped and murdered every night was now
living across the street from her.

"What happened to her? Where's she now? Can I
talk to her?'"

"She's in a mental institute now. She tried to set herself on fire."

"Oh, my God," Josh gasped.

"It was Dale, wasn't it?" Sarah asked. "Dale was her coworker, the one she thought was raping her. Wasn't he?"

"The man she identified as her attacker was Dale McCarthy. We never arrested him. That's why his prints weren't in the system. We didn't have enough to go on and her story didn't make any sense. So we closed the case. We figured she was just crazy. Then when she dumped kerosene all over herself and lit a match, we just figured that that confirmed it. Then I heard about your case from Detective Lassiter. I saw the tape and I heard your neighbor's name. I put two and two together."

"Do you still have the tape? In evidence somewhere? Can I hear it?"

"I don't think that would be a good idea. He did . . . more to her than he did to you. It was pretty violent. On the tape, it sounded like he was tearing her apart."

"I want to meet her."

"She's in really bad shape. That all happened six years ago. She's been in the Nevada Mental Health Institute ever since."

"How is he doing it? How is he able to kill people and bring them back to life?"

"I don't know," Harry said. "Maybe he's like a faith healer."

"But they're all fake. They're all scammers. There's no such thing as a real healer."

"Do you know that for sure?"

"No, but that Amazing Randi guy has been debunking

faith healers and mystics for a couple decades and I've never even heard of a faith healer bringing someone back from the dead. And isn't the deal that you're supposed to be really pious and have strong faith in order to be able to heal the sick and wounded? Like a monk or a minister or something? It's supposed to be like a gift from God, right? Are you trying to say that this perverted fuck is some kind of saint?"

The detective waved him off.

"Jesus did it."

"That piece of shit ain't Jesus!" Josh roared. There was still pain in his voice. His eyes were fierce and wounded. Sarah could tell he was just barely holding it together.

"No. He's definitely not Jesus but maybe he's able to tap into the same type of energy. Maybe it's God. Maybe it's something else. Maybe he's tapping directly into the life force, the force of creation. We assume that that force is intelligent and moral and good. But what if it isn't? What if it's random and chaotic and mindless and somehow your neighbor has found a way to harness its energy? What if the same power that allowed Jesus to raise Lazarus from the dead is allowing Dale to resurrect his victims so he can rape and murder them over and over again?"

Josh shook his head and stood up from the couch. He took a few steps away from the couch and then shook his head again with his back to Detective Malcovich.

"No, Detective. I can't see God giving a power like that to a sex murderer."

"I didn't say anything about God. I said the life force, the force of creation."

Josh turned around and looked at the detective.

"So, are you saying there's no God, Detective? Just some creative force? What are you, one of those New Age hippies?"

Sarah watched her husband swell up. Religion was a topic she tried to stay away from around Josh. He didn't go to church every week, not since everything that had happened to him as a child, and she wasn't sure he'd ever actually read the Bible, but he believed and was more than a little defensive about it. The mere mention of Richard Dawkins would send him off on a tirade. Sarah was a bit more open-minded. She didn't know if God existed and would never say this to Josh but she thought anyone who claimed to know was deluding themselves. She was hoping the grizzled old detective wasn't one of those militant atheists. She had a premonition of Josh tossing him out on his rear.

The detective chuckled but didn't smile. The expression was devoid of mirth.

"Did I tell you I was a vice detective? Twenty years on the force looking at the worst of human nature. Evil and atrocities you could not even imagine. Every day I saw rapists, child molesters, drug dealers, addicts, prostitutes, pornographers, and sex slaves and more than my share of murders and assaults. So, if you're asking me if I question whether whatever force runs this universe has any morality remotely resembling man's, then that answer would be yes. I question it. I doubt it. I disbelieve. If you're asking me if I doubt if an intelligent hand is guiding it all, unless that intelligent hand is even more sick and twisted than the criminals I've been locking up for the past two decades, then I doubt it. I doubt it very much. I can't look at someone like Dale, who can do the things he can do. I can't look at some rich fuck who can molest his kids or murder his wife or sell drugs to teenagers or kidnap young girls and force them into prostitution and get away with it because he can afford the best lawyers, and believe in some omnibenevolent all-powerful father figure up there watching over us. I can buy a mindless force."

"But you believe us about Dale?" Josh asked.

"I do. I believe you. And so does Trina."

"Trina?"

"Detective Lassiter."

"But not Torres, huh?" Sarah asked. "He ain't buyin' none of this, is he?"

"Torres is a bit of a skeptic. Even more so than me. At least he is when it comes to everything but God. He's a Catholic."

Sarah stood up and paced the floor.

"So how can you help us any more than she can, Harry? I mean, no offense, but so far the police department hasn't done shit for us."

"I'm going to help you catch him in the act. I'll set up a stakeout right here in your house."

"Is this another one of those off-the-record deals? That's how Lassiter got in trouble and all the evidence she and Detective Torres gathered got thrown out and rendered inadmissible."

Harry smiled sardonically, almost sneering, and for the first time, for just a moment, Sarah thought he looked more like a gunfighter than a hippie.

"Yeah, well I won't be trying to gather evidence. I'm going to catch him sneaking in here and I'm going to put a bullet right between his beady little eyes."

Hearing him say it made Sarah aware of how transparent the plan was. It was the obvious thing, which meant that Dale would probably be expecting it. But what else could they do? The other part of the plan that bothered her was that it sounded like premeditated murder. It wasn't much different than walking across the street and putting a bullet in Dale's skull right now. She only hoped that a prosecutor would see the difference.

"That's the same plan we had. But shouldn't you be trying to arrest him, Harry? Why would you risk your badge doing something like this? I know it's your job, but officially there's no case. You could just walk away and let us try to catch him ourselves. Why are you here volunteering to give up your time and risk your career?"

Detective Harry Malcovich reached into his sports coat and pulled out his wallet, a tattered brown leather thing with receipts and business cards spilling out of it and bursting its seams. He pulled out a wrinkled photograph and held it up so Sarah and her husband could see it. It was a picture of a beautiful young brunette in her twenties with big smoldering eyes, long thick eyelashes, and full lips just like Sarah's.

"I owe it to Dorothy Madigan . . . for not believing her. If I had stopped him, if I had just believed her, if I hadn't just dismissed the whole case, she might not have tried to kill herself. If I had stopped him then, he might not have attacked you."

Sarah's eyes filled with tears.

"Thank you. Just tell us what we need to do."

CHAPTER TWENTY-FIVE

Detective Harry Malcovich was on the phone with Trina Lassiter, trying to patiently explain what he was doing at the Lincolns' home.

"I'm going to set up a stakeout. Yes, I know, Trina. This is your case. That's why I'm calling you. Starting tonight. No, the captain doesn't know anything about it and I'm not putting in for any overtime. This is all off the record. No. No. I know that. This isn't my first rodeo, Trina. I'm going to drive around the block and then come back on foot. I'll hop the fence and come in through the back door. Yes, I'll let you know if anything happens. I'll call you in the morning. Good night, Trina."

He tucked his cell phone back in the pocket of his jacket.

"Is everything okay?" Sarah asked.

"She wasn't happy. She thinks I'm trying to take over the case. The funny thing is, she admits there's not much of a case. I'll explain the connection to my case to her in the morning. Torres is out. He's got kids and a wife. He's worried about doing something that might get him fired. Jobs are hard to come by right now."

Sarah smirked.

"He doesn't believe me. He thinks I faked the tape

somehow. He wouldn't give a damn about his pension if he thought I was telling the truth."

"It ain't the easiest story to swallow."

"I know." Sarah looked down at her feet, then over her shoulder at the sliding-glass door with the security bar on it.

"I'll need somewhere to camp out here while we wait for him to make his move."

"You can sleep on the couch. How long do you think this will take?"

"I'd love it if he made his move tonight but I'd be surprised. He'll probably try to wait a few days to see if things calm down but eventually he'll do it again. He's obsessed. He can't help himself. Unless he starts fixating on someone else."

Sarah looked at Detective Harry Malcovich without responding. There was something about the man that made him appear wise and worldly in a tragic sort of way. He was like a vagabond uncle who had been back-packing around the world since the sixties and only dropped in once in a while in between trips to Egypt or Tibet. Everything he said seemed to hold some deeper meaning that he was keeping to himself but hoping she would figure out on her own. Sarah didn't know what to say about Dale going after some other woman. She knew she would feel guilty. She would blame herself for not stopping him but she'd also be relieved that her own personal ordeal was over. But Sarah doubted that she'd ever be able to relax knowing he was still out there somewhere and the idea of him getting away with raping her angered her. She wanted him to pay. She wanted to kill him for it.

"So then how many days are you thinking, Detective?"

"Three days. A week at the most."

Sarah thought about living with a relative stranger for a week and sincerely hoped that it would not take that long. She didn't like the idea of having a strange man wandering around the house, even if he was a cop. She could see the same uncertainty on Josh's face but knew he wouldn't say anything. Josh hated verbal confrontations. If it wasn't a disagreement he could settle with his fists he tended to ignore it.

"I'm going to go move my car a few blocks away. I'll come back through the back door so your neighbor doesn't know I'm here. Just don't shoot me when you see me hopping your fence."

Sarah nodded. Josh smirked.

"Don't worry," she said. "We'll hold our fire."

Sarah and Josh walked the detective to the front door and saw him out, locking the door behind him.

"So, what do you think of our new houseguest? He just sort of invited himself, didn't he?" Sarah said.

"Well. I guess it's a better plan than taking NoDoz."

"Well, it's almost four in the morning now. He'll be leaving soon anyway. Then I can finally rest and then get that run in that I've been wanting to do since we left for the hotel. So much for my thirty miles a week. Maybe I'll get so fat that fucker across the street will lose interest."

"You'd still be gorgeous even with thirty or forty extra pounds on you. It would give you some breakneck curves. Just more to love."

"What about sixty pounds?"

"Now, don't push it. I don't even keep that much meat in the freezer."

"You're a big, strong guy. You shouldn't mind lifting a little weight. Might save you a trip to the gym."

Sarah was trying her best to lighten the mood the way she normally did but today it felt strained and false. She wasn't in any mood to laugh and hearing the sound of her own forced laughter only made her feel more miserable. She fell silent and just stared ahead at the empty wall, waiting for the detective to return.

"You think we should call Detective Lassiter? You know, just to check this guy out. Make sure he is who he says he is and isn't some sort of rogue cop?"

"Couldn't hurt. I've still got her on speed dial. Hand me my phone before he comes back. I'll call her."

Sarah took her phone from Josh and dialed eleven. The phone rang three times and then Detective Trina Lassiter answered, sounding groggy and mildly annoyed.

"Hullo?"

"Detective? I'm so sorry to wake you."

"That's okay."

"I just wanted to ask you a few questions about Detective Malcovich. Is he okay? I mean, is he . . ."

"Harry? He's harmless. I know he's a bit unconventional with that whole Columbo act of his and he can be a bit of a know-it-all and that will get on your damn nerves, but that's it."

"It just seems a bit weird that he shows up at our doorstep in the middle of the night and practically moves in."

"Yeah, he has a tendency to get a bit obsessed with a case. He has one of the best closure rates in the department though. He may not always get his man but he gets more than most."

"Okay."

"Look. My shift begins at eight. I'll stop by your

house and check on you. Harry wants to talk to me some more about your case anyway."

"Yeah, he said that my situation reminds him of another case he had a few years ago. He thinks they might be related."

"Really? He didn't mention it to me."

"Oh, shit!"

"What?"

Sarah heard a noise in the backyard and she and Josh both rushed into the kitchen to retrieve their weapons. Sarah reached her Sig Sauer first and already had it cocked when Harry knocked on the sliding door.

"What happened? What's going on? Are you okay? Sarah?" Detective Lassiter asked.

"It's just Harry. I'll see you in the morning."

"Okay. Good night. Everything will be fine."

Sarah hung up the phone and put it in her pocket; then she uncocked her weapon and opened the door for the detective.

"Sorry about the noise. Your back fence was a little higher than I thought. I fell on my ass trying to climb it. I think I might have smashed one of your sage bushes."

"That's okay. Come on in."

Harry dusted himself off and stepped into the kitchen.

"So, I guess we'd better all get some sleep. There's no way he's going to come in with all these lights on."

"I wish it was that simple. He doesn't seem to care if the lights are on or not. He doesn't care if it's day or night. The only thing that seems to matter to him is that we're sleeping. He won't attack while we're awake."

"But how does he know you're sleeping if all the lights are on?"

"That's what we've been trying to figure out. We think he might be sneaking into the house when we're not at home and waiting until we fall asleep. Either that or he's got some kind of monitoring device set up in here somewhere."

"You mean like a camera or a listening device?"

"I don't know. But he always seems to know when we're sleeping."

"We checked the whole house tonight to see if he was hiding in here somewhere," Josh said.

"That would be pretty ballsy of him," Detective Malcovich said.

"He's doing it somehow."

"Maybe he's psychic? We are saying that he can bring people back from the dead, right? Precognition wouldn't be too much of a stretch from that," Sarah said.

"Or maybe he's got some kind of a connection with you both now? Maybe he's psychically linked to you somehow now that he's resurrected you both?"

"I'm sure there's probably something a little less supernatural at work than that," Josh said.

"I don't think we can rule anything out right now. What we're dealing with here is something completely extraordinary."

"Maybe. I'm too tired to think about it right now. I'm going to bed. Good night, Detective."

"Just call me Harry."

"Okay, Harry. Good night." Sarah turned and walked upstairs. She heard Josh downstairs saying good night to Harry and showing him where the bathroom and the refrigerator was. "Josh? Make sure you bring our guns up with you. I don't think I can sleep without mine."

"Okay, I'll bring it. Good night, Harry."

Sarah was about to get in the bed. She had just pulled back the covers when the rancid smell of curdled blood assaulted her nose. She had almost forgotten about the blood in the mattress. The technicians from the crime-scene unit had cut three huge two-foot-by-two-foot squares out of the mattress for evidence but had left the rest of it. They had taken the fitted sheets but left the comforter and had even pulled the covers back up like they were trying to make the bed. It didn't make any sense. There was something almost gruesome about it. Sarah looked down and only then did she notice that they had done the same with the carpet. The big clean spots were gone. Where they had been there was now just bare wood. It was time for a new mattress and a new carpet. There was no way she could sleep on that thing. Sarah collected her pillow and left the room. Josh was coming up the steps when she passed him in the hallway.

"I can't sleep in there. It smells like rot. All the blood in that mattress is starting to reek and the police technicians cut it all up. I don't know why they didn't just take the whole thing. There ain't shit we can do with what's left of it. The whole thing smells like blood."

Goose bumps raced across her flesh as she realized that she was talking about her own blood and remembered how it had been bled out of her. She went into the guest room and crawled into the queen-size bed wondering how Josh was going to fit in there with her. Josh tucked the Sig Sauer under her pillow and put his own weapon on the nightstand.

"Good night, baby. I guess we don't need to get that Rottweiler now."

"Let's just hope that Harry still has some bite left in him," Sarah said, then kissed Josh on the lips and rolled over to go to sleep.

CHAPTER TWENTY-SIX

Dale could hear the detective snoring in the next room. He'd panicked when Sarah and her husband had come home and begun searching the house for him. When the detective had arrived, he was certain that he'd be discovered. But they had missed him. The detective had talked about killing him if he found him in the house and so Dale had decided to slip out as soon as he was able. He'd been waiting ever since for the detective to finally go to sleep. It had taken longer than he had expected.

At some point Dale had fallen asleep and, as usual, he had dreamed of his mother. This dream was different than the rest, however. This one felt more like a latent memory, a recollection of something long-suppressed. He felt the emotions almost immediately, before anything had happened, a crushing fear and sadness came down on him along with the taste of metal and the smell of blood and his mother's tea leaf–scented perfume and perspiration.

"Why are you killing me, Mom?"

Tears raced down his cheeks as Dale watched his mother standing above him, clubbing him in the head with the hammer. He could feel each concussive impact. He could see the world fading into darkness and taste the coppery twang of blood on his tongue, feel it leaking from his ears and plugging his nostrils. He was awakened by the sound of his own sobs.

Dale sat in the dark, worried that he'd given himself away with his crying, expecting to be dragged out from beneath the sink at any moment by Sarah's Neanderthal husband and the detective and murdered right there on the laundry room floor. His face was still wet with tears, the dream still vivid in his mind. But Dale knew that it had been more than just a dream. He knew it with near certainty. His mother had tried to kill him. Somehow, his mother had beat him with a hammer, had nearly murdered him, and he had no memory of it until now. His mother had hated him. She had tried to kill him and then she had burned herself alive and tried to take him with her. No one loved him. No one ever had. The only way he had ever gotten anyone to show him any love was when they were dead or dying, when he had them at his mercy.

So be it. He wiped the tears from his eyes and yawned silently. The past was the past. There were more immediate issues to contend with rather than whining over his dead mother.

She didn't love me, then fuck her. That hateful bitch!

Above him, everything was quiet. He had no way of knowing if Sarah and her big apelike husband were really asleep but he knew they were completely aware of him now. They had caught him on film. They even suspected he had been hiding out in their home. And they had guns. And now there were three of them. He would have to very careful.

Dale's arms and legs were beginning to tingle from the loss of circulation. His limbs had started to go to sleep and now he didn't trust them to hold him when he stood. He had been folded up in the cabinet beneath the laundry sink for hours, waiting for his chance to slip out quietly. Now he was thinking that he might not go so quietly after all.

Dale slowly pushed open the cabinet door. He had folded himself into the small cabinet like a contortionist. He pulled his leg from where it had been bent beneath him and slowly unfurled himself from beneath the sink. His legs tingled maddeningly with pins and needles shooting up and down his limbs. They felt as if they were made of wet tissue, and Dale had to steady himself by holding on to the sink while he waited for the blood to flow back into his extremities.

He thought about Sarah and her perfect body, those big tits with the big swollen nipples, that tight wet pussy, and that gorgeous face. He wanted her so badly every muscle in his body was tensed, sinews pulled tight, trembling with the force of his desire. He could feel the erection surging in his boxers. He didn't care anymore about the detective, about getting caught, or even getting killed. He had to fuck Sarah Lincoln again. He needed her, wanted her more than his next breath, his next heartbeat. He didn't think it was possible for him to live without her. She was perfection.

Dale reached into his pants and began to stroke himself as he remembered fucking Sarah in her sweet little ass, between those big lovely breasts, ejaculating his seed on her perfect porcelain doll face. Dale knew he was not a well-endowed man. The one time a woman had given herself to him willingly it had ended with her laughing at him, ridiculing him for his diminutive size. Well, it hadn't completely ended that way. The real end had come when he'd plunged a knife into her neck and gave her a tracheotomy, carving a hole in her esophagus just big enough for him to stick his little cock in and rape her throat. Then he had brought her back to life and driven her home smiling and grinning the entire time. He had even shaken her father's hand when he dropped her off. That had been the last time he'd allowed himself to try to date a woman the "normal" way. He now saw his talent as what it was, a gift from God. It had been given to him to make up for all the other things God had failed to give him. It was his compensation for being born to parents who were meth addicts, for being so frail and sickly, skinny and pale, for having such a tiny penis. He could fuck anyone he wanted now, no matter what he looked like. All he had to do was sneak up on them . . . and kill them. Then he could bring them back to life just like Jesus did.

Dale took a few steps away from the sink to test his shaky legs. His feet still felt numb but it no longer felt like his legs were going to collapse underneath him. He stretched his arms and wiggled his fingers until all the tingling sensations went away; then he pulled out his hammer and slowly cracked open the laundry room door.

The old, fat detective with the ponytail was sitting on the couch in his wrinkled suit with a pillow behind his head and his face pointed up to the ceiling, mouth open, snoring like a grizzly bear. He was clutching a fleece blanket in his lap. His Glock was still tucked under his arm in a shoulder holster. Dale calculated his chances of creeping out of the laundry room, across the great room and into the living room without waking the detective and then killing him before he could pull out that gun. The chances weren't good. But Dale knew that he was going to try it. There was never a question. He would do anything for one more night with Sarah.

The first floor in the Lincolns' house was all stained concrete with a glossy polyurethane coating. The floor was slippery but at least it didn't squeak like a wooden floor or make that tapping noise that tile floors made when you walked on them in your shoes. But they weren't completely silent. Dale slipped off his shoes and began tiptoeing across the hard floor in his socks. His heartbeat was thundering in his chest and sweat drenched the handle of the claw hammer in his left hand, as well as the curved and serrated diver's knife in his right. The saliva in his mouth had dried up and his eyes felt watery. He stared intently at the detective's face, prepared to bolt for the front door if the man woke and knowing he would never make it.

Halfway across the floor, only three or four yards from the detective, Dale decided that if the man woke up he would rush him with the knife. He was fairly confident that he could gut him like a fish before he could pull that gun from its holster. But Dale had never taken on a grown man before unless he was ambushing him in his sleep. Men intimidated Dale and a guy as big as this detective would probably put up a good fight. He might even wrestle the knife away from Dale and use it on him.

Dale swallowed hard and his legs began to tremble. Perspiration soaked his T-shirt and ran down his forehead into his eyes. He wiped away the sweat with the back of his hand and crept closer. Now he was so close he could have been on top of the detective in three quick steps if he needed to. He was sizing up the big man, trying to decide where to plunge the knife in first if he had to defend himself or where to cut him when he reached him to silence him and take him out before he could fight or make a sound that might wake up the rest of the house. The last thing Dale wanted was a fight.

Two more steps and the detective's eyes opened. Dale almost screamed. He plunged the knife into the side of the detective's neck so hard the blade completely submerged in his flesh up to the hilt. Blood sprayed from the wound and the detective's eyes bulged. Both of his hands flew up to the knife in his throat and a gurgling and wheezing sound came from his mouth. He started to rise up from the couch, groping for his weapon with one hand while holding his throat with the other. Dale clubbed him with the hammer and the detective fell back onto the couch. Dale hit him again and one of the detective's eyes spilled out of the socket and drooled down his cheek like an oyster shucked from its shell. The next blow caved in the left side of his head and the next one dislodged a piece of his skull, flinging it across the room and revealing a patch of the detective's gray matter.

The detective's remaining eye had rolled up into his skull and his body began to convulse. Dale placed a pillow under the detective's feet so his spasmodic fit wouldn't make too much noise and wake Sarah or her husband. The big man was still making that wet, asthmatic wheezing sound. Dale grabbed the knife protruding from the detective's throat and began to saw through his windpipe, cutting his esophagus in half and nearly decapitating him. The corpse finally ceased its Saint Vitus's dance and lay still. Dale put his foot on the man's chest for leverage and then yanked the knife out of his throat. He wiped the blade off in the detective's graying hair and turned toward the stairs.

This was the tricky part. There were two stair treads

that squeaked and Dale could never remember which ones they were. He tried to walk on the edge of each stair instead of stepping in the middle to eliminate the potential for a squeak that would alert Sarah and her husband. If he had to flee the house, he wouldn't be able to bring the detective back to life. That would be murder and Dale knew that murderers went to hell. Worse was the fear that if he murdered someone and defied God's law, then God might take away his gift. He had to make sure that didn't happen.

Dale took another step and felt the stair flex under his weight. He slowly released his weight off his foot and used the railings to lift himself up over the stair, supporting himself on his arms. He took the next few steps without a sound and was soon standing in the upstairs hallway outside the master bedroom.

Dale knew that there was a strong possibility that Sarah and her husband were on the other side of the door with their guns cocked, waiting for him to enter so they could empty their pistols into his face. His pulse had been over a 160 beats per minute since he'd woken under the sink. Now it felt like it was closer to 200. He put his hand on the doorknob and slowly turned the handle. The door crept open slowly and Dale slipped inside.

The room was dark except for the dim illumination from the streetlight outside leaking through the blinds. It was just enough light for Dale to see that the room was empty. The bedsheets had been pulled back revealing a mattress stained with blood. Dale could smell blood in the air, rancid blood. He stood in the doorway for a while trying to figure out where they could be. He spun around and looked in back of him to make sure they hadn't set some sort of trap and weren't sneaking up on him from behind. Then he checked the closet and under the bed. They weren't there. Dale was about to scream when he remembered the other two bedrooms. They had probably slept in one of those.

But why? Was it some kind of trick?

The longer Dale stood in the bedroom, the more overwhelming the smell of fetid blood became. Slowly it dawned on him that the smell was probably the reason why they had not slept in their own bed. He turned around and crept quietly out of the room, closing the bedroom door behind him.

In his socks, still tiptoeing as softly as possible, Dale made his way to the first bedroom and pushed open the door. His heart lightened and an overwhelming feeling of joy rose inside him as he spotted Sarah lying beside her husband, eyes closed, sleeping soundly. Her big husband was making whining and whimpering sounds in his sleep and tossing and turning fitfully. Seeing that videotape of what Dale had done to him had obviously disturbed him greatly.

Dale didn't know what had possessed him that day. He had just wanted to punish the big man. He wanted to emasculate him, humiliate him. Seeing Josh's big cock and knowing that he was fucking Sarah with it every night, that she willingly gave herself to him, that she enjoyed it, loved it, loved him, imagining her sucking it, letting him fuck her in the ass with it, had enraged him. All he could think of was how much he wanted to break Josh down and show him, show her, that Josh was not a better man than Dale just because his penis was twice as big. He wanted Sarah to see her big, strong husband with his porn-star cock, humbled. He wanted to show her who the real man was. Thinking about it had made Dale's cock hard and so he had gone

with it and used it as an instrument of torture. It had
even surprised Dale when he had managed to ejacu-
late. He wondered if they had done a rape kit on Josh.
He wondered how humiliated the big man must have
felt when they swabbed his rectum and found Dale's
semen inside of him.

Dale took a moment to delight in the big man's
misery, watching as the big man moaned and grimaced
in his sleep, reliving his violation; then Dale stepped
inside the room and lifted the hammer over his head.
He brought it down with all of his might and blinked
when the blood spattered his face. Sarah began to
scream almost immediately. She always screamed. Dale
had come to love that sound as much as he loved her.

CHAPTER TWENTY-SEVEN

Sarah woke up when she heard the detective moving around downstairs. She could hear Josh's voice down there too. The two men were talking about something with obvious excitement. Sarah sat up in bed, yawning and stretching, and tried to hear what they were talking about.

"I already called Trina. We've got a CSU team headed over here right now."

Something had happened. Last night. Even with the detective standing guard. Somehow, Dale had gotten into the house again. Sarah swung her legs over the side of the bed and stood up. She felt her feet squish into the carpet and pink foam squeeze up from the carpet padding in between her toes. She ran to the window and opened the blinds. There was a clean spot on the carpet so light that it was almost white. The spot was huge. It surrounded the entire bed. Where she had stepped, pink footsteps trailed all the way to the window. Where Josh had stepped, the footsteps were almost red. Even the sheets on the bed were no longer the white ones that had been on the bed almost since they'd moved into this house. They were a pale blue set she'd had since college and hadn't seen in several years. Sarah began to tremble. This was too much. This was all just way too much.

The room began to tilt and spin and Sarah knew she was about to faint. She began to hyperventilate and her heart felt like it was going to pound its way through her rib cage. She wanted to scream but could not find the voice. Sarah tried to focus, to slow her breathing, slow her heartbeat, do something to fend off the panic attack before it took complete control over her. Now that she knew that this was all real, that it was not some figment of her imagination, it was just too much to deal with.

Sarah took several steps toward the door. When she felt the bloody water squish out of the carpet between her toes again, she could not help herself. Sarah screamed and collapsed onto the floor.

Detective Lassiter, Harry, and her husband were all hovering over, looking down at her with worried expressions on their faces when she woke. She was downstairs in the living room, lying on the couch with a pillow beneath her head.

"Are you okay?" Josh asked. He looked so worried and frightened.

"What happened?"

"He got in again. We've got him on tape walking into our bedroom. But he's disappeared. The police can't find him anywhere."

Sarah looked up and there was a huge reddish brown stain on the ceiling above their heads. She looked down at the floor where there was a similar stain on the concrete.

"He wasn't quite so neat this time," Harry said, wincing in disgust.

That was when Sarah noticed a similar stain in the detective's hair. The whole side of his head was caked with blood. His gray hair was almost completely red on one side. His neck and shirt were stained red-brown as well. Harry was right. Dale had been messy this time.

"What happened?"

"You must have fainted."

"No. I mean what the hell happened? How did he get in? You were supposed to protect us."

"I don't know. I must have fallen asleep. But don't worry. He really fucked up this time. We've got more than enough to arrest him now and this time we can make it stick. We've got him for breaking and entering, felony stalking, trespassing, attacking a police officer, and whatever else the DA can come up with."

Everything but murder and rape. Sarah looked over at Detective Lassiter.

"But you can't find him. Can you? You don't know where he is, do you?"

"We'll find him. In the meantime we're going to move you into protective custody."

"What if you never find him?"

"We will. I promise you we're using every resource at our disposal."

"But you still can't promise me he won't get away, can you? You still can't promise me I won't be looking over my shoulder for the rest of my life, that I won't wake up one night and see that sick fuck standing over me. You can't promise me there won't be any more bloody sheets in my laundry or bleach spots on the carpet, can you? He did it again, with a detective sitting right in my living room! Even with all of us armed with guns he just walked right in here and raped me again!"

"Sarah, I am sorry. I don't know how it happened. I must have fallen asleep and he got in the house somehow and hit me with something."

"No." Josh spoke up. "He didn't get in the house.

He was already here. He was in here hiding some-where, somewhere we didn't look."

"We looked everywhere, Josh. He wasn't in here."

"He had to have been. We must have missed some-thing. Harry was sitting right here on the couch. Look how far that front door is from here. If someone had walked in that door Harry would have had plenty of time to react. And even if he somehow overpowered Harry, which I can't really see happening, we would have at least heard the struggle upstairs."

"So, he must have ambushed me somehow," Harry agreed.

"He might have still come in through a window. You have vinyl window frames. They don't make a lot of noise when you open them and they're notoriously easy to break into. He could have popped open a win-dow and crept into the house without anyone knowing he was here. He used a hammer in that video. If he caught Harry from behind with the hammer there wouldn't have been much of a struggle," Detective Las-siter said.

"I don't know. It just doesn't feel right."

"Well, we'll make sure the boys from CSU are thor-ough when they go over the place. We'll have them dust everything for prints. We're going to have to do an-other rape kit on you . . . and you too, Mr. Lincoln." Detective Lassiter looked over at Harry. "Maybe even you too."

"Awww, fuck. Are you kidding me?"

"You saw the tape. You saw what he did to them. We have to be thorough about this."

"So, you don't think we faked the tape?"

"I never did. I just couldn't explain it any other way."

"And now? Did Harry tell you about the case he worked on like ours?"

"He told me. It still doesn't make sense to me. I mean, I believe in God. I even believe in the supernatural. But I just can't believe that God would let someone like that have that kind of power. I'm sure if we thought about it long enough we could figure out how he's doing it. There's got to be a reason that doesn't involve mystical powers."

Harry shook his head and snorted in disgust.

"How is this any different than the power a parent has over their children? How many times have we seen parents abuse that power, neglect, beat, torture, and molest their own kids? Crackheads, junkies, and meth addicts have kids. Those young, innocent lives in the hands of people who would trade them for a dime bag. God gives immense power to really fucked-up people all the time. This really isn't any different."

Detective Lassiter held up her hand and turned her head away. She closed her eyes like she was trying to compose herself but her eyebrows furrowed and her nostrils flared.

"Harry, I've told you about this before. I'm not going to stand for you bashing my faith. You're free to think what you want, just keep it to yourself because I don't want to hear that shit."

"You asked a question."

"I'm serious, Harry. Back off."

Harry waved his hands in surrender.

"You did ask."

"So what are we going to do?" Sarah asked. "Where will we go? What about Josh's job?"

"He's going to have to miss a few days."

254 WRATH JAMES WHITE

"He's extra-board. He's not technically a full-time employee even though they work him harder than anybody. He can't miss days. He doesn't get any sick time or anything like that. They'll fire him."

"Well, does Dale know where you work?"

"I don't know. I don't think so. I can't remember if we told him when we introduced ourselves or not."

"Because if he does, he can follow you back to Sarah."

Everyone turned to look at Sarah again. She felt more like a victim now than she had in days. Everyone had to look out for poor, poor Sarah. They had to make sure the boogeyman didn't get her.

And did I mention that the boogeyman looks like fucking Don Knotts in The Incredible Mr. Limpet? Sarah thought.

"Well, I have to work or we'll lose our house."

"Let the damn bank have it," Sarah said. "I can't stand to look at that bedroom anymore. And that smell. I'll probably smell that for the rest of my life as it is. The house is worth half of what we paid for it now anyway. We'll never get that equity back. We'll just go back to being renters. This neighborhood is turning into a ghost town anyway."

The two detectives stood beside Sarah's husband, looking at the stain in the ceiling.

"I don't know if I'd cry too much about losing this place now if I was you. No offense but it would creep me the hell out to live here," Harry said, turning his back on the room and buttoning his sports jacket.

"That's real sensitive, Harry."

"No. He's right. Fuck this house. Just give us some time to pack our things."

"You can't lose your job though. We can't even get an apartment without a job and this isn't like it was a few years ago when you could just walk right out and get another job. People are being laid off left and right. You need this job."

Sarah was standing between her husband and the two detectives with her arms folded across her chest. She pointed at Josh's chest as she spoke. Her fingernails had been bitten almost down to the cuticles. Josh withered. His entire body appeared to wilt in front of her.

"She's right. I can't get fired right now. I'm going to have to go to work."

"Okay. Well, you're just going to have to be careful. Watch to see if anyone is following you. Once we decide on what hotel we're going to put you up in you're going to want to make sure you drive past it a few times before you park just to see if anyone is following you. I'll drive you home the first night just to show you what I mean."

"Thanks, Detective. I don't mean to put you out. We just really can't afford for me to lose my job."

"I'll take him. Neither one of you can drive worth a damn."

Detective Mike Torres stood in the doorway eating a bag of spicy Doritos and licking his fingers. He walked into the room swaggering like a B-movie matinee idol. Sarah couldn't hold back her laughter. He looked like such an asshole. Even his melodramatic entrance was overdone and evidence of a massive unchecked ego. Detective Lassiter rolled her eyes.

"So, does that mean you believe us now?" Sarah asked.

Torres shook his head. He was wearing a white short-sleeved shirt and a red silk tie. He was still wearing black jeans with black motorcycle boots. He looked like a member of a Mexican motorcycle gang who'd cleaned up for a job interview or a court appearance.

"It means that I'm going to do my job. There's an APB out for the little geek across the street. He may have attacked a cop. So we've got him for assaulting a police officer. You've got him on tape breaking into the house and there's no other weird shit on the tape that would render it inadmissible. I don't need to know how he's doing this shit. I'm curious but it don't really matter as far as I'm concerned. All I need to do is do my job and bring him in and keep you two safe. This is just another stalker case to me."

Torres took another handful of Doritos and then crumpled up the bag. For a moment Sarah was afraid he was going to toss the empty bag on the floor. Even with the house reeking of curdled blood and decay she still felt protective of her home. This had been her dream home. She and Josh had upgraded everything they could from the stainless-steel Whirlpool refrigerator to the matching stainless-steel KitchenAid convection oven, microwave, and even the dishwasher. The faux cherrywood blinds were all upgrades as well. But the stained concrete floor was the centerpiece of the house. Josh had ripped out all the carpeting on the first floor himself and then brought in a friend to stain the floor a golden tan and then seal it. It was gorgeous and unique. Despite what she'd said earlier about abandoning the house, Sarah felt a queasiness inside at the thought of leaving it all behind.

Detective Torres smiled wanly, then placed the crumpled bag into his pocket.

"So where are we taking them?" Torres asked.

"To one of those extended-vacation hotels on Tropicana."

"Those places are shitholes," Josh said.

"No. These are pretty nice. They're new and they have a kitchen and a laundry in their rooms. They're like studio apartments. They even have one-, two-, and three-bedroom suites. Besides, you won't be staying there long," Detective Lassiter said.

"What if we stayed at the hotel where I work? I'm sure they'd give us a decent rate. They're practically giving rooms away now that the economy is in the toilet."

"Because if Dale McCarthy is still stalking the two of you, and we have every reason to believe that he is, then the hotel where you work would be the first place he would check."

"Then how about the Bellagio?" Sarah asked.

"You're joking right?" Torres said.

"Of course I'm joking. Unless you can swing it."

Detective Lassiter laughed.

"Yeah, we'll see what we can do. But in the meantime you need to get packed."

Sarah and Josh walked upstairs together. Sarah looked around her house when she got to the top of the stairs.

"I know I'm supposed to hate this place now, with all that's happened here. It does creep me out. I almost feel like the house is haunted now. Every time I look at those spots on the carpet I keep thinking about the nightmares in my head that turned out not to be nightmares and the things that were on that tape. I get nauseous just thinking about it and I feel my heart race and I want to scream. But I'd rather get rid of the carpet and throw out the mattress and paint the walls a different color than just leave. I just can't imagine leaving this house. This is our home, Josh. How can we let this monster chase us out of our home? How could we let a few terrible, horrible memories replace years of good memories? Besides, our credit is so fucked up we'll never be able to buy a new house and the president is supposed to be doing something to stop the foreclosures. We need to fight for our home, Josh. We need to fight Dale. We need to fight anyone who tries to force us out of our home."

Sarah looked at Josh and could see the indecision on his face. There was pain in his expression. Sarah could see him wrestling with the idea of staying. He had been relieved when the detectives had suggested they leave the house and Sarah had agreed. Now that she was having second thoughts about leaving, Sarah could see all the tension winding its way back into his muscles. She knew Josh wanted to forget everything that had happened in this house and she couldn't blame him. What had happened to him threatened his entire identity, his whole sense of self. He didn't want to be around anything that would remind him of that humiliation, and this house was the single biggest reminder. She couldn't blame him if he wanted to burn it to the ground and piss on the ashes. But she also couldn't allow it. She had to fight for her home.

"Okay, baby. We'll make it work somehow. We'll figure something out."

They walked into the bedroom and that overpowering smell made Sarah's stomach churn. The odor of death and decay had gotten worse since the night before. There was a fly in the room. Sarah didn't know how it had gotten in but she knew that it was just a matter of time now before the bed would be full of maggots. Josh pinched his nose and turned to look at her with a grimace on his face.

"You sure you still want to live here?"

"We need to get rid of that mattress. It will be okay. This is our home."

"Okay. If you're sure, then I'm sure."

They pulled two suitcases out of the closet and began to pack. Sarah threw in her running shoes and some workout gear along with four changes of clothes. She didn't know how long they would be at the hotel but if it was longer than four days, then she'd have to come back and get more clothes. She looked at Josh's ice skates tucked in the corner and his hockey jersey hanging above it. She had been upset at not being able to run and here Josh hadn't been on the ice in over two weeks and he hadn't said a word. Sarah looked over at Josh and felt a pang of guilt. When all of this was over she had to make sure to give him more time for himself. Brawling with some bartender on the ice was just the sort of thing Josh needed to restore his manhood. Though murdering Dale with his bare hands would have probably been more effective. Sarah really hoped that could be arranged.

CHAPTER TWENTY-EIGHT

Sarah, her husband, and Detective Harry Malcovich sat in the waiting room of the hospital. Waiting for someone to swab their orifices for traces of semen and check them for tearing and bruising. Sarah studied Harry's face. He looked more than embarrassed. He looked enraged.

One by one they were called into the room to see the nurse. Detective Lassiter was there, along with a rape crisis counselor. They walked Sarah into the examination room. Sarah disrobed and the detective helped her into her hospital gown.

The nurse busied herself preparing the rape kit while Trina Lassiter and the counselor tried their best to keep Sarah calm and relaxed. Sarah did not feel anxious at all. She felt numb. This was her second rape kit in a matter of days and she had no idea how many times Dale had actually raped her. At least three times that she knew about and probably closer to five or more. Sarah wondered if the numbness she was feeling was what sex slaves felt like after being raped by one john after another, day after day after day. Thinking about herself in terms of a sex slave made her feel even worse.

"My name is Karen Burns. I'm going to give you my card so we can talk later. Right now I'm just here to answer any questions you might have and to help the detective and the nurse guide you through this process. I know you've been through a terrible ordeal but we are here to help."

The rape counselor was a young blonde woman in her twenties who looked like she was fresh out of college and dressed very conservatively in a plain white shirt and a long blue skirt that came almost to her ankles. Her hair was pulled back in a bun. Sarah guessed that the woman was probably Mormon. There were a lot of Mormons who worked in the hospitals in Las Vegas for some reason. Most of them were volunteers but an almost equal number were health-care professionals.

The counselor spoke calmly to Sarah, explaining everything that was about to happen. Sarah wondered if this woman had ever been raped. She doubted it but it wouldn't have surprised her either. There had to be some reason a woman like her went into a profession like this.

"Just relax. The nurse needs to take a couple samples from your rectum and your uterus. It might be a little uncomfortable but it will be over quickly. Detective Lassiter and I will be right here holding your hands."

"This ain't my first rodeo," Sarah said, borrowing a phrase from Harry. "I was just here last week."

"Oh," the counselor said and looked over at Detective Lassiter. She looked back over at Sarah with a different, somewhat less sympathetic expression on her face.

"She's not a prostitute, Counselor. She's just had one very tough week," the detective offered by way of an explanation.

The woman was clearly confused and more than a

little shocked. Sarah supposed it was shocking. But given everything else she'd seen in the last couple of days, being raped more than once in less than a week no longer felt quite so shocking, though no less degrading and humiliating. She felt no less violated than she had the first time she was here. The only difference was that now she knew what they were going to do and what they would find and she'd had time to prepare herself mentally for it. She was not going to allow herself to break down in tears again, though now would have probably been the appropriate time to do so and she certainly felt like crying, like screaming, and punching the walls. She just didn't know if she'd ever be able to pull herself back together again if she allowed herself to fall apart now. The counselor was still looking at Sarah skeptically and somewhat judgmentally. Sarah could see all the questions on the woman's face. She felt like telling the young counselor that she'd been murdered perhaps half a dozen times as well.

"How many rape victims do you see in here every day?"

"It's hard to say. We see a lot of prostitutes and victims of domestic violence who we would classify as date rapes. Often, those are even more violent than the assaults from strangers. But on average I see about two or three a day."

"Two or three a day?"

The woman nodded.

"And I'm just one counselor."

Sarah didn't know why she found that so surprising. Rape was one of those things she had never thought much about until she'd woken up screaming a week ago. Sarah wondered why the counselor was even there and where she'd been last week when it was just Detective Lassiter and the nurse.

"Aren't you a rape counselor, Trina?" Sarah asked the detective.

"I'm a victims' advocate. It's slightly different. A lot less training."

"So where was the counselor last week?"

"NASCAR was in town last week along with about a hundred thousand fans. It was a busy week for rape counselors."

She said it so matter-of-factly, as if it should have been common knowledge that the incidents of rapes increased during sporting events. Sarah supposed that it should have been obvious. But that was just not ordinarily something you thought about.

The nurse busied herself lubing her rubber-gloved fingers so that she could slide them more easily into Sarah's vagina to get the sample. Detective Lassiter sprayed her with something she called luminol and scanned her with a UV light. There were glowing splotches all over Sarah's breasts. She didn't bother to ask what the splotches were. She was pretty certain she knew.

After the nurse had finished taking her swabs and Trina was done photographing every square inch of her, Sarah wiped herself with wet disposable towels that reminded her of baby wipes, then dressed and walked out into the waiting room. She met her husband's eyes as he was called into the room. He was a wreck. She reached out for his hand and squeezed it. Then she pulled him close and kissed him.

"I love you, Josh."

"I-I love you too," Josh stammered back. He looked so frightened that it was breaking Sarah's heart. As big as he was she still felt like it was her job to protect him. He was fragile in so many ways.

Sarah felt terrible for her husband. She could think of very few worse things that could happen to a man like Josh than being raped by another man. She wished she could have gone into the exam room with him but knew that would have been too humiliating for him. His pride would have never allowed it. She hoped they would find nothing, for the sake of his sanity. She hoped he hadn't been violated again.

Detective Harry Malcovich was sitting with Detective Torres. They were watching TV and Torres was flicking the strap on his gun holster on and off as if he were just itching to pull his weapon. Sarah came and sat with them. She could tell that Harry was dealing with the whole thing no better than Josh was. He looked up at her and manufactured a smile for her. It looked every bit as artificial as it was. His eyes were haunted, swimming with dark shadows.

"Did everything go okay? You okay?" he asked.

Sarah shrugged.

"As good as I can be I guess."

"Don't worry, Sarah. This will all be over soon. If this wasn't personal before, it damn sure is now. And if they find that that sick fuck touched me anywhere I'm going to hurt him as much as I possibly can before I blow his fucking head off. Fuck prison and fuck this badge. If they want it they can have it but I'm going to kill that pervert. You can bet on that."

"And don't worry, I'll help you," Detective Torres said. "This weird-ass case is taking up too much of my damn time. I'm starting to dream about that little motherfucker myself."

"What kind of dreams?" Sarah asked, showing more interest than she'd intended.

"Not *those* kind of dreams. No offense to either of you but ain't nobody raping me no time soon. Just thinking about it makes me want to eat my pistol."

"Will you shut the hell up you insensitive son of a bitch. Sarah has been raped and she doesn't need you sitting there talking about how you'd kill yourself if it happened to you. I don't need that shit either. I don't know what that twisted nutcase might have done to me. I don't even want to think about it until and unless I have to. So, just be quiet would you? Thank you."

Harry leaned his head back, took a deep breath, and closed his eyes.

"Ay, look Harry, I'm sorry. I wasn't thinking."

"Skip it. I know you didn't mean it, you ignorant bastard. Just watch it. I won't launch a complaint against you for that kind of shit but someone else might. Sarah is a victim of something no one should ever have to go through and it's our job to try to make her feel safer, not to make her even more depressed."

"I'm sorry, Sarah . . . uh . . . Mrs. Lincoln. I just wasn't thinking."

"That's okay." Sarah turned away and stared at the television anchored to the wall in the corner of the room. There was a cooking show on with some chef making deep-fried Twinkies and Oreos. Sarah didn't feel the least bit hungry and all the fried junk food flashing across the screen was making her nauseated. She knew Detective Torres hadn't been trying to deliberately offend her but he had nonetheless. She tried her best not to stereotype him as a typical macho, chauvinistic Latino man but she had her prejudices no matter how liberal and enlightened she considered herself to be and guys like Mike Torres brought them all to the fore.

The three of them sat there in a tense, uncomfortable silence. Sarah turned to Detective Malcovich.

"Harry? When we're done here, can you take me to see Dorothy Madigan?"

The detective turned to look at Sarah.

"Why?"

"I just need to see her. I need to speak to her. I want her to know that I believe her."

"You're right. We should go. Okay, I'll take you. You sure you want to go right now? We can wait until tomorrow."

"I think I should see her now. I think . . . for my sanity too."

"Okay. We'll go."

Josh walked out looking shell-shocked. Sarah rushed over to her husband and wrapped her arms around him. They called Harry in next.

"Oh great. I can't fucking believe I'm doing this. I'm going to kill this fucker when I catch him."

He walked to the examination room, grumbling the entire way. Detective Lassiter turned to walk in behind him and he stopped her.

"You must be crazy. Go sit down, Trina. I can hold my own hand. You too," he said to the rape counselor. He walked into the room with the nurse, leaving Trina and the counselor out in the hallway.

Sarah looked up at her husband.

"Is everything okay?"

"They'll have the lab tests back tomorrow but they didn't find any evidence of rape. Not that that means anything. They didn't find any tearing or abrasions on you either. But the detective said that she didn't see anything that looked like semen on the swabs, but you never know until the lab results come back."

"I asked Harry to take me to see Dorothy Madigan, the woman who Dale raped before me, the one who set herself on fire."

"Jesus. Why? I mean, are you sure?"

"I think I have to. I want to hear what he did to her. I want to tell her what he did to me. I want her to know that I believe her. And I want to make her a promise."

"A promise?"

"I want to promise her that I won't let Dale hurt anyone else like he hurt us. I want to promise her that I'm going to stop him."

CHAPTER TWENTY-NINE

The Nevada Mental Health Institute was a drab gray building with dash stucco walls, large bronze tinted windows and an eight-foot sculpture out front that looked like a cross between a brain and a solar system made out of aluminum and stainless steel. The institute sat across from Sunset Hospital on Eastern Avenue, and Sarah must have driven past it more than a dozen times since she'd lived in Las Vegas without ever realizing it was there.

It was nearly the size of the hospital itself and was surrounded by a small private park for the residents with walking paths, a bocce ball court, and even a tennis court. The parking lot in front of the building was cracked and spalling, with weeds growing up through the fissures. There were only a handful of cars in the lot, including an ambulance parked in the red fire-zone directly in front of the building. If it wasn't for the beautifully maintained lawn surrounding the back of the building it would have looked like yet another foreclosed property.

Sarah and her husband parked their Saturn directly in front of the building next to the detectives' vehicles. She was surprised when Trina and Torres stepped out of their car and began walking toward the building with Harry.

"We're all going in?"

"Yeah, I want to hear her story. Try to make some sense of what's going on. I still can't believe this," Detective Lassiter said.

"I damn sure don't believe it," Detective Torres offered.

"Don't tell Dorothy that. We're here to let her know that she's not crazy, not to put even more doubts in her head."

They all walked into the building together. Sarah held Josh's hand tightly. He was still shaken after his exam and Sarah felt like he needed her strength, whatever little strength she had left.

Harry flashed his badge at the receptionist and asked to see Dorothy Madigan. Trina and Detective Torres flashed their shields as well. The obese woman behind the receptionist desk asked them all to sign in and then gave them visitor's passes.

"Room 511. I'll let the nurses know to expect you."

The building looked and smelled just like a hospital except everything that would have been white in a regular hospital was either pale gray or sky blue. Sarah supposed the colors were meant to have a calming effect. She just found them depressing.

When Sarah and her entourage arrived on the second floor the sky blue theme grew increasingly dominant, replacing the gray almost entirely. Even the nurses' uniforms were blue or green. An orderly the size of an NFL linebacker walked by carrying a mop and a bucket and even he was wearing light blue. He looked like a Smurf on steroids.

Sarah had imagined that all the patients would be locked in their rooms, maybe strapped into straitjackets but most of the doors were open and patients lingered here and there in the halls or wandered aimlessly. The few doors that were shut were not locked and Sarah jumped as a door flew open and one of the patients, an old man in his late sixties or early seventies, scurried past her mumbling to himself and scratching the flaking skin on his bald, crinkled scalp.

"Detectives?" Another overweight nurse, this one wearing light green hospital scrubs instead of the traditional nursing uniform, approached and began shaking hands even before she'd introduced herself. She was young and pretty, the kind of pretty that would have been gorgeous minus forty or fifty pounds. Sarah wondered how anyone in the health-care field could allow their own body to fall into such disrepair, but obesity seemed to be an occupational habit in this profession. She shook the woman's hand and smiled, chiding herself for her cattiness.

"I'm Alice Douglass. I'm Dorothy's nurse. She's in the common area right now watching television with some of our other guests."

"Guests" was apparently the PC term for patients.

The nurse shook Detective Torres's hand and he practically drooled all over himself. His smile was wider and more genuine than any Sarah had ever seen on his face since making his acquaintance. He obviously liked big girls.

"Detective Mike Torres, ma'am." He held on to her hand a moment longer than necessary and then winked at her when he released it. She smiled and blushed and when she turned around to lead them to Dorothy Madigan she put a little extra swish in her hips. Sarah looked over at Detective Lassiter and they both rolled their eyes.

Sarah, Josh, and the detectives all marched down the hall following the nurse who was still walking with a pronounced switch in her hips that sent ripples through her formidably sized buttocks. Detective Torres was smiling like he'd just hit the Megabucks jackpot.

They walked into the dayroom and the plump nurse escorted them to a woman with long dark hair sitting in the corner of the room watching a game of chess and a soap opera on the big-screen TV in the center of the room simultaneously. As they approached the woman, Sarah began to make out more of her features, or what was left of them. The pallid, mottled skin on her face and neck was wrinkled and shriveled like the skin of a raisin. Her lips had been completely burned off and despite the best attempts of a plastic surgeon to rebuild them, her mouth was still little more than a gash in her face. Her nose had nearly melted away, leaving two small holes in the center of her face where her nostrils had been, giving her an almost reptilian appearance. Both of her ears were all but gone, merely shriveled flaps of skin and cartilage above her ear canals, which were now just two holes in the side of her head. Her arms and hands had likewise shriveled under the same intense heat that had taken her facial features. Her hands were gnarled like crow's feet and her left hand was missing all but two fingers. Sarah remembered the beautiful woman she had seen in the picture Harry kept in his pocket. That woman was completely gone now.

"Dorothy? These people are from the police department. They're here to ask you a few questions. Is that okay?"

Dorothy looked them over. She paused first at Harry, giving him a wan smile and a nod. Then she stared at Sarah, looking her over from head to toe. Even with so much of her face destroyed, Sarah could see the distress in Dorothy's expression. The woman turned back to look at Harry with eyes filling rapidly with tears.

"He's at it again isn't he? He's doing it to her? Now do you believe me?"

Her voice was surprisingly calm and level. Not the disjointed, semiarticulate rant she had been expecting. Her voice was low and raspy as if she'd been smoking cigarettes and drinking whiskey for decades. It didn't match the woman Sarah had seen in the photograph. It was a sultry, bluesy voice, incongruous with the tragically disfigured woman sitting in the dayroom of a mental hospital.

"I'm sorry, Dorothy. I wanted to believe you. You know that. I tried to keep the case open as long as I could."

"I know, Harry. You were great even after this."

She gestured toward the scars on her face and the countless more hidden beneath her clothing. Sarah knelt beside Dorothy's chair and stuck out her hand.

"My name is Sarah Lincoln. Dale McCarthy lives across the street from me. He's been breaking into my home every night since he moved in and raping and murdering me and my husband, Josh. We're going to catch him and we're going to kill him."

Dorothy stared down at Sarah's hand and reached out for it with her good hand.

She shook hands firmly, then looked up at the other two detectives.

"Who are they?"

"Detectives Trina Lassiter and Mike Torres."

"Detectives? Why? How? How did you make them believe?"

"I have a video."

The woman's eyes widened.

"You-you have a video? I want to see it. Can I see it? What's on it?"

"It shows Dale breaking into their house, clubbing Sarah and Josh in the head with a hammer, raping them both, and then stabbing them both to death. Then he apparently resuscitated them both or resurrected them."

"Both of you?"

Dorothy looked at Josh, who looked away.

"How? I mean, how did he bring them back to life? How does he do it?"

"He breathed into their mouths like he was doing pulmonary resuscitation, mouth-to-mouth, and they both just healed up. Their wounds went away and they were alive again."

"You have that on tape? All of it?"

"Yes. It's all on tape."

"But he got away. He's still out there?"

"Yes."

"So, why are you here then? He's not here is he?"

Dorothy looked around. Her eyes widened in panic and she tried to lift herself from her chair. Harry put his hand on her shoulder and eased her back into her chair.

"No. He's not here. I just wanted you to know that I was wrong and that I'm sorry and I'm going to make it right. I'm going to catch him. I'm going to finally put a stop to this."

"Can I ask you a question, Dorothy?"

Dorothy looked down at Sarah, who was still crouched beside her chair.

"Yes?"

"What did he do to you?"

"I don't remember. I can't remember hardly any of it. I would wake up with these pictures in my head, these terrible images of being raped, being stabbed, being skinned alive. Then they would just go away and I wouldn't be able to remember anything. I would walk around all day feeling violated and wounded but not knowing why. I was terrified, especially when I would see Dale at work. Then I started keeping a dream diary. I would write down everything I could remember as soon as I woke up. Some of the things were . . . they were just unimaginable. I would have never thought anyone capable . . . it was inhuman some of the things I dreamed. Then one night I put a tape recorder under my bed and I caught it all on tape. It was just the audio but I had written it down that morning too. I wrote that he had skinned me alive and that's what I heard on the tape. I heard myself screaming, I heard the sound of flesh and skin tearing. And I heard him laughing."

Sarah didn't know what to say. She didn't think anything could have been worse than what she'd seen on that tape but the tape had been silent. She couldn't imagine what it must have sounded like. She couldn't imagine hearing herself being skinned alive and remembering it.

"That's terrible. My God."

"It's in the past now. Or at least it was until you five walked in here."

"I'm sorry. I really am. I didn't mean to make you relive all of that."

"Like I said, it's all in the past now."

Sarah wondered if she should ask the next question. She tried to think of how to phrase it or if she should ask it all. She knew that it would worry her if she didn't.

"Do you mind if I ask you one more question?"

Dorothy looked fearful. She was still recomposing herself from the last question. She took a long, deep breath and blew it out slowly.

"Okay, go ahead."

Sarah picked her words carefully.

"You just . . . you sound so sane. I mean, you don't sound . . . you don't seem, you know, mentally disturbed. Why are you here? Why did you do this to yourself?"

Dorothy turned away. She looked down at her fingers, then drew her hands up into the sleeves of her robe and looked over at the TV, where a clip of Barack Obama was on talking about economic recovery.

"Was it because I didn't believe you?" Harry asked. "Did you have some sort of nervous breakdown or something?"

Dorothy shook her head. Tears began to run down her face, traveling the maze of crinkled skin to the corner of her mouth.

"I didn't want him to touch me again. I figured I would either die or look like this. Either way he'd never touch me again. I was right. I haven't seen him since."

Sarah stood, smiling bitterly.

"I've seen him. He left you and came straight to me."

Detective Lassiter shook her head.

"No, he didn't. There were six years between the two of you. I'm pretty sure he didn't stop for six years."

"No way a guy like that takes a six-year hiatus," Torres added.

"You're right. There are other victims out there," Harry said. "And they probably don't even know it."

CHAPTER THIRTY

When the detectives dropped Sarah and Josh off at the "safe house," she had been expecting at least one of them to stay. She was quite surprised when they all left.

"Torres will be back to drive Josh to work."

"I need to call in to make sure I'm working. I don't have a set schedule yet."

"Okay, just let Trina know," Harry said.

"Um, excuse me. Trina?"

"Yes?"

"Who's staying with us?"

Detective Lassiter looked at Harry and Torres before she answered, and Sarah knew that no one had been assigned to them. They were being left on their own.

"Unfortunately, we all have other cases we're working on as well as this one so we can't stay here with you but I assure you that you're safe. We need to be out there hitting the street looking for McCarthy anyway. The sooner we catch him the sooner you can go back to your home. We can't catch him sitting around here. Besides, he's not the Mafia. He has no way of finding out where you're staying unless he follows one of you back here. As long as you're cautious, you'll be safe," Lassiter said.

"Okay."

"Don't worry. We'll catch him," Harry said and

then, just like that, they all filed out of the apartment, leaving Sarah alone with her husband and their combined fears and anxieties.

True to the detective's word, the Extended Vacation Suites was a brand-new sprawling motel that looked more like an apartment complex. It rented out rooms by the week and the month and there were more families and couples living there than she ever would have expected. Most of them, Sarah guessed, had probably lost their homes to foreclosure. Looking at the single moms, the single dads, the married couples with two, three, four, and five kids all crammed into these little rooms, Sarah made up her mind that she would not abandon her home.

In addition to the families there were the obvious prostitutes, the drug dealers, the gamblers, and con men, the solitary men and women living transient, secretive lives better suited to motel life than permanent residence. They made Sarah nervous but curious in a voyeuristic way. She knew she'd be spending many days peeking through the curtains to spy on her neighbors. She never thought of herself as one of those types of people but then she hadn't lived in an apartment since college.

There were twelve buildings separated by a parking lot and landscaped courtyards. There was a gated pool just a few buildings away and a clubhouse with a modest fitness center that was just two treadmills, an exercise bike, an elliptical machine, and some free weights.

The buildings were only two stories high, stucco, painted tan with orange accents. If it wasn't for the marquee-size neon sign at the front of the complex it would have looked like just another apartment or condominium complex. Sarah sat on the bed staring at her suitcases. It was still hard to believe everything that had happened to her in the last few days. It seemed like only yesterday that she was waking up to the smell of burned pancakes and frying bacon, eager to finish breakfast so she could have sex with her husband. Now, sex was the furthest thing from her mind and she was hiding out in a motel from a sadistic psychopath with the power to resurrect the dead. It was hard to believe and even harder to accept. She looked over at Josh, who was sitting beside her, staring at the blank TV screen with vacant eyes. She wondered if Josh would ever recover from what he had seen on that tape. She wondered if either of them would.

She stood up from the bed and began to undress. Sarah needed a shower. Her muscles felt tired and achy. She could feel the tension bound up in her sinews like coiled springs. She felt dirty. She imagined that she could still feel Dale's sweat and semen on her. She could feel blood in her hair, on her skin. She knew it was all in her head but that did not change the fact that she felt grimy.

Standing there naked in front of Josh, she wondered if they would ever regain their sex drives. Josh was not even looking at her. He continued to stare off into space. A week ago Sarah would have been offended and probably would have given him head just to prove to herself that he still found her desirable. Today she was relieved that he wasn't interested.

Sarah walked into the bathroom and turned on the shower. The water was hot almost immediately and Sarah stepped in. She closed the shower curtain, but then memories of all the horror movies she'd watched as a kid came flooding back, along with the very real fact that she was now being stalked by her very own psycho, and she ripped the curtain open again. Water sprayed all over the bathroom tiles as Sarah scrubbed the memory of her assault from her skin. Taking a shower with the curtain closed was yet one more thing she knew she would not be able to do again for some time.

When she walked out of the bathroom wrapped in towels, Sarah found Josh sitting on the edge of the bed with his nine-millimeter in his hand. It was cocked and Sarah could only assume that it was loaded. The way he stared at the gun, Sarah knew she had come out of the shower just in time.

"Josh? What are you doing with that gun? What were you about to do, Josh? Were you going to leave me?"

"I can't take this. I'm sorry." Josh raised the gun to his head and tears began to stream from his eyes.

"Don't you fucking dare! Don't you fucking dare, Josh! Don't! Don't!"

Sarah held out her hands for the gun as she rushed forward, dropping her towel and pausing just short of snatching the gun away from his head. She was afraid he would pull the trigger if she tried to take the gun from him and one of them might get hit.

"You don't know, Sarah. You don't know what it's like. That twisted fucker, what he did to me. I can't get it out of my head. I keep thinking about . . . about . . ."

Sarah shook her head. Her eyes were wide, staring, unblinking at Josh, darting from the gun in his hand to his eyes and back to the gun. "No, Josh. No. Put the gun down."

She inched closer and sat beside him. She placed a hand on his thigh and turned to look at his face.

"Let's talk about it, Josh. Talk to me. But you can't leave, okay? We have to stay together. I need you, Josh. I can't go through this alone. You're supposed to protect me."

"But I can't! I can't protect you! That skinny little geek walked right into our house and raped you while I was lying right beside you. He raped me, Sarah! He raped me! I can't even protect myself."

Josh's eyes were wild. He looked scared. But more than that, he was ashamed. Sarah could see the humiliation written all over him. Dale had shattered his pride, his self-esteem that he had worked so hard to rebuild after what had happened to him as a boy. Dale had huffed and puffed and blown it all away. He had broken him, just like he had set out to do.

"When I was a kid, I was a baseball player, a good one. Did I ever tell you that?"

Sarah nodded. He had.

"That priest, Father Steve. That's what we called him, Father Steve. Steve Miller was his name. He was the head camp counselor and coach of our baseball team. I was the star. I was better at baseball than I ever was at hockey. Father Steve would always try to get me to stay after practice or after the game to work on my pitch or my swing or help put away the equipment. He would try to touch me but he was a little guy, about five-four. A little skinny guy like Dale. I was almost as big as he was when I was ten. I would just push him away and tell him to stop playing. I would even laugh about it. I laughed about it with the other guys at camp too. He had tried stuff with most of them too. We thought it was a joke. We used to talk about how we would kick his scrawny ass if he ever tried anything. Then one day, we were alone after a game, and he just attacked me. I tried to fight him off but he was too strong. He raped me. I couldn't stop him. After that I left baseball. When I got back home at the end of the summer I left the church. I didn't tell anyone what happened at first. I was too embarrassed. I started lifting weights when I was eleven. I used to dream about finding Father Steve and strangling him to death. But I never did. I never confronted him. Then one day I told my parents. My dad slapped me and yelled at me. They put me in reform school where I was raped by a bigger boy and one of the counselors. I started lifting weights until I was too big for anyone to fuck with. I started playing hockey in high school and power-lifting to make myself even bigger and stronger.

"When I was in college, there was a news story about a Father Steve Miller who'd been indicted for child molestation. He was accused of molesting over a hundred boys over the course of twenty years with the church. They were asking for other victims to come forward to testify. I recognized a couple of the witnesses from summer camp. They had been on the baseball team with me. I turned the TV off. I couldn't watch it and I never came forward. I just tried to forget it all. I started drinking. I was a roaring drunk when you met me. That's why I started skating so badly. It wasn't because I didn't have the killer instinct. It was because I was usually playing drunk. That's why I got kicked off the team. I started going to AA while we were dating. I wanted to get better for you. I didn't want to lose you."

It was the most Josh had ever told her about what had happened. Sarah was sobbing hard when he was done. She hugged him as he lowered the gun from his temple and dropped it into his lap. She could feel him sobbing hard against her. They sat like that for several minutes, releasing all of their pain.

"If you didn't want to lose me, then don't lose me now. Stay with me. Let's fight this thing together."

Josh sat back and uncocked his pistol.

CHAPTER THIRTY-ONE

Not knowing where to find Sarah was driving Dale crazy. He had become obsessed with her. He kept sneaking back to her house to check for her, wary of the police who drove by periodically to check the house, sometimes parking in front for hours at a time, watching his house as well. Dale would simply wait until dark and sneak around back and jimmy one of the windows.

At night they would shine the big spotlight on their side mirror on his house as they drove by, looking for Dale. Sometimes they would get out and check the backyard with a flashlight. Luckily, the yard adjacent to theirs belonged to a house that had been foreclosed on. It was abandoned and Dale would sit in the window behind a sheet he had tacked up as a curtain, watching until the cops went away. Then he would break in. He'd gone into the house three times before he was convinced they had fled. Their luggage was gone and Dale wondered if they had taken some kind of emergency vacation. But something didn't seem right about that. If the cops had managed to catch Dale they would need a witness. They would have ordered them to stay in town. They had to still be in Vegas somewhere. They were probably in witness protection. Somewhere where only the police knew where to find them.

Dale slipped back out of the Lincolns' house and

hopped back over into the adjoining yard just as the next patrol car pulled up. By the time the police officer wandered around the rear of the house with his flashlight, Dale was back in the abandoned house, watching him from the window. The car sat in front of Sarah's house for nearly an hour. When it finally drove off, Dale watched its headlights turn the corner, then watched until its taillights disappeared down the street. He waited another ten minutes to be certain that no other patrol cars would be coming to take its place before he climbed into the new Hyundai Sonata he'd picked up at the auction and drove off toward the police station. If the police were the only people who knew where Sarah was, then that's where he would start.

Dale drove up Washburn Street doing thirty-five miles an hour, and not a mile over. His eyes repeatedly checked the rearview mirror for police cruisers. Getting caught now would ruin everything. He would never see Sarah again if he went to prison.

Crossing Lossee Street was nerve-racking both because of the number of police cars that traveled this stretch of road, breaking the very speeding laws they were sworn to protect, and because of the traffic and the lack of a stoplight. Crossing the four lanes of traffic became a game of high-speed chicken. Dale got lucky and drove across all four lanes without stopping, narrowly missing a battered old truck full of construction workers.

Dale pulled up outside of the North Las Vegas police headquarters on Washburn, parked across the street from the police parking lot, and waited. He watched as police officers, a couple of ATF agents, and even one car that he could have sworn was marked FEDERAL BUREAU OF INVESTIGATION came and went. After an hour neither the black woman nor the old detective with the ponytail had appeared. Dale was growing impatient. The thought of walking into the station and asking for them crossed his mind several times and he might have been desperate enough to try if he had remembered either of their names. He sat there for a moment trying to recall the name the black woman had given him when she'd come to his house to arrest him. He could even picture the business card she'd left him sitting on the top of his desktop computer. He just could not make out the name.

Another hour went by. Dale watched policemen dragging in spitting, cursing, fighting, drunken prisoners. He watched them leave in their civilian clothes and head home to their wives, girlfriends, or a bar stool and a bottle. Dale was getting anxious. Patience had never been one of his virtues and this waiting was testing every ounce of will he possessed. He wished that he had a gun. He wanted to grab any cop at random and force them to tell him where Sarah was. The only thing holding him back was not knowing whether just any cop would know where they were or would even be able to locate them. He'd watched *Law & Order* enough to know that when the police took someone into protective custody, they kept the location of the witness secret from all but a very limited few.

A black Crown Victoria pulled into the parking lot and as soon as it passed Dale's car he spotted the pony-tailed silhouette. It was the old cop, the one whose throat he had cut in Sarah's living room. Dale tried to restrain himself from running across the street and tackling him in the parking lot. He watched the old cop walk into the station and Dale sat back and waited a bit longer. The man would be coming out again soon and Dale would have to be ready when he did.

Dale hadn't really thought of a plan. He didn't know how he planned on kidnapping the cop or getting the Lincolns' whereabouts out of him. He didn't have a gun and he didn't know if he could get close enough to use the knife. The old detective would shoot him on sight. He still had the hammer but that again meant getting close. Even if he did manage to ambush him again he would still have to drag him off the street and into his car without being seen or stopped. Dale hoped that he could simply follow him right to where Sarah was staying without having to confront the old detective at all. That would have been far easier. Dale was still sitting there trying to figure out how he would get close enough to make the detective tell him where Sarah was when the detective walked out of the station and climbed into an old gray F-150.

The truck left the police station and Dale followed in his Hyundai, wishing that he'd had the foresight to tint the windows or at least wear some sort of disguise. His mind was not working right. He still could not figure out how he was going to get what he wanted from the old detective. He looked at the savage-looking diver's blade sitting on the seat beside him, rusting with dried blood, the hammer on the floor with bits of skull and brain matter matted onto it. He followed two car lengths behind the old Ford, even though the detective seemed completely oblivious to everyone around him.

The old detective pulled into the parking lot of a bar and grill, hopped out of the truck, slamming the door behind him, and strode toward the bar, eyes fixed like lasers, like a man on a mission. Dale followed. The old

hippie cop was either going to pull his old lady out of
the bar by her hair or he was a drunk about to go on a
serious binge. Dale sincerely hoped it was the latter. It
would make his job so much easier if the old detective was barely conscious when he left the bar. The only
drawback was that it meant another long wait. Dale
turned the radio to an oldies station and laughed when
they began playing a tune by the Spice Girls. *Who
would have ever thought that they would be considered oldies?* Dale wondered. Two songs later Milli Vanilli came
on the radio, blaming it on the rain. Dale wanted to
take the knife and pierce his own eardrums with it.
Dale had never been into goth music but when De-
peche Mode came on and declared that they gave in to
sin because they had to make this life livable, he
couldn't help but sing along. He knew exactly how they
felt. Dale's eyes closed and he sat back and listened to
the music. Before the end of the song he was dreaming
again.

His mother was standing above him. He could see
the claw hammer pull back, raised high above her head.
There was blood on the hammer. It was saturated in
it. And there were bits of brain, his brain. The hammer began to fall again. Everything went black. Dale
woke up.

There were tears on his face, and his clothes were
drenched in sweat. Run DMC was playing on the car
radio and the old detective was leaving the bar. Dale
drove the Sonata over to the detective's truck. His hand
gripped the hammer as he inched closer. He was per-
spiring again, hoping the detective wouldn't turn around
and see him behind the wheel and start shooting. He
pulled up beside the detective's truck, watching as the

old cop staggered as if sleepwalking to his car. Dale slipped out of his SUV with the hammer in his hand. The old cop had his back turned, fumbling with his keys, trying to find the key to the truck. Dale hit him once with the hammer at the base of the skull and the detective folded and went down.

The detective lay on the gravel-top parking lot, snoring loudly as if he had just fallen peacefully asleep. Dale dragged him into the SUV, fished in the detective's pockets for handcuffs, and locked his wrists together behind his back; then he took the detective's gun out of the shoulder holster and placed it under the driver's seat along with the hammer and the knife. He reached across the detective and strapped his seat belt across his chest.

Dale put the car in drive and headed back to the abandoned house. He pulled the pistol from beneath the seat and sat it on his lap as he passed Lossee Road, heading back up Washburn Street. Dale checked the rearview mirrors repeatedly. If a police officer tried to pull him over he would have gunned him down without hesitation. He was so close now. Soon he would be back in the cold, dead arms of the woman he loved.

The detective woke up as Dale pulled into the driveway. Dale pointed the gun in his face and put a finger to his lips.

"Shhhhh. You stay nice and quiet or this gun is going to start making a lot of noise. Now, we're going to get out of the car. I mean, you're going to get out first. No. I'm going to get out first. Then I'll come around and get you out. If you yell or scream I'm going to shoot you in the face and leave you bleeding on the sidewalk.

Then I'm going to go after that black detective with the big tits and the big ass. Do you understand?"

The old detective looked at Dale without speaking, his bloodshot eyes out of focus and uncomprehending.

"Where is Sarah? You can tell me now and avoid a lot of pain. I know all about pain. I've killed more people than anyone you've ever met. No serial killer in history has murdered more often than I have. I just bring them back to life. No harm. No foul. But before I bring them back, I make them scream, just like I'm going to make you scream. I'm going to skin you alive, Detective. I'm going to tear you apart piece by piece. But if you just tell me where Sarah is I'll kill you quickly and then I'll bring you back and you won't remember a thing. It'll be like nothing ever happened."

"Fuck off, you little twerp."

The detective spit in Dale's face and Dale lashed out and smashed him across the face with the butt of the pistol. This time, the detective took it well. He spit blood onto the windshield and then turned and smiled at Dale with his teeth stained red with blood.

"I was in Vietnam in the seventies and Grenada in the eighties. I have killed a lot of people too and I've seen even more death. You, my friend, are a lightweight, a pussy. And you can kiss my ass."

Dale hopped out of the car and ran over to open the passenger-side door. The detective fell out of the car and Dale caught him. Just as the detective fell into his arms, Dale felt searing pain in his neck and shoulder. Dale tried his best not to scream.

"Stop. Stop. Stop it! Fuck. Stop it!"

The cop was biting him, trying to tear out his jugular with his teeth. Dale cocked the pistol and placed it under the detective's chin.

"I *will* kill you. And this time I won't bring you back. Now, let go."

The detective released his hold on Dale's throat. His bite had broken the skin and blood dripped down Dale's chest and shoulder. Dale wiped the blood from his neck. He was okay. The old detective hadn't gnawed through any major arteries.

Dale wanted to beat down the detective right on the driveway but he didn't know if the neighbors were watching and he didn't want to have to drag the big man into the house by himself. There were also cops still patrolling the neighborhood so the sooner he could get the big man inside the better. Dale walked the detective around to the side of the garage at gunpoint. There was a service door put there by the previous owners that was unlocked. Dale pushed the big man inside.

He walked the long-haired detective into the kitchen where Dale had set up a card table and a couple of chairs.

"Sit down, Detective."

"Harry. My name is Harry."

"I don't give a fuck what your name is. All I want to know is where Sarah is."

Detective Harry Malcovich laughed.

"So, what are you going to do? Beat it out of me? Waterboard me? Shove toothpicks under my finger-nails?"

Harry laughed again. Dale felt his anger rising, taking over.

"What if I do to you what I did to Sarah's husband?"

The old detective snorted.

"What if I fuckin' enjoy it, you sick piece of shit?"

"I promise you, Detective, whatever I decide to do to you, you will not enjoy it."

Dale sat Harry down in the chair and began wrapping his ankles with duct tape. He wound the tape around Harry's chest a few times, strapping him to the chair. He put another piece of tape over the detective's mouth. Once Harry was tied tight to the chair, Dale pulled out his diver's blade, straddled Harry's lap, and began sawing off the detective's nose with the serrated knife. Even Dale winced at the sound of the knife ripping through flesh and cartilage. He was disappointed that he couldn't hear the detective's screams. Even muffled, they were excruciating.

Blood poured from Harry's face in a steady downpour. The ragged hole where Harry's nose had been was now a bleeding crater in the center of the detective's face.

"You ready to talk now, Detective Harry? Or do I have to pull out my cock and fuck that hole in your face? With all that blood and mucus, I bet it feels just like pussy. Come on, Detective. Don't make me keep hurting you. Just tell me what I want to know. Tell me where Sarah is."

The detective shook his head. Dale began to unzip his pants and unbuckle his belt.

"I guess you're going to get skull-fucked then. Please, don't think I'm enjoying this. Well, actually, I'm loving every fucking minute of it."

The detective began thrashing his head back and forth and trying to break free from his bonds. The chair rocked forward and backward and then fell over. Dale straddled the chair and looked down at Harry. The detective was still shaking his head back and forth. Dale knelt on the detective's chest with his stubby, stiffening cock bobbing above the old cop's face.

"Don't worry. I cum quick."

Dale grabbed Harry's face in both hands and held it still. The old detective's screams vibrated up through his nostrils sending tremors up through Dale's organ. True to his word, Dale ejaculated after a few quick strokes. The detective began gagging and choking as Dale's seed obstructed his breathing. With the tape still covering his mouth the detective could not spit out Dale's semen, neither could he breathe through his mouth. First he tried to sneeze out but without nostrils he only succeeded in making cum bubbles. He began making a snorting sound and Dale realized that the detective was trying to suck Dale's semen down his throat and swallow it so he could breathe again. As Dale watched, the old detective began to heave and wretch. He regurgitated with the tape still covering his mouth and began to spasm and convulse. Dale stood up and tucked his blood- and mucus-slickened cock back into his pants. He started to reach down and pull the tape off the detective's mouth but then he hesitated.

There was no way the detective was going to tell him where Sarah was. If he hadn't talked after getting his nose cut off, then he wasn't going to talk no matter what Dale did to him. He would hunt him down and tell the rest of the police where to find him. But not if he was dead. All Dale had to do was let him choke on his own vomit and he would be out of the way. Dale knew that he could always bring him back to life later, after he had Sarah back.

Dale stood silently, watching. The old cop thrashed about on the floor, slowly asphyxiating, lungs filling with vomit, drowning, arms still handcuffed behind him, still bound to the chair with duct tape, unable to

move. His struggles increased in their intensity, then
came to a halt. His chest ceased its rise and fall. Dale
checked Harry's pulse. Nothing. He removed the handcuffs from the detective's wrists, picked up the pistol,
and walked back out the door, hoping that he would
have better luck with the black detective.

He drove slowly back up Washburn Street to the
police station, wondering if he could be stopped for
driving too slowly. He speeded up a bit so that he was
just a mile or two over the speed limit. The night shift
and morning shift were just changing when he arrived. He wasn't sure what shift the black woman
worked or if she even had any set hours. On TV, it
looked like the detectives were always on duty. If that
was the case, Dale knew that he could be waiting all
day. She could be anywhere in North Las Vegas, probably out looking for him.

Hours went by. Dale sat still for a while listening to
everything from Stevie Wonder to The Doors to
Guns N' Roses to Michael Jackson on the oldies station. Every once in a while a cop would start eyeing
his car suspiciously and Dale would drive off and circle
the block once or twice before parking again. There
was no sign of the black detective and Dale was getting anxious again. Several times a black woman
would leave the police station and Dale would start up
his car and prepare to follow, only to realize that it
wasn't her. The longer he sat there the more he began
to wonder if he would recognize the detective from
every other black lady cop that came out of the station. Luckily, there weren't many of them.

Maybe that black cunt isn't even working today, Dale
thought and he felt a sudden pang of sorrow. Tears
filled his eyes and he wiped them away with the back

of his hand. *What the fuck is wrong with me?* He wondered if he was falling in love with Sarah Lincoln but knew that was impossible. He barely knew her, except for the glimpses of her life he stole hiding out in her laundry room and the feel of her flesh, the sound of her screams. Certainly not enough to fall in love with but yet that's what it felt like. The very fact that the cops were scouring the street looking for him and he was risking his freedom by parking in front of a police station waiting to kidnap one of the detectives assigned to track him down was proof enough that he had developed a dangerous obsession. He couldn't help himself though. He had to have her. But if he couldn't find the black detective he'd never find Sarah. He would have to leave town without her or stay and continue looking for her himself and risk getting caught. If he got caught there would be no more Sarah and no hope of finding a replacement for her.

There are a lot of fish in the sea, Dale thought. *If I leave now I might find someone even more beautiful than Sarah.* But Dale had never seen a woman more beautiful than Sarah, not even on television. *She should be mine*, Dale thought. *It isn't fair. Why can't I have a woman like that? Why does that big hockey-playing blackjack dealer get to have her? It isn't fair!*

Dale punched the dashboard and wiped more tears from his eyes. He knew he was falling apart, losing his grip. All he needed was Sarah and he would be okay. Everything would be good again. Maybe he could kidnap her and take her away with him somewhere. Maybe he would just make love to her one last time. No violence this time. At least not until the end. Then he would strangle her sweetly, lovingly and this time when she woke up, Dale would be gone forever. It

sounded perfect. Almost romantic, but Dale wasn't
sure he could really leave her. It was too much to think
about now.

The sun was high in the sky before the black detective finally appeared. It was nearly noon. He had been
sitting in front of the police station for over six hours.
He was hungry and dehydrated. His mouth felt like he
had been drinking dust. He licked his chapped lips
and squinted through eyes blurred from lack of sleep.
The detective was wearing a pair of tan high-waisted
pants and a white blouse with billowing sleeves buttoned all the way to the top. She was wearing a pair
of black pumps. She looked like she should have been
carrying a riding crop. It was definitely her. Dale
started his engine.

The detective pulled out of the parking lot in a sleek
black BMW sports car with large chrome rims on the
tires. If he hadn't known that she was a cop he would
have thought she was a drug dealer or a stripper. She
had obviously picked up her taste in cars from the sus-
pects she dealt with.

Dale followed her to the 215 freeway staying two or
three car lengths behind as they traveled south toward
Henderson. The BMW exited at Green Valley Parkway,
then continued south past the Green Valley Ranch
Casino and The District retail shops and restaurants.
Dale studied the happy couples, the families, the
groups of teenage friends, all enjoying themselves
shopping, talking, laughing, and embracing. It was a
life that Dale could scarcely imagine. He had never had
a best friend let alone a group of friends to hang out
with. He had never been part of a couple. His family
had never gone out for a fun afternoon of dining and
shopping. His mother and father had been too busy

chasing the next high to take him on any fun family outings.

The BMW turned into a small gated community on Horizon Ridge. Dale waited until she'd turned the corner before stepping on the accelerator and racing to catch the gate before it closed. He just barely made it through the gate and caught a glimpse of the BMW as it turned the next corner. Dale piloted the Sonata through the maze of cul-de-sacs one block behind the detective's BMW. Dale spotted the BMW pulling into a garage and he stopped his car at the end of the block. He hopped out of the car and jogged down the street toward the detective's house. The garage door began to close and Dale broke into a full sprint. He slipped under the door just before it closed. The detective wasn't in the garage. The fire door slammed shut and Dale jumped, startled. She had gone into the house. Dale crept slowly toward the fire door. His hand trembled as he reached for the handle and his heart pounded like a *taiko* drum. He could not be sure that she had not seen him slipping under the garage door. The detective could have been crouched on the other side, aiming her weapon, prepared to shoot him the minute he opened the door.

Dale placed his ear against the door. He could hear water running in the kitchen and the detective humming and singing some gospel song. Dale inched open the door. The detective had her back to him. She was washing dishes and singing. It was not the gospel tune Dale had thought it was. You didn't shake your ass like that to gospel.

The door was open a quarter of the way. Dale knew he couldn't open it much wider without the tightly wound springs in the bomber hinges squealing. He stood in the doorway, a few short feet from the detective, breathing hard. He had the old hippie cop's .40-caliber Glock in his hand. He could have just shot her in the back. He pulled the hammer down on the pistol and the detective whirled around, reaching for the pistol on her belt.

"Don't do it, Detective. I *will* kill you."

The detective had her gun out of the holster. All she had to do was raise it six inches and it would have been pointing directly at Dale's chest. He knew she was probably a better shot than he was. Dale had never even fired a gun before but he already had his gun aimed at her stomach, and with her so close, he could hardly miss. All he had to do was pull the trigger. He could tell by the look in her eyes, the doubt, the fear, that she knew he had her. Dale wished that he was a sharpshooter like the cowboys on TV and could have shot her in the arm or something just to get her to drop the gun.

He saw the look in her eyes change from fear to anger.

"Aw, shit!" He knew she was about to shoot him. He knew it beyond the shadow of a doubt. This was why he preferred to ambush his victims rather than confront them face-to-face. You could never guess how someone would react to being attacked. Some became terrified, passive, and compliant. Others, like this detective, fought.

The detective raised the gun. Dale closed his eyes and pulled the trigger. The bullet went low, hitting the detective in the belly instead of the chest. The detective paused for a second, wincing and grimacing and belching up blood. Dale waited for her to fall or scream or run. He was still pointing the gun at her.

The black woman's eyes widened in shock, then hardened.

"Oh fuck."

She started moving forward again, aiming her nine-millimeter at Dale and pulling the trigger. Bullets struck the fire door, the doorjamb, and whizzed past Dale into the garage. One dug a searing furrow along the side of Dale's head, barely missing his left eyeball. She was aiming at his head. Dale dove behind the kitchen island and returned fire. He struck her in the chest, the thigh, her right arm. She continued moving forward. The large woman dove on top of Dale and began punching and clawing at his face. He felt her hands clamp down on his throat and squeeze his windpipe shut. He was already breathing heavily from the adrenaline racing through his veins after being shot at. With the large black woman's hands clamped down on his esophagus he could not get any air into his lungs. He still had the gun in his hand and he aimed it at the detective's chest and pulled the trigger until the hammer fell on an empty chamber. Blood sprayed Dale's face and arms as each bullet bore a new hole in the detective's torso. Finally, she rolled off him and collapsed onto the kitchen floor, bleeding out on the ceramic tiles, dead.

Dale coughed and wheezed, then took several deep breaths trying to slow his breathing. His lungs burned with each breath. His heart hammered in his chest. Dale's arms and legs trembled uncontrollably. He tried to stand but the trembling in his legs almost dropped him back to the floor. He held on to the kitchen island and waited for the trembling to stop. Dale looked down at the dead detective.

Jesus, that was one tough bitch, Dale thought. Even with

almost an entire clip in her chest and stomach she
had nearly killed him. Dale grabbed her by her legs
and dragged her toward the fire door. He spotted her
car keys on the kitchen island and grabbed them. He
dragged the detective out into the garage, opened the
rear door of her BMW, and pulled her up onto the backseat. Dale shut the rear door, slid into the driver's seat
and shoved the detective's key into the ignition. There
was a garage-door opener attached to the visor and
Dale pressed the remote. The garage door rattled and
squealed in its tracks as it rose. Dale started the engine and put the BMW in reverse. He pulled out of
the garage and drove off down the street. Several of
the neighbors had come out of their houses. An elderly couple carrying a dachshund and wearing what
looked like matching pajamas and slippers tried to
wave him down as he sped off down the street. He was
less than two blocks away when two police cars raced
by him heading back toward the detective's house with
their sirens and lights blaring. If he had been even two
minutes slower, they would have caught him.

Three more police cars raced by as Dale exited
through the gate and turned back onto Horizon Ridge.
Soon he was back on the freeway, headed home, the
dead detective bouncing around on the backseat.
Blood rolled out from beneath the driver's seat and
pooled under Dale's feet, sloshing onto his shoes. Dale
took the 215 and headed toward North Las Vegas.
Back to the abandoned house where he'd left the old
detective with the ponytail.

The road began to blur as the pain in Dale's skull
roared like a forest fire. Blood dripped into his eye and
Dale wiped it away quickly, squinting to try to bring
the road back into focus. Another white-hot flare of

agony tore through Dale's skull and he struggled to keep the BMW from swerving into the opposite lane. Another drop of blood dribbled down Dale's forehead into his left eye. He wiped the blood away with his wrist and then reached up to touch his forehead. The entire left side of his head was wet with matted blood and there was a neat round hole in his skull just above his temple. The detective hadn't missed after all. Dale felt around and found the exit wound, a jagged hole in the back of his skull on the right side of his head. The bullet had gone straight through his skull and come back out on the other side. He should have been dead. Dale smiled and rolled his eyes skyward.

"Thank you, God," he whispered.

Dale looked over his shoulder at the body rolling around the backseat. That black bitch had almost killed him. He had gotten lucky. Not lucky—blessed. God had been on his side. He was on a mission of love, and love was the most powerful force in the universe. He would bring the black detective back and then he would make her talk and then he and Sarah Lincoln would be reunited. He didn't care if it took all night. This time he would be patient. He wouldn't rush it. He would start with her fingers and keep cutting until she told him everything he wanted to know. She was tough, but everyone had their limits and he was determined.

CHAPTER THIRTY-TWO

Sarah watched a couple fighting in the courtyard only a few feet from her door. The woman had an infant in her arms and was feeding him a bottle even as she continued to berate the man Sarah assumed was the baby's father. The man was clearly intoxicated and was swaying and staggering as the woman poked a finger at his face and yelled in a shrill voice that felt like it was peeling the skin off the inside of Sarah's ears. The woman had apparently found another woman's phone number on her husband's cell phone and then he had come home several hours late from work reeking of perfume and alcohol. The woman was so angry she was practically screaming. Her voice rose to such a high pitch that Sarah could not understand a single word and doubted that the woman's husband could either.

The man smiled drunkenly and closed his eyes as if reliving some pleasant memory, clearly not listening to whatever the woman was trying to communicate to him. That further aggravated the woman, who slapped him hard across the mouth with the baby's bottle, splitting his lip and dropping him down onto the seat of his pants. That woke him up. He staggered to his feet and began shouting back at her. That was apparently what the woman had wanted. She continued to yell at her husband, pointing the bottle she had just slapped him with as she berated him about all his failures as a man, only now she was smiling.

Sarah watched a little longer, then turned back to her empty room. Detective Torres had come to the room a couple hours ago to drive Josh to work. Sarah had been trying to amuse herself and keep her mind off her situation ever since. She had tried to work on her dissertation but still could not get into it, so she had given up on it after writing, and then deleting, two pages of research notes. Then she had gone to the window to spy on the neighbors. She watched a short Latino woman with gorgeous legs and a pair of breasts every bit as full and perky as her own lead a middle-aged man in a crinkled suit into her room. The man in the suit was nervously looking around to make sure no one was watching him as he crossed the courtyard with the woman. Sarah was pretty sure that the Latino woman was a prostitute working out of her motel room. She watched kids playing soccer and Frisbee in the courtyard and mothers carrying armloads of laundry and groceries. Then the couple had started fighting and the entire courtyard had stopped to watch.

Sarah was scared. This was about the worst time she could have ever imagined for her to be alone in a strange motel room. Sarah picked up her cell phone and dialed eleven for Detective Lassiter. The phone rang five times before the voice mail answered.

"Hello, you have reached Detective Trina Lassiter with the North Las Vegas Metropolitan Police Department. I am unavailable right now. Please leave your name, number, and a brief message and I will return your call."

Sarah hung up the phone and hit redial. Again the phone rang five times.

"Hello, you have reached Detective Trina Lassiter with the North Las Vegas . . ."

Sarah hung up the phone and tossed it onto the bed. She looked at her running shoes and sighed. It had been days since she had gotten in a good run. She still did not really feel like running but sitting around the motel room was driving her crazy. Sarah grabbed her Asics running shoes and sat down on the edge of the bed. She considered calling Josh to tell him that she would be out jogging in case he called and could not get a hold of her, but she knew that his cell phone would probably be in his locker at work and by the time he got the message she would already be done with her run. She decided to try Detective Lassiter one more time. She picked up the phone and hit the speed dial. Once again she got the voice mail greeting. This time she left a message.

"Hello Trina, this is Sarah Lincoln. I just wanted you to know that I was going out for a jog. I didn't want you to panic if you called or came by and I wasn't here. I'll be back in an hour. It's almost six o'clock now. I'll call you back when I get in."

She called Detective Malcovich next. He didn't answer either. Sarah guessed that they might have both been in the same meeting somewhere or working on a case or in court or whatever else cops did when they weren't protecting her from supernatural sex murderers. She left a message for him as well.

"Hello, Harry. It's Sarah Lincoln. I just wanted you to know that I was going out for a jog in case you dropped by to check on me. I'll be back by seven. It's six o'clock now."

Sarah hung up, picked up her keys, and walked out the door. She had forgotten to pack her water bottles. Luckily, she had remembered her Garmin. She turned

it on, then waited for it to locate a satellite. She quickly
keyed in a six-mile course and began jogging up Tropicana, away from the strip. She passed the Adult
Superstore and tried not to think about how long it
had been since she'd had sex with her husband, let
alone did anything freaky with him. She didn't know
if she could ever walk into a store like that again without thinking about what that pervert had done to her.
She jogged up toward the Orleans Hotel and almost
got hit by a car trying to cross Arville Street. There
was another sex-toy and apparel shop on the next
block. Sarah had never realized before how many of
these shops there were in Vegas. She guessed that it
was like smoking. You never realized how many smok-
ers there were in the city until you quit and were con-
stantly being accosted by their smoke. That's how she
felt now, accosted by all the commercialized fetishistic
sex.

   She barely looked at the new strip club that had just
opened up across the street from the Orleans as she
picked up her pace, enjoying the feel of the wind on
her face even if the air was warm and congested with
car exhaust fumes. It was better than being cooped up
in a motel room worried about being raped and murdered. The Garmin beeped, telling her to pick up her
speed, and Sarah lengthened her stride.

CHAPTER THIRTY-THREE

Detective Lassiter was a ruin. Dale had skinned the fingers on her right hand one by one, cutting around the base of each digit with a scalpel and then jerking the skin off with a pair of Robogrip pliers like he were removing a condom. She still had not told him where Sarah was. So Dale had gotten more creative. He boiled a pot of water and stuck her other hand in it until it began to blister. Then he took the scalpel and the pliers and de-gloved her entire hand. He wished that he could have removed the gag from her mouth so he could have listened to her screams. They must have been exquisite, he thought.

The detective was strapped to the chair with silver duct tape. Her arms, legs, and head were completely immobilized. She had been almost mummified in tape. He had ripped open her shirt and torn off her bra. Then he had begun cutting on her breasts. He tried to imagine that she were Sarah but her breasts were bigger and flabbier than Sarah's. They looked more like his mother's, only in a different, darker color. Dale remembered what his father had done to his mother's breasts on the night he died.

He cut a line from one shoulder to the other, then down her sides and across her belly in a perfect square. He peeled up the edges of the square with the scalpel and began slowly flaying the skin from her torso. He lifted a flap of skin at her shoulder and grabbed it with the pliers, stripping her skin from the muscle and fat like the peel of an orange. He didn't care if she talked or not. He was having fun now.

Over the course of an hour Dale had excoriated all the skin from Detective Lassiter's chest. Her mammary glands were a bloody mass of fatty tissue, lobules, and connective tissue. Dale removed the tape from around her mouth and head. Mucus, saliva, and tears drooled down her face onto her exposed muscles and sinews. Her breath stuttered out in jerks and starts, spraying saliva and blood. She was shivering from shock and the loss of blood. She would be dead soon. But not before she told him where Sarah was. He didn't care if he had to bring her back and torture her all over again.

Dale grabbed Detective Lassiter by the chin and lifted her head until her eyes met his. Her pupils had narrowed to pin dots.

"Tell me where she is." He ran the scalpel up the detective's inner thigh all the way to her vulva. "Or I start cutting down there."

CHAPTER THIRTY-FOUR

The sky was beginning to darken as Sarah passed Jones Street. Storm clouds rolled in from the south, blanketing the sky. Sarah considered turning back but she felt good. Her lungs felt strong, like she could run forever, and the chances of an actual rainstorm were slim. It only rained two or three weeks out of the year and this was not the season. She decided to keep running.

Tropicana was a long, slow, steady incline, not a steep hill but a gradual ascent that filled your quadriceps with lactic acid and kept the burn going through the entire run. Sarah ignored the persistent burn in her thighs and ran another long block to Rainbow Boulevard. She slowed down for just a moment and checked the clouds above. The sky was completely gray now but still not a drop of rain had fallen. The Garmin began to beep again, urging her on. Sarah took one more glance at the skies, then charged forward. It had been a week since her last run and she had missed it more than she knew. She continued running up Tropicana Avenue another mile. She could see Buffalo ahead, less than a block away.

A black BMW pulled up beside her. Sarah spotted it out of the corner of her eye but ignored it. The Garmin was beeping again, telling her to speed up. She broke into a full sprint for the last block. She knew that she would still have to turn around and run the four miles back to the motel once she reached Buffalo but right now she didn't care. Pushing herself to her limit felt good.

Sarah reached Decatur Boulevard with her lungs feeling like they were about to burst. She checked her time on her Garmin. It was a personal record. Four miles in thirty-one minutes. She leaned up against the street sign to catch her breath and celebrate her victory. She was just about to begin that long jog back down Tropicana when that same black BMW she had spotted out of the corner of her eye stopped at the corner. An alarm went off in her head too late to escape as the car door opened and Dale stepped out of the BMW aiming a pistol at Sarah's head.

"Get in the car."

Sarah looked down Tropicana Boulevard and considered running. The street was packed with traffic. She could take a chance and hope that Dale wouldn't shoot her in front of so many witnesses. Then she remembered that he was already wanted by the police. There was no longer any need for him to be discreet. If she ran maybe a police car would happen by before he could catch her again. Maybe someone would stop their car and help her. Dale was already coming around the car toward her. It was too late now. He had the gun pointed at her face now.

"If you run I will shoot you dead. Now get in the car."

He opened the car door and grabbed Sarah by the arm, dragging her inside. Sarah began to scream and punch at Dale. There was blood leaking from Dale's head and Sarah tried to aim a punch at the wound. Someone shouted something at Dale from a passing car and Sarah hoped that they would call the police, that someone would save her before he got her alone. Sarah felt Dale crack her over the head with the pistol and her legs wobbled. She was thrown into the car and the door was slammed shut behind her. Dale ran around the car and Sarah tried to reach up and lock the door before he could open it. Dale ripped open the door and pushed her back into her seat. He shoved the pistol into her ribs and pulled the BMW back out into traffic.

"Why are you doing this?"

"I don't know. Shut up. Don't talk."

There was a desperation to Dale's movement that Sarah hadn't noticed before. This was not the careful, meticulous killer who had bathed her and her husband after murdering them both, washed her sheets, and scrubbed the walls and floor. The impulsive madman who had just snatched her off a busy street in the middle of rush hour was an entirely different breed of killer. Something had changed him.

"You could have gotten away. The police let you go. They didn't have anything on you. Why did you come back?"

"I said shut the fuck up!" Dale slapped her and Sarah's head spun.

Sarah knew that she was going to be raped and tortured no matter what she did. There was nothing he could threaten her with. No matter what she did the pain would be the same.

"Why me? You could have any woman you wanted, a woman of your own who would love you. I'm married. Why do you want me?"

Dale turned quickly and Sarah braced for another blow but instead he gritted his teeth and answered her question. His face was twisted in anger and some deep emotional pain.

"Any woman? Is that what you think? I can have any woman? Women hate me. My own mother hated me. This is the only way I have ever gotten anyone to pay attention to me. That's why God gave me this power, so I wouldn't be alone, so I could make whores like you love me without violating his law. Thou shalt not kill. I can bring them back."

Dale smiled smugly, proudly.

"But the Bible also says, 'Thou shalt not covet thy neighbor's wife.' I'm married. I have a husband. You're sinning right now, Dale. You've been sinning all along. You have to let me go and turn yourself in. You need help." Sarah was trying her best to control her panic. Tears were streaming from her eyes.

"It doesn't matter. God will forgive me. He knows what I feel."

"What do you feel, Dale?"

Dale's face twitched. He licked his lips and stared straight ahead through the windshield, avoiding Sarah's inquisitive eyes.

"Do you love me, Dale? Do you think you actually love me? This isn't love. You don't hurt the people you love. This is sick. This is twisted and evil."

"You have to be quiet now."

"I want to know, Dale. I want you to tell me what you think you feel for me."

"I loved my mother. She was the first person I ever brought back to life. My dad murdered her right in front of me. But I brought her back. She hated me ever since. She hated what I could do. She kept trying to kill herself and I kept bringing her back. Then she tried to kill me, beat me to death with a hammer. I mean, she tried to. She tried again on the day she died. She poured gasoline all over herself and burned herself up. She tried to take me with her. She poured gasoline outside my bedroom door while I was sleeping and set it and herself on fire." He turned to look at Sarah again; his face was a riot of twitches and tics as he struggled to suppress his pain. "That's it. No more talking now. I'll shoot you if I have to. I can always bring you back. But no more talking."

This time Sarah listened. She recognized the neighborhood as they pulled up to the gate. She even knew the code on the keypad. One, two, four, three. He was taking her home.

CHAPTER THIRTY-FIVE

"How do you see this ending, Dale? You see us being together forever or are you just going to fuck me one last time and run?"

Sarah was trying to get under his skin. She wanted to ruin whatever sick fantasy was driving him. Take away any satisfaction she could from what he was about to do to her. He seemed to be coming unhinged. Nothing about what he was doing made any sense. He had taken her back to her own house to do what? Rape her? And then what?

"Shut the fuck up and get out of the car."

"You haven't thought about it, have you? You're just making this all up as you go, aren't you? What are you going to do? The cops will be looking for me. They'll put you in prison. Then you'll be the one getting raped every night. You'll be the one waking up screaming."

"Get the fuck in the house!"

He grabbed her by the hair and shoved the barrel of the Glock against her temple. Sarah walked with him to her front door, knowing that she was in for unfathomable pain once that door shut behind her. She considered trying to fight him, forcing Dale to kill her now before he could hurt her, but that would only stall the pain. He would just drag her back into the house, revive her, and torture and rape her anyway. She stepped through the door into her home, hoping that someone would find her before Dale could hurt her.

Dale took her up to her own bedroom and pushed her down on the bed. The mattress seethed beneath her, crawling with thousands of maggots and flies. The entire room smelled like death and madness.

"You've never had a real woman, have you, Dale?"

Dale clamped his hands over his ears and winced. Blood trickled down his face from the wound in his head, which had started to bleed again. He wiped it away quickly. He squinted and swayed a little. For a moment, Sarah thought he was about to faint or perhaps even die on the spot. She rose from the bed.

"What the fuck are you doing? Get back on the bed!"

He pointed the gun at her and for a moment Sarah thought he was going to pull the trigger. Then he winced and grabbed his head with his left hand, still pointing the gun at her with the right. Blood was seeping from the wound and trickling down his forehead steadily now. He blinked repeatedly, trying to keep the blood out of his eye.

"I'm getting ready for you, Dale. You can't fuck me if I'm fully dressed. Isn't this what you wanted? You don't have to rape me. I'll let you have whatever you want. Maybe I'll even rape you."

She reached out for his belt buckle and he pulled away from her. She guessed he probably couldn't get it up with a woman he hadn't tortured and abused. That was part of his ritual, his fantasy. A willing victim ruined the fantasy for him.

"Come on, don't you want to cum on my tits? Isn't that what you told the detectives you wanted to do to me? Here I am, Dale. Let's fuck!"

She reached out for him again and he pulled away again.

"Stop that! Not like that. Get back on the bed."

Sarah heard a tire screech outside. She glanced out the window and saw Detective Torres pull into the driveway of Dale's house, throw open his car door, and charge up the walkway to Dale's front door, his gun pulled. He kicked down the front door and went inside.

Fucking idiot, Sarah thought. Didn't he notice the car in her driveway?

Moments later the street filled with black-and-white patrol vehicles and one Saturn hybrid SUV. *Josh!* If anyone had the sense to check their house it would be he. The cavalry had arrived.

"They're coming for you, Dale. You don't have much time. You'd better get it up if you want to get in one last fuck before they send your crazy ass to the gas chamber."

She reached out for him again. This time he had both hands on his bleeding head, eyes closed, grimacing in pain. She grabbed his cock, testicles and all, and twisted as hard as she could. When Dale cried out, she balled up a fist and punched him in the mouth as hard as she could. The gun flew and Dale dropped to his knees. Sarah never let go of his testicles. She was trying to tear them clean off his body. She punched him again, aiming for his bleeding head, and then again in the face. Then she grabbed his testicles with both hands and twisted his cock in one direction and his balls in another. Dale screamed like a woman.

The bedroom door flew open and Josh burst inside. He took one look at Dale lying on the floor with Sarah tugging at his crotch and an expression of white-hot rage twisted his features. He grabbed Dale by the throat and lifted him from the floor as effortlessly as a mother would have lifted a newborn. He began strangling Dale. Sarah did not object. She did not implore him to stop as she would have thought she might have. She remained on the floor, watching her big, strong husband, the love of her life, strangle her tormentor to death, waiting for Dale to die. She wished she had a cigarette. Revenge was even better than sex. Then Detective Torres walked in and ruined everything.

"Put him down, Josh. Let him go."

The detective was pointing a gun at her husband.

"He tried to kill me! He kidnapped me and was going to rape me!"

"I know, Sarah. But I can't let him do this. This ain't the way. You said it yourself, you don't want Josh going to jail for you and that's what will happen if he kills him."

Torres was right. She didn't want to lose Josh. She needed him.

"Then you kill him. Just shoot him. You kill him!"

"I can't do that, Sarah. I'm a cop."

"Where's Harry?"

"I don't know. I can't get a hold of him or Trina. I thought they were at the motel. That's why I went there looking for them. That's Trina's car out front. I need to find out what this piece of shit did to her and I can't do that if he's dead. Let him go, Josh! Now!"

Dale was turning blue and had passed out. He would be dead soon. A bunch of uniformed cops spilled into the room. Two of them tackled Josh. He tossed them aside like they were rag dolls and went after Dale again. Three more cops jumped on top of him but Josh continued to fight, almost managing to break free again.

"Don't hurt him. He's the victim here. Just get him under control. Calm down, Josh. It's over. You and your wife are safe."

Josh stopped struggling but the police officers continued to hold him. One of them had his cuffs out and was reaching down to slap them onto Josh's wrists. Sarah scrambled over to her husband and pushed the officer away.

"Cuff *him*, not him!"

The officer looked over at Detective Torres, who raised an eyebrow and gestured toward Dale, who was lying unconscious on the floor by the window. His head wound was bleeding profusely now and only then did Sarah realize that it was a bullet wound.

They rolled Dale onto his stomach and handcuffed him. Then they began to search him, finding the diver's knife, a cell phone, and the keys to the BMW.

"Wake him up! Throw some water on him or something. Bring him here!"

The officers dragged Dale's limp, unconscious body over to Detective Torres, who led them into the master bathroom. Torres pulled Dale into the tub, then stepped out and turned on the shower. Dale woke up immediately, swallowed a mouthful of water, and began to cough. Torres shut off the water.

"Where the fuck is Detective Lassiter? What did you do to her?"

Dale smiled.

"They're dead, both of them. They were trying to keep me from Sarah."

Sarah's heart sank. Harry and Trina had died because of her.

Detective Torres fell back against the bathroom cabinet, eyes wide, stunned.

"I should have let him kill you, you sick bastard. Where are they? Show me."

Dale pointed toward the back of the house.

"The house next door."

Torres nodded to the other officers.

"Go check the house. I've got him. All of you, go!"

The officers filed out, leaving Sarah, Josh, and Torres alone with Dale. Detective Torres withdrew his pistol from his holster again. It was a Glock .40 just like the one Harry carried. Just like the one Dale had been carrying. He pointed the weapon at Dale's head.

"Don't. He can bring them back."

Torres paused. Tears were streaming down his face. He no longer looked like the macho asshole Sarah had taken him for, the one he always pretended to be.

"Bullshit. I don't believe all the magic bullshit."

"He can. You saw it on the tape. He can do it and if there's a chance you have to let him."

The detective's radio squawked and he removed it from his belt clip, still pointing his gun at Dale.

"Detective Torres? We found Lassiter and Malcovich. They're dead. He killed them. He tore them apart. It's awful."

Torres looked at Sarah, then back at Dale.

"Can you really do it?"

"I have to. Murder is a sin."

Torres called back over the radio.

"Get everybody out of there. I don't want anyone touching anything. Wait for me outside."

"Should we call CSU or the ME?"

The detective looked at Dale with obvious suspicion, then held the radio to his mouth again.

"No. Don't do anything until I get over there. Just wait."

He grabbed Dale by the shirt and dragged him out of the shower.

"Come on."

Together they walked out of the bedroom, out the front door, and into the detective's car. They drove around the corner in silence. Sarah didn't want to see what Dale had done to the detectives but knew she had to. She had to see it, but more important, she had to see him bring them back.

They pulled into the driveway where a dozen cops stood in front of the house. The neighbors had come out of their houses to see what was going on and the police were already having a hard time trying to manage them.

"Get some yellow tape up and get all these people behind it. Where are they?"

"In the kitchen," one of the officers, a short black cop shaped like a fireplug with arms almost the size of his clean-shaven head, replied. Torres nodded and began walking up to the front door, dragging Dale with him.

"You can't take them in there. It's horrible. You can't let civilians see that."

Torres whirled around, his face twisted into a scowl, tears in his eyes, obviously trying hard but having a difficult time suppressing his emotions.

"That's my partner in there and a guy I've known since I've been on the force. Don't tell me what I can and can't do. Just shut the fuck up and keep these people away from the crime scene. I'll handle the witnesses however the fuck I want to."

He stormed up the walkway and into the house. Sarah and her husband followed.

The officer on the radio had not been exaggerating.

Dale had torn the two detectives to pieces. He had cut Harry's nose off his face, though Sarah could not see any other wounds or what had exactly killed him, but with Trina, he had taken out all of his fury.

Her torso had been flayed of all skin, as were both hands. Between her legs looked even worse. He had carved out her vagina like he were coring an apple. Sarah could not have imagined the pain she must have gone through.

Torres turned and punched Dale in the stomach, doubling him over.

"If you can bring them back, then you'd better do it right now, and you'd better hope you can do it because if you can't I'm going to do to you everything you did to them."

Dale dropped to his knees and vomited onto the floor. Torres kicked him in the ribs, knocking him into his own vomit.

"Get the fuck up and bring my friends back!" Torres pulled out his gun and pointed it at Dale's head. "Do it now!"

Dale struggled to his feet. His eyes rolled up in his head and he looked again like he was going to lose consciousness but then he steadied himself. He walked over to Harry and placed his lips against the detective's lips. He took one long breath and breathed into Harry's mouth. Then he did it again, taking an even deeper breath this time and fully expanding the detective's lungs. The third time he breathed in and Harry breathed out. The detective began breathing on his own in a fast, panting breath like he was hyperventilating. As Sarah watched his nose began to regenerate, like a film running in reverse. Detective Torres made the sign of the cross and continued to stare as Harry began to blink and open his eyes.

"Oh *mi Dios!* He did it. This little piece of shit can really do it!"

He removed the gag from the detective's mouth and Harry bent over and threw up onto the floor.

"Cut him loose!" Detective Torres said, and Sarah began opening drawers, looking for something to cut the detective free with.

Torres grabbed Dale by the shirt and dragged him over to Detective Lassiter.

"Do her now. Bring her back."

Dale put his lips to Trina's lips and began breathing into her lungs. Her chest rose and fell with each exhalation. Sarah and Josh stopped what they were doing to watch. The detective's skin began to reknit itself, growing back up over her chest. The skin on her hands began to grow back also, starting at the wrists and spreading back down over her fingers. Between her legs, the ragged hole Dale had carved in her sex began to sew itself shut and her vulva gradually reformed. When Dale removed his lips from the detective's she was completely whole again though still unconscious. Dale dropped to his knees at her feet, kneeling in a small pool of congealed blood.

"I can't fucking believe it. He did it," Torres said in an awed whisper.

"Cut me the fuck loose."

It was Harry. He was fully conscious now and struggling to free himself from the tape still binding him to the chair. Josh finally found a butter knife and went to work trying to cut through the duct tape around Harry's arms. Sarah used a key from her key chain to saw through the tape on Harry's ankles. It took a while but they finally managed to cut Harry free.

"Where's my fucking gun? I'm going to put a bullet in this freak's brain." Harry stepped forward and Detective Torres grabbed him by both arms to hold him back.

"Wait. Wait, Harry. Wait. Will you wait a second! We have a problem."

"There's no problem, Mike. Give me your gun and I'll fix the problem right now!"

"You don't understand, Harry. There are about a dozen officers outside who just saw you lying dead on the floor in here. What the hell am I supposed to tell them when you walk out of here looking as healthy as a horse?"

"Dead? What the fuck are you talking about?"

"This piece of shit murdered you and Trina. He tortured you to find out where we were keeping Mrs. Lincoln. I just made him bring you back. You should have seen it, Harry. I've never seen anything like it. You were dead as disco, bro, and he just breathed into you and you were alive again. You don't remember it? Were you in heaven?"

"Heaven? Fuck no! I don't remember shit except waking up tied to a chair and seeing you three all standing around looking at me. I went for a drink after work. I was walking to my car and then I woke up here. You're saying I was dead?"

"You were in full rigor. He had cut your nose off and then I think you choked on your own vomit. He had a gag over your mouth and you must have thrown up."

Sarah and Josh went to cut Detective Lassiter free. She was still unconscious, snoring soundly as if she were merely asleep and not reanimated. Josh took the butter knife to the tape around her arms and shoulders while Sarah squatted down in Lassiter's blood to cut her ankles free. Harry and Torres were still debating whether to shoot Dale and how to explain to the cops outside why Harry and Trina were walking out instead of being carted out in body bags. Dale had lost consciousness and was lying on his side with his face in the detective's blood. Sarah had the urge to take the butter knife from Josh and try to cut Dale's throat with it but it was too dull. She considered stabbing him in the eye with it instead. She removed the last strip of tape from Trina's ankles just as the woman woke.

Detective Lassiter looked around in a panic. She was breathing hard and struggling to free herself from the rest of the tape while trying to reorient herself. Before anyone could react, she leaped up from the chair and ran over to Detective Torres. She snatched the Glock out of his hand and pointed the gun down at Dale.

"Motherfucker!"

She pulled the trigger, once, twice, three times, four times, until Torres finally wrenched it back out of her hands. All four shots had gone directly into Dale's skull, scattering his brains across the floor.

The front door opened and police officers rushed into the room with guns drawn. Torres turned his back and held up his hands to tell the officers to hold their fire.

"Hold it. Hold it. I got this. It's all under control. I got this."

Sarah felt the pain even before her body began to fly apart. She looked over at Josh as his head began to bleed and his throat tore open in the same spot where Dale had cut him in the video they had taken on their spy camera. Harry collapsed first, convulsing on the floor and choking. His nose fell off, leaving a hollow crater in the center of his face like there had been before Dale had resurrected him.

Trina began losing chunks of flesh and skin. She stumbled around screaming as her skin sloughed off in sheets and her vagina fell apart.

Sarah looked down at her body as her chest tore open. One of her breasts fell off and the other lost a nipple and most of its skin. Her stomach ripped open and her intestines spilled out onto the floor; then she began to choke as her throat split wide and blood filled her throat and lungs. She collapsed between her dead husband and her murderer.

As she lost consciousness, she heard Dale beside her begin breathing rapidly. She turned her head and tried to focus her eyes as her vision began to darken. She could make out what was left of Dale's skull as it began to knit itself back together.

☐ **YES!**

Sign me up for the Leisure Horror Book Club and send my FREE BOOKS! If I choose to stay in the club, I will pay only $8.50* each month, a savings of $7.48!

NAME: _____

ADDRESS: _____

TELEPHONE: _____

EMAIL: _____

☐ I want to pay by credit card.

☐  ☐ ☐

ACCOUNT #: _____

EXPIRATION DATE: _____

SIGNATURE: _____

Mail this page along with $2.00 shipping and handling to:
Leisure Horror Book Club
PO Box 6640
Wayne, PA 19087
Or fax (must include credit card information) to:
610-995-9274
You can also sign up online at **www.dorchesterpub.com**.
*Plus $2.00 for shipping. Offer open to residents of the U.S. and Canada only.
Canadian residents please call 1-800-481-9191 for pricing information.
If under 18, a parent or guardian must sign. Terms, prices and conditions subject to change. Subscription subject to acceptance. Dorchester Publishing reserves the right to reject any order or cancel any subscription.